MW00938650

STAY INFORMED

I'd love to stay in touch! You can email me at kathleen@ kathleentroy.com

For updates about new releases, as well as exclusive promotions, visit my website and sign up for the VIP mailing list. Head there now to receive a free story

www.kathleentroy.com

Enjoying the series? Help others discover *Dylan's Dog Squad* by sharing with a friend.

ALSO BY KATHLEEN TROY

Dylan's Dog Squad Series

Dylan's Dilemma

Dylan's Dream

Dylan's Villain

Coming soon: Dylan's Hawaiian Ghost

Never Believe Series

Never Believe in Luck Twice

(Prologue/short story to Never Believe a Lie Twice)

Never Believe a Lie Twice

Coming soon: Never Believe a Con Artist Twice

DYLAN'S VILLIAN

KATHLEEN TROY

DYLAN AND FRIENDS PUBLISHING COMPANY

To Dylan,
I know you by heart.

A world-class snooze is the only way to
start the day.
-Dylan

CHAPTER ONE

"Are you sure you weren't followed?"

Casey and Sumo exchanged looks and shook their heads.

You're our first client. Dylan gave a happy tongue-hanging-out-of-his-mouth grin to the small girl sitting cross-legged on the floor of the tree house. *Dylan's Dog Squad is officially in business!*

Holly hunched forward, put her elbows on her knees, and whispered, "Let's get one thing straight. Everything we say is confidential. You know, like between a lawyer and a client."

Casey squirmed. "Are you in trouble?"

Holly's dark eyes darted left and right. "If you don't find Bailey, I'm dead." Her eyes bugged out and she slashed her right index finger across her throat.

"Whoa." Sumo's thumbs paused midair above his iPad. "When you called, you said Bailey was gone. You didn't say anything about dead."

"Stay on track," Holly ordered. "He's gone and I'm going to be dead if you don't get him back."

Yikes. Dylan wiggled his buns and nudged Casey. *This is a big case. Good thing we're on the job!*

"So, are we straight here? Everything is confidential?" Holly glanced over her shoulder before dropping her voice an octave. "If it's not, I'm outta here."

Dylan pawed Casey's leg. *We're sitting in Holly's tree house. Where would she go?*

"You bet. Everything is confidential," Sumo agreed. "We'll need some information from you." His fingers returned to his iPad, ready to go to work.

Casey cleared his throat. "How long has Bailey been missing?"

Holly squeezed her eyes shut, gave a small shake of her head, and counted fast to ten. When she opened her eyes, she zeroed in on them. "Bailey's been *gone* since breakfast."

Casey checked his cell phone for the time. "That's not very long to be missing."

Holly tossed her hands into the air. "Bailey is *gone*, not *missing*."

"I don't get it," Sumo said. "What's the difference?"

Holly slapped both palms onto her knees. "Is English a second language for you? Bailey is *gone*. That means he's not *here*." She paused. "He always comes back. Eventually." She hitched a shoulder and let it fall. "Sometimes he's gone for days." She pointed her finger at them. "Your job is to get him back now."

"All right." Casey moved on. "How old is he?"

Holly sat up straight. "Ten, like me."

"Okay. What color is his hair?"

"Black, like mine." Each hand grabbed a fistful of hair and pulled it away from her face. "Kind of spiky."

"Eyes?"

Her thumbs and index fingers formed two circles around her eyes. "Black, like mine."

Sumo looked up from his iPad. "How tall is he?"

She fluttered a hand over her head. "Same size as me."

Are you twins?

"Got it." Sumo nodded and thumb-tapped the info into the iPad. "What was Bailey wearing?"

She chewed on her lower lip. "A red and blue cape."

"That's it?" Casey frowned.

Holly tipped her head, thought, and nodded once. "Yeah."

Bailey must be very cold.

"Uh," Casey looked to Sumo but got no help, "do you have a picture?"

"Sure." Holly pulled a cell phone out of her back pocket, scrolled through her pictures, and worked the screen. "I just sent it to you."

Sumo's cell phone pinged, and Casey, Sumo, and Dylan leaned together to look at the screen.

Dylan studied Bailey's picture—short spiky black hair, big ears, pale round-moon face, black beady eyes, big lips, big feet, long arms, and a yellow toothy grin.

"Whoa," Casey said. "Bailey is."

A really ugly kid.

"A chimp," Sumo blurted out.

"A kleptomaniac," Holly corrected.

Dylan looked up at Casey. *Huh?*

"Steals things," Casey explained.

Dylan took in the tree house crammed with stuff. A striped hammock, strung from corner-to-corner, was heaped with stuffed animal toys. A guitar was propped in the corner next to a tennis racket and boogie board. Backpacks were everywhere. Flip-flops, straw hats, and sweatshirts were piled next to a tricycle and bike helmet. Stacks of Amazon deliveries and mail lined the walls, blocking out the sun from the windows. *Bailey is one sticky-fingered chimp.*

"Look, I'm staying with my grandfather while Rachel, that's my mom, is on tour with her latest book."

Casey interrupted, "Why do you call your mom Rachel?"

Holly narrowed her eyes. "Do I really have to explain every little thing to you?"

It would help.

"Anyway, the San Diego Zoo has this big ribbon-cutting ceremony thing coming up and Rachel is coming home on Wednesday. I'm supposed to be watching Bailey. So far, she and my grandfather don't know Bailey is gone." She sucked in a ragged breath. "I want to keep it that way. If they find out," the finger slashed across her throat again.

"You're dead," Casey finished.

"Hey!" Sumo waved both hands in the air. "I've got it! Your mom, your mom," he stammered, "is Rachel Langdon. Wow!" Sumo turned to Casey. "Remember when she spoke to our class last year? Hey, she never mentioned she had a daughter."

Holly gritted her teeth and muttered, "Never does."

"Wow, your mom is famous." Casey thought hard. "She's called something weird. Primo? Prima?"

"Primatologist," Holly and Sumo said together.

"Yeah." Casey elbowed Sumo. "You kept asking her all those dumb questions."

"They weren't dumb." Sumo elbowed him back. "Chimpanzees are so cool. They can see colors and details. They can run up to like twenty-five miles an hour and they're four times stronger than humans their size."

I can run faster than Casey.

Sumo went back to Holly. "Man, you're so lucky. You get to live up here with Bailey."

Holly blinked once. "Only Bailey lives in the tree house."

"Really?"

She scowled. "You think *I* live here?"

Sumo's cheeks burned. "Uh," he mumbled, "I mean it'd be so cool to have a chimp."

"Are you nuts?" Her black eyes flashed. "I'm a *servant* to that chimp. I've gotta eat my meals with him. Watch TV with him—*Animal Planet.* Like how many times can I watch that? I gotta take him for walks. Do you know what it's like to walk down the street with a chimp? Every time Rachel writes a new book, I gotta go on talk shows with him." She shuddered. "Rachel even makes me answer his fan mail." She tossed her hands into the air. "You wouldn't believe the dumb questions people ask."

Dylan, Casey, and Sumo kept quiet.

"Stuff like Does Bailey like Chunky Monkey Ice Cream? Who's Bailey's best friend? Does Bailey play on monkey bars? Does Bailey snore? What's Bailey's favorite color?" She narrowed her eyes. "My all-time favorite is when people ask if Bailey's my brother. Grr!"

Dylan flinched and wiggled closer to Casey. *She's kind of scary.*

"You're kidding!" Casey smirked. "People really ask that?"

You do look alike, same hair, same eyes. Dylan whined. *Same teeth.*

"Oh yeah, it's a riot having the other kids make fun of me. Calling me banana breath." She leaned closer. "When we were little, Rachel used to think it was fun to dress us alike."

Casey, Sumo, and I have matching Angels T-shirts.

"Your mom travels all over the world. It's pretty cool," Casey shrugged, "and you get to go, too."

"With a *chimp?*" She started tearing at the cuticle on her right index finger. "You don't know what it's like to have a famous mom. Everyone expects me to become a primatologist—just like her. *She* expects me to become a primatologist—just like her."

"We get it." Sumo pointed at Casey. "His mom was the same way. She has a children's book company and represents authors and illustrators. She was always telling Casey he had to go to college and then into business with her."

Dylan sighed. *Casey hates reading.*

"I finally got the guts to tell her I didn't want to." Casey pulled Dylan close. "Right, Little Buddy?"

Dylan put his muzzle on Casey's lap and licked his knee. *Right!*

Casey turned Dylan's bandana around and showed Holly the Dylan's Dog Squad logo. "So, Sumo, Dylan, and I started Dylan's Dog Squad. Dylan's going to take his American Kennel Club Canine Good Citizen test this week and he'll be certified."

Dylan pulled himself into a sitting position and puffed his chest out with pride. *I'll have my own vest with an AKC Canine Good Citizen patch.* Then Dylan's shoulders sagged. *Last time I didn't pass. I've got to pass. I can't let Casey down. He's counting on me.*

"Later," Casey stroked Dylan's ears, "we're going to have a dog training business. Do Search and Rescue. At first, I was scared to tell my mom but now she gets it."

"I told you she would," Sumo said. "Your mom's cool."

Casey, Dylan, and Sumo smiled.

"How nice for *you*." Holly stabbed the air between them with her bloody finger. "Where were we? Oh yeah, I'm supposed to be watching Bailey. Now he's gone and I'm going to be dead." She sat back. "Can you do the job or not?"

Arf!

Sumo waved his iPad. "Absolutely. Just a few more questions."

Casey started again. "How did Bailey, uh, become gone?"

Holly shrugged. "I guess I accidentally, sort of maybe, forgot to shut the tree house door this morning and he got out." She shrugged again. "When he gets out, he likes to," her voice trailed off, "collect things."

Dylan looked around. *The tree house is jammed full of stuff. You must forget a lot.*

Sumo considered this. "It's not like chimps run around Brea every day. Is he microchipped? Does he have a collar?"

"Just a collar. No chip."

No chip for the chimp.

"Great," Sumo said. "You could wait until someone finds him and then pick him up."

Arf! Pipe down, Sumo. This is our first case!

"You don't know much, do you? Only dogs and cats are domestic animals—not chimpanzees. Doesn't matter Bailey is famous. Doesn't matter Rachel is famous. If Animal Control gets ahold of Bailey, they'll toss him into the slammer."

Dylan pawed Casey's knee. *Slammer?*

Casey leaned down. "Jail."

"That might not be so bad," Sumo said slowly. "At least you'd get him back."

Holly's voice shot up. "Are you crazy or just dumb? How'd that look if Bailey gets arrested? My grandfather is Frank Matias—*Mayor* Matias."

Casey lifted his eyebrows. "You never said your grandfather is Mayor Matias."

Holly glared at him. "Well, I'm saying it now."

Oh-oh. Mom is friends with Mayor Matias.

"Well," Casey said lamely, "Bailey's been lucky so far. No one has seen him. Maybe he'll just come home."

"Yeah, well, Bailey has to get back quick. Like I said, the San Diego Zoo is having a big ribbon-cutting ceremony. Rachel has this whole thing set up for the press. It's a really big deal," she huffed out a breath, "and Bailey—not me— gets to do the ribbon cutting."

You really don't like Bailey.

"Hey, that sounds fun." Sumo turned to Casey. "We should go."

Holly ignored Sumo and fisted a hand on her hip. "It's kind of hard to have a ribbon cutting ceremony with Bailey if there's no Bailey. We're running out of time."

Dylan whined. *Holly is making some excellent points.*

Casey nodded. "Have you thought of calling the police? My Uncle Rory is a Detective Lieutenant with Brea PD. I could ask him to put out a Be On the Look Out."

"Do I have to spell this out for you?" Holly swept a hand around the tree house. "Bailey has been on a crime spree, ripping off the neighbors." She clapped her hands together happily and leaned closer, "Lucky for me, no one will ever know. I've got a plan to get rid of all this."

"That's great," Casey nodded. "What's your plan?"

She smiled for the first time. "I'm donating it all to the Goodwill Society. There's a store by Stater Brothers on Imperial Highway."

Uh-oh. That's not a very nice plan.

Casey shifted his buns on the hard floor. "I'm pretty sure that's illegal."

Uh, yeah.

"So what? I'm desperate."

"You don't want to do that." Sumo looked up from his iPad and showed them the screen. "Google says messing with the US mail is a federal offense. You and Bailey would both end up in jail."

Just then a padded envelope slid off a tall stack of mail and thumped to the floor. Dylan pawed at Casey's leg. *It's too late for Holly to worry about jail. Bailey has already messed with the mail.*

"Bummer." Holly frowned. "I'll have to think of something else." She reached into the pocket of her shorts and put a fistful of twenties on the floor between them. "So how about it, Dylan's Dog Squad? Are you going to help me? Otherwise, I'm," she frowned.

"Dead," Casey and Sumo said together.

Whine.

CHAPTER TWO

"What now?" Holly pushed to her feet.

"I need something of Bailey's to give to Dylan." Casey scanned the crowded treehouse. "That's how Dylan will pick up Bailey's scent and be able to track him."

Arf! That's my job.

"Tracking. Okay. Great. Sure," Holly nodded, "tracking is good. Only," she raised a warning finger, "when you find Bailey, *don't* chase him. That's his idea of a fun game."

I like it when Casey chases me. Hmm. I've tracked a dog and little boy before but never a chimp. Dylan cocked his head. *No problem! Bailey is kind of like a little boy—just hairy.*

Holly cracked her knuckles. "You'll never catch him anyway. That chimp can really move." She went over to Bailey's hammock, grabbed its edge, and gave it a quick shake. Stuffed elephants, rabbits, bears, and ducks flew off.

Wow! Bailey has almost as many woobies as me.

She lifted the pillow on the hammock, rummaged underneath, and pulled out a Mickey Mouse T-shirt. "Last summer Bailey got to ride on the float in the Disneyland

Main Street Electrical Parade," she said and then muttered under her breath, "not me."

Lucky chimp! The Disneyland fireworks are the best. We can see them from our house every night at nine o'clock.

She held up the shirt. "This is Bailey's favorite shirt. Disneyland gave it to him to wear in the parade." Another mutter, "I didn't get one."

Wow! Bailey has his own Mickey Mouse T-shirt. Dylan leaned against Casey's leg and whined. *You said we could go to Disneyland sometime.* Dylan added a muzzle rub. *I've always wanted a Mickey Mouse T-shirt.*

Holly wadded up the shirt and sent it sailing over her shoulder. Sumo caught it. She focused on the floor, kicked through the stuffed woobies, and came up with a pair of Mickey Mouse ears. "Need these?"

Bailey has his own Mickey Mouse ears—no way! Dylan put his head down low, his ears flopped over his eyes. Dylan tossed his head in reverse, his ears flopped back. He shook them out. *How does Mickey Mouse get his ears to stand up?*

"Nah." Sumo tossed the T-shirt to Casey. "This works."

Casey put the shirt in a plastic bag and then into his backpack. "Does Bailey have a leash?"

"No," Holly said.

"Okay," Casey hesitated, "does he come when he's called?"

Holly cracked up. "Get serious."

This is getting hard, guys.

Sumo threw his hands up. "Forget it, Casey. How are we supposed to bring Bailey back if he doesn't have a leash, we can't chase him, and he won't come when he's called? We can't do this." Sumo turned away. "Uh-uh."

Casey grabbed Sumo's arm. "Hold on."

"If this was going to be easy," Holly pointed to the

money in Casey's hand, "Dylan's Dog Squad wouldn't be getting two hundred bucks."

Whine. C'mon, guys. This is our first case.

"Right." Casey put the money in his shorts pocket and gave her his best grin. "Dylan's Dog Squad needs to consult."

Sumo, Casey, and Dylan huddled together. Sumo whispered, "How are we going to pull this off? We need a plan."

Dylan shifted on his paws. *A really good plan.*

"No problem," Casey insisted. "A chimp roaming around Brea will be easy to spot. We'll talk to the neighbors —someone must've seen him. All we have to do is find Bailey and follow him around until he gets tired. Chimps have to sleep sometime," Casey reasoned. "When Bailey conks out, we'll throw a blanket over him and tie him up with bungee cords. A chimp weighs, what, a hundred pounds? Maybe a little more? We can carry him back."

Sumo and Dylan stared at Casey.

"That's the dumbest plan I've ever heard."

Whine. Dylan got on his hind legs and pawed Casey's leg. *It could use some work.*

"Look," Casey patted Dylan's head, "Dylan's Dog Squad's reputation is on the line. We've got to do this."

"I don't know." Sumo made a face. "Bailey's been ripping off neighbors and stealing mail. He's a criminal chimp."

"Not our problem. Our problem is finding Bailey. Besides, Holly said she'd take care of the stuff Bailey collected."

"You mean get rid of the evidence."

"Whatever." Casey dropped his voice, "This is our first case and it's a big one. If we find Bailey, we could get more business."

"If we help Bailey, we could get arrested," Sumo corrected.

Dylan yipped and dropped down to all four paws. *I don't want to get arrested.*

"We'll figure it out as we go." Casey shrugged.

"All right." Sumo scrubbed his hands over his eyes and then pointed at Casey. "We'd better not end up in the slammer."

I don't want to end up in the slammer.

"I heard you the first time."

"I can't believe I'm doing this," Sumo complained and headed toward the tree house ladder. "See you downstairs."

Casey turned back to Holly and gave a thumbs up. "Dylan's Dog Squad is on the case."

"Great. Remember, *don't* chase Bailey."

"Got it. It might be a good idea to leave the tree house door open for Bailey," Casey said, "in case he comes home."

"Sure."

Casey waited for Dylan to look at him. Casey held both hands out in front of him and closed both hands into fists. Then he tapped his right fist on top of his left fist twice in the wrist area, signing Work. "Ready to go to work, Little Buddy?"

Arf! Dylan scampered over to the tree ladder. *Ready to find Bailey.*

Casey picked Dylan up and started down the ladder. "We'll text you as soon as we have something."

Holly followed them over to the opening and watched them go down.

When they made it to the bottom, Casey put Dylan on the ground, got the plastic bag out of his backpack, and pulled out Bailey's shirt. He held it close to Dylan's nose. "This is Bailey. Dylan, find Bailey."

Arf! Arf! Dylan danced in a circle, tugged on his leash, and then cocked his head. *This way.*

"Good boy, Dylan." Casey looked up at Holly and then motioned toward Dylan. "He's got Bailey's scent."

"Great." Holly gave them a cheery wave. "Remember, *don't* chase Bailey."

CHAPTER THREE

Three hours later Dylan heaved a big sigh, sniffed the air, put his snout to the sidewalk, and followed Bailey's trail to a big tree. Getting on his hind legs, he put his paws on its trunk and danced once around the tree. *Arf!*

"Got something?" Casey called.

Sore paws. Dylan lifted his head to catch the hot summer breeze. *I've tracked Bailey to every house, front porch, backyard, and driveway. I've been in every bush and out of every bush. This Dylan's Dog Squad business isn't so easy.*

Dylan gave up, slid to the ground, and whined. *I can't climb a tree.* He went over to Casey and plunked his butt on the ground. *Now what?*

"Dylan's lost the scent," Casey told Sumo.

No, I didn't. Stupid Bailey went up that tree.

Sumo plopped onto the grass, kicked off his flip-flops, and wiggled his toes. "I'm tired of walking."

Me, too.

Casey tipped his head back and searched the tree

branches. "Bailey probably climbed this tree and swung over to one of those trees."

Stupid, dumb Bailey.

"Did you know chimpanzees are great at climbing trees?" Sumo leaned back on his hands. "They like to rest in trees at night. That's why they like tree houses. But chimps prefer to spend the day on the ground."

I don't climb trees and I like to sleep on Casey's bed at night. Stupid, dumb, lamebrained Bailey.

"Why do you know about chimps when you don't have to?"

Sumo shrugged. "I read a lot."

Not Casey.

"Okay, Little Buddy." Casey shoved Bailey's T-shirt back into the plastic bag before putting it into his backpack. "We've covered most of Holly's neighborhood. I want to try the Brea Sports Park next."

Dylan stretched his front paws out in front of him and belly dropped onto the sidewalk. *I want air conditioning.*

"This is nuts. And it's humiliating." Sumo took a long drink from his water bottle. "Our client is a chimp. Why couldn't Dylan's Dog Squad's first case be something easy? Like a kidnapped baby or someone's grandfather wandering off the front porch."

Casey got Dylan's water dish out of his backpack, put it in front of Dylan, and filled it. "Here you go, Little Buddy."

Dylan stuck his muzzle in and lapped the bowl dry. *Arf!*

"Holly was right," Casey added more water to Dylan's dish. "If finding Bailey were easy, she wouldn't need us."

"No wonder she paid in advance," Sumo grumbled. He lifted his Angels cap up and used the back of his hand to wipe his damp hair off his forehead. "Where do you think she got the two hundred bucks?"

Dylan shook the water off his muzzle and blinked up at Sumo and Casey. *Seriously? You don't know?*

"Bailey," Casey and Sumo said together.

Duh.

Sumo went back to grumbling. "I don't have the guts to figure out how many laws Bailey has broken."

"It's not breaking the law if a chimp does it," Casey argued. "Pretty sure about that one. Maybe."

Maybe not.

Casey's cell phone vibrated. He took it out of his pocket and read the text. "Mom says if we want lunch, be home in fifteen minutes."

Arf! Arf! Dylan jumped to his paws and danced around Casey's legs. *I do.*

Sumo rubbed his stomach with one hand. "I need food."

Casey started texting but stopped. "What about Bailey? We can't just quit now."

Yeah, we can. Dylan shifted from paw to paw. *Dylan's Dog Squad must eat!*

Sumo brightened. "I've got an idea. We'll send a Be On The Look Out to the Dylan's Dog Squad volunteers. With all of them looking, we'll find Bailey in no time." Sumo wiped his forehead again and turned his Angels cap around backward. "We should've asked them to help us in the first place."

"Uh-uh. No volunteers. We told Holly we'd keep this confidential."

Listen to Sumo.

"We are." Sumo pulled out his cell phone and his thumbs attacked the screen. "The volunteers are cool. I'll tell them it's a top-secret assignment."

"No."

Yes.

Sumo ignored him and read over his text before looking up. "I told them to be on the lookout for a five-foot, hairy male with black hair wearing a red and blue cape."

"Won't they think the cape part is weird?"

Uh, yeah.

"Nah. When they figure out Bailey is a chimp, they'll think it's awesome." Sumo's thumbs went back to his screen. "I'm telling them to ask around about missing Amazon packages and mail, too."

"Okay, I guess."

Sumo hit Send and smiled. "Lunchtime."

Casey put Dylan's dish and the empty water bottle into his backpack. "I wanted to go home anyway. Dylan has a forty-foot training leash we used in his agility class. If we can hook the leash onto Bailey's collar, I think it would be easier than using bungee cords to bring him back."

Dylan rolled his eyes up to Casey. *You think?*

They walked back to their bikes and Casey unzipped Dylan's bike trailer. "Let's go home, Little Buddy."

Dylan hopped in, circled once, then plopped onto the comfy cushion. *My feet are tired. I'm tired.* He laid his muzzle on his front paws and closed his eyes. *Just enough time for a world class snooze before lunch.*

"When we get to my house," Casey zipped up the front screen of the bike trailer, "Mom is going to ask what we've been doing."

Dylan's eyes flew open. *Uh-oh. Mom.*

"Are you going to tell her Dylan's Dog Squad got its first case?"

"Uh-uh. Mom would ask a zillion questions about the case. If I tell her our client is a kleptomaniac chimp, she'll freak."

Right.

Sumo put on his bike helmet and hooked the strap. "What are you going to say?"

Casey swung a leg over his bike and pushed off. "I'll think of something."

Dylan heaved out a sigh and rolled over onto his side. *Oh boy.*

CHAPTER FOUR

"Hey," Sumo yelped when he saw the patrol car parked in front of Casey's house, "how'd the cops find out about Bailey so fast? I told you we shouldn't have taken this case."

Dylan pressed his nose against the side screen of the bike trailer and studied the shiny patrol car. *Are we going to the slammer?*

"Suck it up, Sumo." Casey pedaled past him. At the top of his driveway, Casey took off his bike helmet and waited for Sumo to catch up.

Sumo skidded to a stop beside him. "You wouldn't listen and now we're in trouble."

"Relax. It's probably Uncle Rory."

"Your uncle is a Detective Lieutenant with Brea PD." Sumo chewed on his lower lip. "If he finds out we're mixed up with Bailey, he'll have to arrest us. We'd be accomplices. Or Accessories. Or something. Maybe I should go home before he sees me."

Does Uncle Rory arrest little dogs? Whine.

"If we're in trouble and you split, Uncle Rory would just go get you." Casey unzipped the screen on Dylan's bike trailer and ruffled his ears. "We're home, Little Buddy. Get out."

No. Dylan squinted up at Casey. *I don't want to go to the slammer.*

Casey hooked Dylan's leash onto his collar and dragged him out. "C'mon. You're always hungry."

Dylan trooped along behind him. *This may be my last meal as a free dog.*

Casey eased the front door open, peeked inside, and checked out the living room. He waited a moment and then motioned for Sumo and Dylan to follow. They slipped in and Casey closed the door.

Sumo whispered, "The coast is clear."

A rattle of dishes came from the kitchen. "Casey. Sumo. Go wash your hands."

"Yikes!" Sumo jumped and grabbed Casey's arm. "Do you have cameras in your house? How did your mom know we were here?"

Casey raised both hands palm up and mouthed, "Dunno."

Mom knows everything.

Casey called back, "Hi, Mom."

More rattle of dishes. "We're having lunch on the deck. It's a beautiful day."

"It's only a beautiful day if you haven't been tromping around Brea hunting for a criminal chimp," Sumo griped.

Dylan lifted his snout to the air and sucked in yummy smells. *Lunch makes every day beautiful.*

"Great, Mom." Casey leaned down and unhooked Dylan's leash. "We're hungry."

"Rory is here."

"Told you," Sumo hissed. "Your uncle is here to arrest us. Maybe I'm not so hungry."

I am. Dylan broke away from them, raced through the living room, did a bun burn on the hardwood floors, and skidded to a stop at the deck door. He scratched once. *Arf!*

"Hurry up and wash your hands." The fridge opened and closed.

"Mom would never let Uncle Rory arrest us on an empty stomach. She'd make us eat first."

"That's good." Sumo sighed.

"I hope," Casey added under his breath and started walking toward the powder room. "Anyway, you heard Mom. We need to wash our hands."

Two minutes later Casey and Sumo were outside and sliding into their chairs. French dip sandwiches were already on their plates.

Dylan was prancing back and forth between Casey's and Sumo's chairs. *Mom promised me a sandwich.*

"Hi, guys," Rory said when they sat down. He reached for the pitcher of lemonade and filled their glasses. "I wanted to see you."

"Why?" Sumo blurted out.

"It's been a while." Rory's eyebrows drew together, and he said slowly. "I was in the neighborhood. I thought I'd stop in, see my favorite sister."

"I'm your only sister," Mom laughed, coming out with a basket of French fries and Dylan's lunch. "I haven't heard from you all morning, Casey. What have you been doing?"

Looking for a stupid chimp. Melting in the hot sun. Worrying about getting arrested. Pick one.

Mom put the French fries on the table and showed Dylan his lunch.

Arf! Thanks, Mom! Dylan dove in as soon as his dish hit the ground.

"Uh," Casey slid French fries onto his plate before

passing the basket to Sumo, "looking around. Took Dylan for a walk." He grabbed the catsup bottle, shook it, and drowned the fries under a red puddle. "The usual."

Mom looked at Sumo.

"Yeah." Sumo waved his sandwich. "Thanks for lunch, Ms. D."

"Of course." She helped herself to French fries. "What are you doing this afternoon?"

Casey sat up straighter. "We're going to hang out at Sumo's."

Mom went on Mom Alert. "Is Ingrid at home, Sumo?"

"Yeah."

Mom filled Rory in. "Sumo's mom is on her honeymoon. Ingrid is the housekeeper. You've met her. She takes care of Sumo when his mom is gone."

Which is all the time.

"I heard your mom got married again." Rory reached for the catsup. "Who is it this time?"

"The guy who owns the winery in Paso Robles. He's got tons of money. Mason somebody."

Dylan scratched at Sumo's chair. *Michael.*

"Michael," Mom corrected.

Sumo never gets the guy's name right.

"Whatever. Anyway," Sumo put his cell phone next to his plate, "after Italy they're going to Paso Robles. They've got to see an architect about the new house Mom wants."

"You're moving to Paso Robles?" Rory asked.

Sumo wiped his greasy fingers on his shorts. "That's what Mom says."

You should live with us. Whine.

Rory bit into his sandwich and his cell phone went off. He wiped his mouth with a napkin, looked at the screen, and groaned. "Mrs. Purdue."

Casey made a face. "The crazy old lady with purple hair who lives near Olinda Elementary School?"

Rory nodded, put his sandwich down, and sent the call to voice mail. "The very one."

"Why does Mrs. Purdue have your cell phone number, Lieutenant Kellan?"

Rory clenched his jaw. "She was my second-grade teacher."

Mom shuddered. "Mine, too. Longest year of my life." Another shudder. "Everyone called her Purple Purdue because everything about her was purple."

Dylan was snuffling around Casey's chair for crumbs. He stopped and raised his head up. *What's purple?*

Casey gave him a French fry. "Purple is a color, Little Buddy. Grapes are purple."

Dylan gulped down the French fry and whined. *What are grapes?*

"Her clothes and shoes were purple," Mom explained. "Her hair was purple. All her pens, pencils, and paper were purple. The flowers on her desk were always purple. All day long she drank some nasty purple liquid from a purple coffee cup." She covered her eyes with both hands. "She gave me nightmares."

That's a lot of purple. Whatever that is. Dylan took another French fry from Casey and chomped it open-mouthed.

"Me, too," Rory said, picking up his sandwich again. "She's even crazier now, Sis. Somehow, she got my cell phone number and calls me all the time. Last week she reported seeing a snowman in her neighbor's yard."

"Get out," Sumo said through a mouthful of roast beef sandwich. "Really?"

Rory gave a half laugh. "Her neighbors had been

invaded by bees and they'd called the exterminator. Mrs. Purdue saw the guy in their backyard. The woman is never without her binoculars—they're purple, of course. The guy was wearing one of those white suits," Rory's free hand made a circle around his head, "with a protective head covering. Mrs. Purdue was convinced he was a snowman. She called me every three minutes until I responded." Rory traded his sandwich for his glass of lemonade. "Captain Rizzoli is at the end of her patience with the woman," he took a swallow, "but we are here to protect and to serve."

"What's her problem now, Uncle Rory?"

"This is almost funny." He started to take another sip of lemonade but smirked instead. "Mrs. Purdue is certain your neighborhood has—these are her words, a roving vigilante."

Dylan pawed Casey's leg. *What's a vigilante?*

Casey stroked Dylan's head. "That's someone who runs around fighting crime."

Uncle Rory does that.

"This person takes the law into his own hands, Little Buddy. Can't do that."

Oh. Dylan thought about that. *Sounds kind of fun.*

Mom started laughing. "How did she come up with the vigilante idea? That's pretty wild even for her."

Rory's cell phone went off again and he read the screen. "Guess who?" He sent it to voicemail. "Mrs. Purdue claims she saw a short, hairy man in a red and blue cape running through her backyard. When she yelled at him to stop, he scampered up a tree and disappeared." He rolled his eyes. "Must be too much purple in her hair dye."

Guys! Dylan swung his head from Sumo to Casey. *It's Bailey!*

"Yeah," Casey scratched Dylan's head and locked eyes with Sumo, "she sounds crazy to me."

"A red and blue cape?" Mom was laughing so hard she was holding a hand over her heart. "Stop! Really?"

Oh yeah, Mom. Really.

Rory's radio went off. He got up from the table and walked away. When he came back, his face was grim. "That was Captain Rizzoli. Now Mrs. Purdue is calling her." He pushed his chair in. "Thanks for lunch, Sis. I've got to see Mrs. Purdue. Captain's orders."

"Do you have to go? We have brownies and vanilla ice cream for dessert." She waited a moment and added, "I made them just for you."

"Sorry, Sis." He gave her a kiss on the cheek. "Next time."

Too bad for you but not for me. I love vanilla ice cream!

"Awesome, Ms. D." Sumo rubbed his stomach. "Your brownies are the best."

"Sorry, Mom," Casey kicked Sumo under the table, "we can't stay. Got to go to Sumo's house."

Her eyebrows shot up. "You two are giving up dessert? Since when?" When she got no response, she gave them a pretty smile. "I'll call Ingrid. I'm sure it will be all right."

"No! Uh, I mean," Sumo stammered, "she's busy."

Casey nudged Dylan out of the way and scooted his chair back. "Are you going to check out Mrs. Purdue now, Uncle Rory?"

"Yes, although I really hate to miss those brownies." Rory sighed and hitched up his gun belt. "Oh, Sis. I meant to tell you to be careful. We've gotten several reports about stolen mail and packages in this area."

Bailey is on a crime spree.

Mom put her napkin beside her plate. "That is serious."

"No kidding." Sumo crammed his last French fry into his mouth and held up his cell phone. "In California messing with the mail is a misdemeanor and has a one-year jail sentence. Under Federal law, the punishment is more serious."

Rory slid his cop eyes Sumo's way. "You know this because?"

Sumo swallowed hard and gave his cell phone a weak pat. "Google. I like to keep up."

CHAPTER FIVE

Dylan felt Casey's bike slow to a stop and then heard him unzip the front screen of his bike trailer. His muzzle twitched on his paws.

Casey tapped him lightly on the shoulder. "Wake up, Little Buddy."

His back leg kicked out once. *Why?*

"We're here."

Dylan stirred, brought his face up, gave a huge yawn, and let his mouth snap shut. He blinked at Casey. *My snooze was just getting good.*

"You gotta see this, Dylan. Mrs. Purdue has the only purple house in Brea."

Purple is a very strange word. When you say purple, your lips move up and down. Dylan tried moving his mouth up and down a few times. No sound came out. *Forget it. Sign language is easier.*

"She's so weird." Sumo's thumbs were tapping the screen of his cell phone. "I'm letting Dylan's Dog Squad volunteers know Mrs. Purdue spotted Bailey."

"Okay."

Dylan padded out of his trailer and heavy flower scents bombarded him. *Achoo!* His ears flopped over his eyes, and he shook them off. Big flower bushes ran along the sidewalk. Little flower bushes lined the driveway. Fat flowers spilled out of pots on the porch. *That's a lot of flowers. Achoo! Achoo!* Dylan swiped at his wet nose with his paw. *Yikes!* Dylan looked up at Casey. *My nose is leaking.*

"I know, Little Buddy. She really likes purple flowers."

Dylan hauled his head back and sneezed again. *Achoo!* He dropped down, buried his face in his paws, and rubbed his snout back and forth. *Much better.*

"Check out the purple Tesla in her driveway," Casey said.

Sumo looked up from his cell phone, gave the Tesla the once over, and then went back to work. "Must be a custom paint job. Tesla's colors are boring."

Dylan studied the car for some clue but gave up. *I really need to find out what purple is.*

"Uncle Rory is here." Casey nodded toward the patrol car. "But I don't see him."

"Mrs. Purdue's side gate is open," Sumo said. "Maybe he's in the backyard."

"Maybe." Casey slipped off his backpack. "This is so awesome, Little Buddy." Casey pulled a container of brownies out and showed it to Dylan. "This is how we're going to find Bailey. It's my best idea yet."

Dylan blinked and looked away. *I don't think so.*

Sumo snorted. "More like the stupidest idea."

I'm with Sumo.

"I can't believe Ms. D fell for it."

Me, either. Mom's pretty smart.

"It's genius," Casey insisted.

Dylan whined. *I don't think genius means what you think it means.*

"Look, Mom felt bad Uncle Rory had to leave and miss his favorite dessert. She made it just for him. So, when I said we'd drop the brownies off at Mrs. Purdue's," Casey grinned, "Mom was all for it. Besides, Mrs. Purdue's house is on the way to your house."

"Won't your uncle think it's weird we show up at a crime scene with a bunch of brownies?"

Good point, Sumo. Uncle Rory is pretty smart, too.

"You watch too much TV. There's no crime scene. Uncle Rory is responding to a call from crazy Mrs. Purdue." Casey went on, "I'll tell him Mom sent us. While we're talking, Dylan will just happen to be off leash and wandering around." Casey shrugged. "Dylan will pick up Bailey's scent and find him." Casey patted his backpack. "I have Dylan's forty-foot training leash. We'll hook it onto Bailey's collar and have him back to Holly in no time."

Sumo wasn't so sure. "Won't your uncle tell us to go home?"

"Not when I show him the brownies." Casey's grin got bigger. "Mom makes the best triple chocolate brownies in the world. There's no way Uncle Rory will pass them up."

"Me neither." Sumo took the container from Casey and looked inside. "Wow! Five brownies." He jammed a brownie into his mouth, held the container out, and mumbled, "Want one?"

"Yeah." Casey took a brownie and bit into it.

Dylan got up on his hind legs and pawed Casey's thigh. *Where's mine?*

"You can't have chocolate, Little Buddy. It'll make you sick." Casey reached into his shorts pocket for Dylan's treat bag and gave him one. "Sorry, it's not vanilla ice cream. I owe you."

Dylan chomped the treat down. *You bet you do.*

"Oh man," Sumo closed his eyes and rubbed his stomach, "that was awesome." He helped himself to another brownie.

"Hey! Now there are only two brownies left."

"Relax." Sumo broke the remaining brownies in half. "See? Four brownies. That's almost five." Sumo snapped the lid back on. "He'll never know."

Casey took the container back and tucked it under his arm. Then he closed both hands into fists and tapped his right fist on his left wrist. "Ready to go to work, Dylan?"

Ready!

Casey opened his backpack and found the plastic bag with Bailey's shirt. He took the shirt out and brought it close to Dylan's nose. "This is Bailey. Dylan, find Bailey."

Dylan sniffed the shirt once and his upper lip curled. *Brownies smell better.*

Casey said, "Let's go."

Casey, Dylan, and Sumo headed for the backyard but stopped when they heard the screams of sirens.

"Sounds like they're coming this way," Sumo turned back to the street. "What's going on?"

Two patrol cars rounded the corner and raced to the curb in front of Mrs. Purdue's house. Officers jumped out and sprinted for the backyard.

Casey tugged slightly on Dylan's leash. "Let's go see."

They found Mrs. Purdue lying on the grass, surrounded by Rory and two officers.

Sumo grabbed Casey's arm, pulled him back, and whispered, "Are you thinking what I'm thinking?"

I'm thinking it's not fair if Uncle Rory gets to arrest Bailey. Bailey is our client. We have first dibs.

"Yeah," Casey whispered back. "Bailey."

Rory was crouched beside Mrs. Purdue. "You're bleeding. Please lie still." He pressed a cloth to her forehead before giving orders to his officers. "Morrison, check around the house. Tanaka, check the garage."

"Who are we looking for, Lieutenant?" Morrison put his hand on his gun, a scowl on his face, and surveyed the yard.

Rory cleared his throat but didn't look up. "The suspect is a short, hairy male wearing a red and blue cape."

Dylan pawed Casey's leg. *Yup. That's Bailey.*

Morrison started to say something but changed his mind. "Right." He turned to Tanaka. "You heard the Lieutenant. Follow me."

Tanaka only nodded and sprinted after Morrison.

Casey and Dylan walked closer. "Hey, Uncle Rory." Casey unhooked Dylan's leash and put it in his shorts pocket. "There you go, Little Buddy."

Rory frowned. "What are you boys doing here?"

Dylan wiggled his butt. *Tracking our first client in Dylan's Dog Squad's first big case.*

Sumo mumbled, "We, uh."

Casey jumped in, "Mom sent us."

"Leave me alone." Mrs. Purdue swatted Rory's hand away and the cloth went flying. She smoothed her long, purple muumuu over skinny, white legs. Purple sturdy shoes peeked out from under the hem of her dress.

Rory put a hand on Mrs. Purdue's shoulder to keep her still. "Your head is bleeding, and you may have a concussion."

"What I have, Rory Donovan, is a lowlife vigilante skulking around my house," she griped. "He knocked me down. That's assault and battery. You, the police, have failed to protect me."

Rory returned to the boys and sucked in a breath. "I'm a little busy right now. Whatever it is, can it wait?"

"Mom sent us," Casey repeated and held out the container. "Brownies."

Chatter came from Rory's radio. He pressed a button and whispered to the boys, "Hold on." After a few seconds, he clicked off and said to Mrs. Purdue, "Paramedics are on their way."

"What are you waiting for?" she snapped and raised up on one elbow. "The vigilante is hiding in my garage. Go after him!"

Dylan sniffed the air. *No, he isn't.*

A lone siren wailed in the distance and amped up.

"My officers are investigating," Rory soothed, trying one more time to settle Mrs. Purdue back down. "Please lie still."

"Don't you use that patronizing tone with me, Rory Donovan!" She glared at him and jabbed a purple fingernail in his face. "You were a mouthy kid in my second-grade class and now you're a mouthy adult." She sniffed loudly. "I can't believe you're the police and carry a gun. You could shoot someone."

"Don't tempt me," Rory said under his breath.

"What?" she crabbed.

The siren cut off, ending in a whoop. Doors slammed and footsteps pounded their way. Two paramedics in navy pants and white shirts hustled ahead of an attendant pushing a gurney.

"I said, here are the paramedics." Rory stood up and moved aside to let the paramedics get to work. He walked over to Casey and Sumo and raked a hand through his dark hair. "She hasn't changed a bit since I was in her class." He crossed his arms over his chest and sighed. "So, why are you here again?"

"Mom told me to give these to you."

"Right!" He smiled happily and grabbed the container. "Colleen makes the best brownies. I'll share them with the other officers." Rory removed the lid, squinted at the four, tiny brownies, and frowned. "Maybe not."

Dylan rubbed against Casey's leg and panted. *It's hot out here.*

Casey reached down and ran a hand along Dylan's muzzle. "Thirsty, Little Buddy?" He rooted through his backpack, found a bottle of water and Dylan's collapsible water dish. He poured some water into it.

Dylan drank the water, lifted his face, and let his ears flap in the summer breeze. *Ah, nice.* Dylan shook his ears. A blur of black ran across the lawn behind Rory and dove behind a huge palm tree. Dylan whined. *Bailey?*

Casey saw Bailey, too, and nudged Sumo. "Uh, Sumo."

Sumo stood on tiptoe and looked over Lieutenant Kellan's shoulder. "Uh, yeah."

Bailey jumped out from behind the palm tree, spread his legs wide on the ground, waved his hands in the air, and bared his teeth.

Casey, Dylan, and Sumo gulped.

Bailey jumped back, behind the tree.

"What?" asked Rory. He turned around, slowly swept the backyard, and came back to them. "Did you see something?"

"Nuh-uh." Casey shrugged, not taking his eyes off the palm tree. "I, uh, I've never been in Mrs. Purdue's backyard. It's really big."

A second passed before Bailey leaped out again. He waved his hands in the air and gave another toothy grin.

Whine. Dylan cocked his head.

Bailey disappeared behind the palm tree again but not for long. He hugged the big tree with both hands and stuck a hairy foot out to one side. Then he wiggled his toes. The toes were followed by his hairy leg inching out bit-by-bit. Bailey gave a few scissor kicks in the air and peeked around the tree.

Bailey's a funny chimp. Whine.

"Yeah," Sumo agreed, bobbing his head up and down. "It's a big yard, Lieutenant Kellan. A *really* big yard. We could, uh, play baseball in it. It's so big."

Rory pinned them both with his cop eyes. "Uh-huh."

Casey and Sumo kept quiet.

Bailey leaned slowly to his left, letting half his face appear from behind the tree. He stared at Dylan.

Dylan leaned to his right and stared back at Bailey.

Bailey slowly drew his lips back.

You have very big teeth. Dylan let his mouth hang open. *I have forty-two teeth.*

Bailey stayed very still. His red and blue cape danced around him in the summer breeze.

Dylan sighed. *I wish I had a cape like yours. Arf!*

"Lieutenant," an officer called, "we're clear here."

Rory nodded to the officer and hitched up his gun belt. "Want to hang out for a while, boys? I can take a break." He shook the container. "We have brownies."

"That's okay," Sumo mumbled, "we had some."

Casey started laughing but stopped when Bailey jumped out from behind the palm tree. He landed on both feet and made a face.

Whine. Dylan wiggled his butt and turned in a circle. *Casey! Sumo! Let's go!*

"Oh, hey, Sumo," Casey said taking his cell phone out of his shorts pocket and checking the time. "Aren't you supposed to call Ingrid?"

"What?" Sumo spotted Bailey. "Uh, yeah. That's right. I need to call Ingrid." He held his cell phone up. "Tell her we're coming."

Rory had his cop stare on them. "What are you boys doing today?"

"Going to Sumo's." Casey fumbled in his shorts pocket for Dylan's leash and pulled it out. "The usual."

"Okay," Rory dragged the two syllables out. He waited but got nothing else. "Thanks for bringing the brownies."

Dylan planted his front legs on the ground, but he kept his rump in the air. *Bailey! Arf! Arf!*

Bailey returned Dylan's arf! with rapid gibber and screeching.

"What's that noise?" Rory looked up, searching the sky. "Birds?"

Bailey dropped to all fours. In a heartbeat, he covered the distance from the palm tree to the long row of bushes separating Mrs. Purdue's yard from her neighbor's yard.

"Wow," Casey and Sumo said softly.

Dylan shot off, following the black flash and billowing cape.

When Bailey reached the bushes, he bounded over them without slowing down.

"Sorry, Uncle Rory. Dylan!" Casey raced after Dylan. "Come back here."

"Dylan," Sumo yelled, "stop."

"Do you need help?" Rory called after them.

"No. Thanks!" Casey waved a goodbye and kept going. "Hurry up, Sumo."

Sumo came alongside him. "Remember what Holly said?" he panted, his short legs struggling to keep up with Casey's long legs. "Don't chase Bailey."

"Oh, yeah." Casey picked up the pace. "Too late now." He yelled, "Dylan!"

Dylan was rocketing across the yard, his ears flying away from his face. *This way, guys!* He reached the bushes ahead of Casey and Sumo, dropped down, and bellycrawled under the bushes after Bailey.

CHAPTER SIX

Dylan kept low to the ground and worked his way through the thick bushes. Branches tore at his ears and scratched his face. *Ow! Maybe tracking Bailey isn't such a good idea.* Dylan dug in with his back paws anyway and pushed himself toward daylight. He struggled out and stood up, shaking dirt and leaves from his ears.

Dylan started to sniff the air for Bailey but stopped. The chimp and his red and blue cape were easy to spot. Bailey was zipping across the huge backyard and heading straight for a swimming pool surrounded by umbrellas and chaise lounges.

Do chimpanzees like to go swimming? Dylan tried to imagine Bailey splashing and having fun in the pool. *Seems kind of strange but it's a hot day.* Dylan started running after Bailey. *Casey and I go to swim parties all the time. They're fun.*

When Dylan got closer to the pool, he noticed two girls in swimsuits stretched out on chaise lounges. Dylan started to circle around the girls.

Not Bailey.

Arf! Bailey, go around the girls! Arf!

Bailey ignored Dylan and kept going straight. He was a chimp on a mission.

Arf! Arf!

"Did you hear that?" One of the girls sat up and started to take a sip from a drink in a frosty plastic tumbler. "Sounds like a dog barking." She paused, still holding the tumbler close to her lips, and searched the yard. When she saw Bailey running toward them, she reached over and shook her sister's arm. "Alexa!"

Alexa kept her face turned up to the sun but managed to mumble, "What, Nicole?"

Bailey leapfrogged over Nicole.

Nicole ducked and spilled the cold drink down the front of her. "Yeck!" she sucked in a breath and sputtered, "I'm sitting in lemonade!"

Bailey landed on the little table next to Nicole. The table rocked and bottles of suntan lotion fell over. He chattered, jumped down, and ran away.

Oh no.

"Help, Alexa!" Nicole screamed and scrunched her legs up close to her body. She pointed to Bailey as he skipped over beach towels and flip-flops on the ground. "It's some big hairy thing!"

Alexa sat up and tossed off her sunglasses. "Oh, wow."

Dylan ran faster but he was getting tired. *Holly was right. Bailey can really move.*

"This is so awesome." Alexa dug her cell phone out of her tote bag and aimed it at Bailey. "I think it's a monkey. Or a chimp. Ape, maybe." She followed Bailey with her cell phone, getting him on video as he headed toward the pool. "Why is he wearing a cape?"

Dylan reached the girls, dropped down, and stomach-crawled under their chaise lounges. When he came out the other side, he gave a shake and went after Bailey.

"Yeck," Nicole said. "Now I've got dirt on me."

Bailey was making good time. He raced along the edge of the pool until he came to the low diving board at the deep end. Bailey put one foot on the diving board and then hopped up. He walked to the middle of the diving board.

Dylan padded up to the diving board, panting hard. *Arf! Come back, Bailey.* Dylan looked toward Mrs. Purdue's yard. *Hurry up, Casey. I could really use your help.*

Bailey looked over his shoulder and his cape billowed around him.

I don't know how to dive. Dylan put his front paws on the board and waggled his buns. *I only know how to swim. Whine.*

"Look at that," Nicole said. "He, whatever he is, has a friend."

"The dog is cute," Alexa said keeping her cell phone aimed at Dylan and Bailey. "He can run pretty fast for a little guy."

Casey and Sumo sprinted into the backyard, looking left and right.

"There," Casey pointed to Dylan and Bailey before taking off in their direction.

Nicole waved. "Sumo! Casey! What are you doing here?"

Sumo saw them, waved, but didn't slow down. "We'll be back."

"Do you need help?" Alexa shouted, "Want us to call the police? They're next door at Mrs. Purdue's."

"No!" Casey and Sumo shouted.

"Stay there, Dylan," Casey called. "We're coming."

Dylan saw Casey and wiggled in place. *Hurry up! I've got Bailey!*

Bailey disagreed. When he saw Casey and Sumo running toward him, he bared his teeth and erupted into hitch-pitched gibberish.

Sumo grabbed Casey by the arm and pulled him back. "This isn't good. Chimpanzees show their teeth when they feel threatened. The sound Bailey is making means he's afraid."

"How do you know this?" Casey frowned. "Have you been reading again?"

"Bailey is Dylan's Dog Squad's first client." Sumo rolled his eyes. "One of us needed to know more about chimps. That would be me since you hate to read."

"Yeah, okay, fine." Casey let it go. "What should we do?"

Bailey didn't wait for them to figure it out. He ran to the end of the diving board and gave it a two-foot bounce. He and his cape went flying. His rump landed hard in the middle of the pool. Water shot up four feet in the air and sloshed over the sides of the pool.

Dylan dropped down to the ground and raced along the tiled edge of the pool. He slipped on some water and his paws went out from under him. Dylan skidded on his butt and landed in the pool.

Dylan surfaced and dogpaddled slowly in place. *Ah! The water feels good.* He shook out his muzzle and looked around for Bailey. *Yikes!*

Bailey was still in the middle of the pool, flailing his arms. His mouth was wide open and his round, black eyes were darting everywhere. When he saw Dylan, he cried out.

Oh no! You can't swim! Dylan dogpaddled in a circle, searching for Casey.

"Dylan!" Casey shouted. He dropped his backpack on the ground and kicked off his flip-flops. "Sumo! Help me!"

I'm coming, Bailey! Dylan dogpaddled closer to Bailey. Bailey slapped the water with both hands, sending a mini tsunami Dylan's way. *Agh! Stop splashing.*

Bailey began to sink. The water went up to Bailey's shoulders. Then up to Bailey's chin. Then Bailey's round face disappeared.

Hurry, guys! Dylan dogpaddled in place. *Bailey's in trouble!*

For a moment Bailey's red and blue cape floated on the surface of the pool. Then it sank, too.

Arf! Arf! Dylan saw Casey and Sumo dive into the pool. *Follow me, guys!* Dylan plunged his face deep into the water and latched onto Bailey's collar. Dylan tried to pull back and dogpaddle.

Bailey had other ideas. His long arms waved about, and his legs kicked out.

Stop! You'll drown us. Help, Casey!

Casey yanked Dylan up by his middle, bringing Bailey with him. "Sumo, get in here. Grab Bailey."

Sumo got between them and hooked an arm around Bailey's chest. Sumo leaned back with Bailey and struggled to do a sidestroke. "It's okay, Bailey. Calm down. You're safe."

Bailey clobbered Sumo in the face and got free.

Dylan wiggled away from Casey. *I'm coming, Bailey!* Dylan dogpaddled over to Bailey, got his collar, and a mouthful of cape between his teeth. Dylan gave it everything he had and did his best to tug Bailey backward.

Bailey gave up the fight and went limp.

"Good job, Little Buddy." Casey joined them, holding onto Dylan, and bringing them both into the shallow end of the pool. Casey tucked Dylan under his arm and helped Bailey sit on the top step of the pool.

Bailey stayed put and wrapped his arms around himself. His silent grin came and went but his black eyes never left Dylan.

"I heard you got a dog." Nicole stood at the edge of the pool, holding a stack of beach towels. "Is this Dylan?"

"Yeah." Casey lifted Dylan up and put him next to Nicole. "This is, uh, his friend Bailey."

"That's cool." Nicole smiled and nodded. "Our little brother has an invisible friend."

Dylan thought about that. *How does Nicole's brother know he has a friend if the friend is invisible?*

"Look this way, Dylan! Social media needs to see this." Alexa was holding her cell phone up and not missing a thing. "Social media fans we come to you live from Brea, California. You've just witnessed the harrowing rescue of Bailey the—what is Bailey?" She looked to Casey.

"A chimp," Casey grimaced.

"What happened to keeping this confidential?" Sumo said out of the corner of his mouth. "Holly is going to kill us dead if this video gets out."

Too late, guys.

Alexa nodded and went on. "Bailey the chimp was rescued by Dylan. Dylan is a very brave pup." She knelt and brought her cell phone closer to Dylan's face. "Do you have a few words to say to your fans?"

Arf!

She laughed and blew Dylan a kiss. "You heard it first, Dylan fans!"

Sumo took Bailey's hand and helped him out of the

pool. Nicole handed Sumo a towel. "Thanks." Sumo draped the towel over Bailey's shoulders and started to rub.

Casey climbed out of the pool, took a towel from Nicole, and used it to wipe Dylan's face and ears. He ran the towel over Dylan's back and legs. "It's so hot, Little Buddy. You'll be dry in no time."

Dylan shook himself, sending his ears slapping around his face.

"You scared me, Little Buddy." Casey hugged him close. "I'm glad you're safe."

Dylan rubbed against Casey and then slurped canine kisses on his cheek. *I'm glad you saved us.*

"Check this out, everybody," Nicole said, pointing to Sumo and Bailey.

Sumo was drying Bailey with the towel and the chimp was making soft mewing noises.

Bailey smiled at Sumo but didn't show his teeth.

"Hey," Sumo smiled back and worked the towel over Bailey's shoulders, "he's not showing his teeth. That's good. That means he's liking this."

"We need to get going, Sumo." Casey brushed Dylan's topknot out of his eyes. "Time to get Bailey home."

"How are you going to do that?" Nicole asked.

"Oh, yeah," Sumo said slowly and stopped drying Bailey. "Our bikes are next door."

Casey, Dylan, and Sumo looked at Bailey.

Bailey was sitting on his haunches, his thumb and index finger in his mouth. He rolled his black marble eyes up at them.

"Since you two are best buds," Casey grinned, "Bailey can ride on your handlebars."

Sumo made a face. "Get serious." He tipped his head. "We could ask your uncle to give us a ride to Holly's."

Two boys, a dog, and a chimp riding in a patrol car in Brea? No way.

"Nuh-uh." Casey shook his head. "Uncle Rory might figure out Mrs. Purdue isn't crazy after all."

Yup.

"So, what's your brilliant idea?"

Casey picked up his backpack and rooted around inside. He brought out Dylan's forty-foot training leash. "Holly said Bailey likes to go for walks. We'll walk him to her house."

Sumo's eyebrows shot up. "Are you nuts? This is Brea. People will think it's weird we're out walking with a chimp."

True.

"Bailey's had good luck so far today. No one's seen him." Casey shrugged. "Holly's house is pretty close." Casey shrugged again. "We'll walk fast. Right, Little Buddy?"

Dylan pawed Casey's thigh. *Do I get vanilla ice cream after this?*

Casey handed the wet towels to Nicole. "Thanks for helping."

"No problem. It was fun." She bent down and patted Dylan on his head. "You can come back any time." She hesitated and then gave Bailey a light pat on his head. "You, too."

Bailey clapped his hands together and gave her a tight-lipped smile.

"Hey, Bailey likes you." Casey hooked the training leash onto Bailey's collar.

Alexa waved her cell phone. "You can't believe how many hits the video has already gotten on social media. Dylan and Bailey are famous."

Uh-oh. I hope Holly doesn't follow social media.

Casey and Sumo exchanged looks.

"Uh, let's go, Sumo." Casey gave the training leash to Sumo. "You can walk Bailey."

"Aw, man." Sumo screwed up his face. "Why me?"

Bailey shrieked and hopped up and down.

"You've upset your new best friend." Casey picked up Dylan's leash. "That's not nice. Besides, you need to walk Bailey because I've got Dylan. Right, Little Buddy?"

Right.

They left the girls and walked to the front yard. When they got to the sidewalk, Bailey reached out with one hand and latched onto the middle of Dylan's leash. He grinned at Dylan, gave the leash a little shake, and started to walk.

Dylan put it in reverse and sat down.

"Hey," Sumo said, "Bailey wants to walk Dylan."

Grr.

Casey tried to pry Bailey's hairy fingers off Dylan's leash. Not possible.

Casey, do something! Dylan shook his head, trying to get free. *This is embarrassing.*

Casey crouched down and whispered, "Listen, Little Buddy. We have to get Bailey home fast before anyone sees him." He pointed down the street to Holly's house. "Also, we have to give Bailey back to Holly before she sees the video on social media."

Dylan stared at him. *What's in it for me?*

Casey dug into his shorts pocket and opened Dylan's treat bag. "Want a treat?"

Dylan swallowed the treat but didn't budge.

"All right, all right." Casey gave Dylan two more treats and waited until he'd finished them. "You drive a hard bargain."

Dylan body-bumped Casey's leg. *I would've let Bailey hold my leash for two treats.*

Casey, Dylan, Sumo, and Bailey started walking. Bailey looked all around him and gibbered nonstop.

"I can't believe no one's out," Sumo said. "It's the middle of the afternoon."

"Nothing ever happens in Brea." Casey waggled Dylan's leash. "Right, Little Buddy?"

Dylan flicked his ears and glanced up at Casey. *What do you call two boys and a dog walking down Lambert Road with a chimp on a leash?*

They turned onto Holly's sidewalk and Bailey took off, his cape flapping behind him. He was still attached to Dylan's training leash, but he made it to the front door. Bailey pounded on the door, waited a second, and then hopped in front of the bay window. He pressed both hands flat on the window, put his face up close to the glass, and looked in. Another hop and he was back on the front doorstep, banging with both fists.

The front door opened slowly, and Holly poked her head out.

"Here's Bailey." Casey reached down and unhooked the training leash. "Told you Dylan's Dog Squad would find him."

Bailey launched into chimpanzee gibberish, waved his hands in the air, and darted past Holly.

Holly glared at Casey. "Bummer," and she slammed the door.

CHAPTER SEVEN

Casey stared at Holly's closed door. "Dylan. Sumo. There's only one thing for us to do."

Dylan didn't wait. He turned and trotted down the front walk. *Follow me, guys.*

Twenty minutes later they were sitting at a small table outside Brea's Ice Cream. Casey was rocking back on his chair, working on a dish of chocolate chip ice cream. Sumo was slurping up a pistachio milkshake.

Dylan stretched out on his blanket and nuzzled his empty dish of vanilla ice cream. *That was good.* He angled his muzzle up to Casey and whined. *How about seconds?*

"Actually," Casey used his spoon to swirl the ice cream around in its dish, "today went okay. Dylan's Dog Squad solved its first case."

"Are you crazy?" Sumo waved his straw in the air and a glop of pistachio ice cream flew off.

Dylan caught it midair. *Hmm. Not bad.*

"Our client nearly drowned," Sumo reminded him.

"Well, yeah." Casey licked his spoon. "What's with

that? If chimps can't swim, why did Bailey jump into the pool?"

"Chimpanzees can see color. Kind of like the way we do. Bailey probably saw the blue water and went for it."

Casey reached down and ruffled Dylan's ears. "Good thing Dylan came along and saved Bailey."

Sumo tipped his milkshake up and drained the last of it. "Good thing Dylan can swim."

Dogpaddle.

The front doors of Brea's Ice Cream opened and Crystal, the manager, walked over to their table. She clicked her pen and held up her pad. "Anything else, guys?"

Dylan sat up straight. *I'd like some more.*

"I'm still hungry." Casey dropped his chair to the ground and checked his cell phone. "Dinner isn't for a long time. Want to split a vanilla milkshake, Little Buddy?"

Arf!

"What about you, Sumo?" Crystal gestured toward the ice cream shop. "Our special today is black cherry ice cream."

Sumo considered this. "A scoop of black cherry and a scoop of cookie dough with," he paused, "walnuts, Oreo crumbles, M&Ms, and," he thought some more, "coconut."

Crystal scribbled it down. "Very healthy. Coconuts are a fruit, nut, and a seed."

Dominick came out of the ice cream shop and walked over to their table. "Crystal, I put the delivery away." He took off his Brea's Ice Cream plaid vest and handed it to her. "I'll see you tomorrow."

Dylan sighed. *I've always wanted a vest.*

Crystal nodded. "Thanks."

"Hi, guys." Dominick reached down and petted Dylan. "I see Dylan's Dog Squad had a busy day."

Casey exchanged looks with Sumo. "What do you mean?"

Dominick pulled his cell phone out of his pocket. "Dylan's all over social media." He gave Dylan another pet. "I can't believe Dylan saved Bailey the chimp."

"How do you know Bailey's name?" Sumo asked.

Uh-oh.

"Are you kidding? Bailey's famous. His owner Rachel Langdon is famous. She's like," Dominick waved his hands in the air and searched for words, "*the* most famous prima-tologist *in the world.* She lectured at my class at Cal State, Fullerton last semester."

That's really famous!

Dominick was on a roll. "The San Diego Zoo is having a special event. It's sold out," he grinned happily, "but I've had my ticket for a week."

"No kidding," Casey mumbled.

"I can't wait." Dominick lifted a hand. "Bye, Dylan. See you tomorrow, Crystal."

Crystal nodded. "I'll get your orders, guys." She put her pen in her vest pocket and left.

"Oh man," Sumo groaned and fell back into his chair. "This isn't good."

"Relax." Casey tossed it off. "Holly's ten years old. She probably doesn't follow social media."

Casey's cell phone started vibrating on the table.

Want to bet?

Sumo leaned over and checked the screen. "That's Holly! Do you think she knows?"

Casey touched the screen on his cell phone, hitting Facetime. Holly's angry face filled the screen. "Hi."

"What did you do to me?" She screamed.

I think she knows.

"What's the matter?" Casey kept his voice calm but raised his eyebrows. "Is Bailey gone again?"

"No, you idiot," Holly raged. "Thanks to you, my grandfather found out Bailey was gone. He says because I was irresponsible—can you believe that crock—Bailey can't sleep in the tree house at night anymore. He says Bailey has to be with me all the time until Rachel gets home."

"That might be a good idea," Casey agreed. "You'll be able to watch him."

"Are you insane? Now I have to share *my room* with Bailey."

I share Casey's room and sleep on his bed. What's wrong with that? Dylan rolled onto his stomach and wagged his short tail. *I get most of the bed.*

"Look, it's just for a few days," Casey said. "How bad can it be?"

The screen on Casey's cell phone lurched. A second later Holly's cell phone slammed into a wall. Casey's cell phone screen went black.

"Uh, I'm guessing Holly thinks it'll be bad," Sumo offered.

The doors to Brea's Ice Cream parted and Crystal walked over with their order on a tray. She set the ice cream on the table and wiped her hands on her apron.

Dylan popped up and put his paws on the table. He pushed his snout closer and sucked in the scent of vanilla milkshake. *Yum.* He wiggled his buns.

"The video of Dylan saving Bailey just went viral." Crystal smiled. "Isn't that great?"

Casey poured some vanilla milkshake into Dylan's collapsible dish and put it on the ground. "Oh, yeah," he said without looking up. "Great."

"Great," Sumo echoed and reached for his ice cream.

Dylan slid his paws off the table and pounced on his milkshake. When he'd finished, he looked from Casey to Sumo. Both were sitting still, staring straight ahead. Neither one had started on their ice cream. Dylan licked his lips and whined. *Guys?*

CHAPTER EIGHT

Arf! Dylan jumped up and planted both paws on their front door. *We're home!*

"Hold on, Little Buddy." Casey gently grabbed Dylan's shoulders and pulled him away from the door.

What?

Casey crouched beside him. "We have to get our stories straight."

Uh-oh. Dylan sat on his rump and sent his brown eyes Casey's way. *You mean our lying.*

"Don't look at me like that. You know it's not nice to judge."

It's not nice to lie to Mom.

"You know how Mom is. As soon as she sees us, she'll start out the way she does, all casual-like, and ask us about our day."

It was an awesome day! We found Bailey. Dylan danced in place. *Dylan's Dog Squad solved its first case.*

"Listen," Casey cupped Dylan's muzzle in his two hands, "here's the thing. Dylan's Dog Squad promised Holly we'd keep the case confidential. Thanks to Alexa and the video she posted on social media, now the whole world knows Bailey got out."

Crazy chimp.

"So, we've got to keep quiet about today so nobody else finds out about Bailey. Especially Mom. You know how snoopy she is." Casey chewed on his lower lip. "I hope Holly got rid of the stuff Bailey, uh, found and brought home."

Bailey didn't find anything. He stole that stuff.

"I know you're thinking we should've told Uncle Rory that Bailey took the mail and the packages." Casey shook his head. "We couldn't tell Uncle Rory because then he would've told Mom. Anyway," Casey went on, "Holly can worry about that. Right now, we have to worry about Mom. Got it?"

What came after we should've told Uncle Rory?

"One more thing. You can't look like you've been swimming. Don't tell Mom anything about that."

Why not?

"We told Mom we were going to Sumo's. If she found out we went swimming, she'd ask where." Casey got Dylan's brush out of his backpack and brushed Dylan's topknot out of his eyes. "Then she'd call Alexa and Nicole's mom. Then she'd find out about Bailey."

Mom's pretty smart.

Casey huffed out a breath. "We can't let that happen." He went to work on Dylan's ears with the brush. "There. Nice and smooth."

Dylan shook his head and his ears fluffed out.

Casey sat back on his heels and inspected Dylan all over. "Okay, you'll do." Casey stood up and opened the door a crack. "I don't hear anything. Mom must be in her office. Just remember, go along with everything I say. Got it?"

Sort of.

"Remember, let me do all the talking."

I can't talk.

Casey crossed the foyer and headed for the stairs. He stopped suddenly and Dylan ran into him.

Yip!

"Sorry, Little Buddy. One more thing, don't tell Mom we had ice cream."

Dylan padded along behind Casey on the stairs. *What about the milkshake?*

Outside of Mom's office, they stopped and listened. "Sounds like she's in a Zoom conference with Cranky Pants," Casey whispered. He put his index finger to his lips, signing Quiet.

They slipped inside Mom's office.

Mom glanced over and gave them a little finger wave before turning back to her computer screen. "A cookbook for teens is a delightful idea, Cranston." She reached for her cell phone. "I can get Gina and Priscilla working on the illustrations right away."

Cranky Pants's ancient face scowled into the monitor. "I'm counting on you, Colleen."

"Of course," Mom smiled sweetly.

"This younger generation knows nothing about day-to-day living." The old man leaned forward in his leather wingback chair and pounded a gnarly fist on his mahogany desk. A crystal paperweight jumped. "The younger generation needs to learn to be self-sufficient. They need to learn skills that matter." His bony chin nodded once. "They need to learn useful skills like cooking." Cranston's faded blue eyes look skyward and he murmured, "I remember so vividly, as a small lad, Cook teaching me to make my first souffle."

Casey snorted.

Mom shot Casey The Look.

Cranston bowed his head slightly and gave a rare smile. "Mother and Father were so proud of my accomplishment."

"Every parent's dream," Mom agreed.

"What?" Cranston's happy memory was gone, and his cranky self was back.

"I said of course they were." Mom opened the calendar app on her cell phone. "Let's get together at the end of the week. I'll have some ideas for you then."

Cranston scowled. "Ideas are useless." He slammed his palm down flat on his desk, narrowly missing a porcelain figurine. It rocked back and forth. "You need to create a marketing plan to make the cookbook sell."

"I've never let you down." Mom hit End of Meeting. She reached for Dylan and settled him beside her in her big chair. "Ugh. That man."

Dylan whined and Mom scooted over, giving him more room. *Thanks, Mom.*

"Cranky Pants wants to publish a cookbook for kids?" Casey leaned against the door jamb. "That's dumb."

"Cranston Pantswick," Mom corrected and ran a hand down Dylan's back. "You need to be respectful."

Dylan kicked out a back leg. *Tickles.*

"Right," Casey smirked. "Like you never call him that."

"Let's put it this way. Cranston owns the biggest children's publishing company in North America. I represent talented writers and illustrators, so we're a match." She cocked her head and drummed her fingers on her desk. "Children's cookbooks have been done to death. This one needs a gimmick to make it sell." She shrugged and changed the subject. "What did you do today?"

"Went to Sumo's. Hung out."

Mom waited.

"The usual."

Mom waited some more and then hugged Dylan close to her. "Why does Dylan smell like chlorine and vanilla ice cream?"

Dylan wiggled out of Mom's arms. He stretched across her lap and put his muzzle on her keyboard. *You're on your own, Casey.*

Casey came closer and sniffed Dylan. "Really, Little Buddy? What's with that?"

"Hmm." Mom tapped the screen on her cell phone and held it up. "Frank Matias called me today." She arched an eyebrow at Casey. "*Mayor* Matias."

"I know who he is."

Dylan blinked up at Casey. *I know he's Holly's grandfather.*

"Frank called with a wonderful invitation."

"Oh yeah?"

"Yes," Mom dragged it out. "Not only for you, me, and Dylan, but Sumo, too."

"No kidding."

No kidding.

Mom propped her cell phone up on her desk and turned it so Casey could see the screen.

Dylan swiveled in the chair and shoved his face closer to the cell phone. *What are we looking at?*

"Social media fans we come to you live from Brea, California. You've just witnessed the harrowing rescue of Bailey the—what is Bailey?" Alexa looked to Casey.

"A chimp."

Alexa nodded and went on. "Bailey the chimp was

rescued by Dylan. Dylan is a very brave pup." She knelt and brought her cell phone closer to Dylan's face.

"Do you have a few words for your fans?"

Arf!

That's me! Dylan wiggled his buns and slid off the chair. *Ow!*

Mom picked Dylan up and put him back in the chair.

"Mom."

She held her right hand up and cut him off. "Casey, I know more than you think I do."

I hope not.

Mom took a deep breath. "I'm proud of you and Dylan's Dog Squad. It took a lot of courage for you to start this business. I know how much you want to become a dog trainer and eventually have your own school. I'm on your side all the way."

Dylan leaned against her and rubbed his muzzle across her shoulder. *You're the best mom.*

Mom hesitated. "I'm *disappointed* you didn't tell me you'd gotten your first case." She ran a hand through Dylan's ears and snuggled him close to her. "You know you can tell me anything."

Anything but not everything. Dylan slurped a kiss on Mom's cheek. *Like Bailey is a criminal chimp.*

"Frank is extremely grateful you returned Bailey. Bailey means the world to his daughter Rachel."

But not to Holly.

"For some reason," Mom reached for a tissue and wiped off Dylan's slobber, "Bailey seems to have a habit of getting lost."

Dylan flicked his ears. *Try running away.*

"Anyway, Frank would like to extend Dylan's Dog Squad's," she paused, searching for the right word, "employment. Frank has asked all of us to go with him, his grand-daughter Holly, and Bailey to the San Diego Zoo for the big ribbon-cutting ceremony. Rachel will meet us there."

Wow! I get to go. Dylan looked up at Mom. *What's a San Diego Zoo? What's a ribbon-cutting ceremony?*

"What would we do?"

"He wants Dylan's Dog Squad to keep tabs on Bailey. Make sure he doesn't run off."

Casey made a face. "You mean like be a chimp bodyguard?"

Mom laughed. "I guess you would call it that."

Casey laughed, too. "See, Little Buddy. I told you having Bailey for a client was no problem. You worried for nothing."

Not me.

"We've got to call Sumo." Casey reached for Dylan and put him on the ground. "I can't wait to tell him about this."

Which part?

"Congratulations, Casey and Dylan." Mom leaned back in her chair and swiveled. "Dylan's Dog Squad has another case."

Whine.

CHAPTER NINE

Dylan belly-flopped onto the grass at Dream Big K-9 Academy. *Whew! I need a world-class snooze.* He heaved over onto his back, sent his paws straight up in the air, and then let them drop onto his chest. His tongue flopped onto the grass. After a moment, Dylan gave life another thought. *I really need vanilla ice cream.*

"Man, this American Kennel Club Canine Good Citizen Test is brutal." Casey dropped onto the ground next to Dylan and kicked off his flip-flops. "Seems like we've been here a hundred years."

No joke. Dylan wiggled his tongue, spit out some grass, and rolled over onto his stomach. He shook his ears out and looked up at Casey. *How long is that in dog years?*

"I'm proud of you, Little Buddy. You're doing great."

Dylan scooted closer and stretched his muzzle across Casey's lap to study the exercise field. *Rottweilers, German Shepherds, Great Danes, Labradors, Golden Doodles, Golden Retrievers, Belgian Malinois, and Australian Shepherds are everywhere.* Dylan's heart sank. *I'm always the little guy.*

"There's got to be like a zillion dogs here," Casey said.

I can only count to ten.

Evaluators wearing armbands and carrying iPads moved between the dogs and their handlers and made notes.

"I don't get why there has to be ten parts to the AKC test," Casey grumbled. "I don't get why it's such a big deal to do each one right the first time."

I don't get why I don't get treats during the test. Dylan whined. *This is a lot of pressure.*

Casey pulled Dylan onto his lap. "I know you're thinking about the last time you took the test."

I flunked.

"That was then, and this is now. You've worked hard and you know your stuff." Casey gave him a hug. "Cheer up. You've already passed the first eight parts. There are only two more to go. You've got this."

Dylan huffed out a breath. *I haven't gotten my vest yet.*

"I can't believe it. There's got to be like forty evaluators here and who do we get stuck with? Grouchy old Roger. Talk about rotten luck."

Roger says mean things to me. He says I'm not a dog because I'm short and fluffy.

"Since Roger owns Dream Big K-9 Academy, you'd think he'd at least pretend to be friendly."

He doesn't like people.

"What's really wild is that he tells everyone else how smart you are. Remember it was his idea for you to take this test?" Casey eased Dylan off his lap and onto the grass. "You'd think it'd kill him to say something nice to you." Casey laughed, stood up, and stepped into his flip-flops. "No wonder he's always covered with scabs and bandages. Even dogs don't like him."

I don't like Roger. He yelled at me all morning and now

my ears hurt. Dylan leaned against Casey and looked up. *When you become a dog trainer, everyone will like you.*

Casey and Dylan watched a young woman put a vest with the AKC Canine Good Citizen patch on her Siberian Husky. The Husky gave a happy yip and wagged its furry butt. Then it jumped up, put its paws on the woman's shoulders, and covered her face with sloppy kisses. The woman hugged her dog.

Casey waggled Dylan's leash. "Are you checking out that dog's vest?"

Dylan was still glued to the dog. *The vest is awesome. Whine.*

"When we leave today, you're going to be wearing a vest with your very own AKC Canine Good Citizen patch on it."

Dylan's heart sighed. *I need to pass the AKC Canine Good Citizen test today, so I can get a vest with an AKC patch. If I get a patch, then Dylan's Dog Squad will get more business. If we get more business, then someday you can become a dog trainer.* Dylan pawed Casey's leg. *We will always be together.*

"Today's the day," Casey promised.

Yes! I won't let you down.

Casey checked his cell phone. "Okay, Little Buddy. Break time is over." Casey reached down and ruffled Dylan's ears. "Let's go show mean old Roger what you've got."

Aren't you forgetting something? Dylan danced in a circle. *Arf!*

"You're right." Casey opened a plastic bag and held out a treat. "This is for good luck."

Dylan chomped it open-mouthed and body-bumped Casey. *I feel better now about the whole thing.*

When they reached the office, a new group of dogs and handlers were waiting to check in.

Hey! Dylan dodged a Saint Bernard.

"Hold on." Casey stopped and picked Dylan up. "It's mobbed in here today. I don't want you to get stepped on."

Dylan hooked his muzzle over Casey's shoulder and watched a Doberman and his handler get in line behind them. Dylan turned back around and snuggled against Casey's chest. *Sometimes it's okay to be the little guy.*

Dylan stared at the backs of the people's heads in front of them. *This is taking forever.* When Dylan's stomach rumbled, he nuzzled Casey's cheek. *I need another snack.*

"Sorry, Little Buddy. I heard your stomach growl. You can have a treat after we finish. You know the AKC rules."

The AKC rules stink.

When they got to the front of the line, Casey said, "Hi, Jean. It's really crowded today."

"We've been testing since eight o'clock this morning." Jean found their names on her iPad and touched the screen. "Okay, I'll let Roger know you're back from your break." She reached up and petted Dylan. "Only two parts left to pass, Dylan. Ready?"

Dylan slurped a kiss on her hand and looked up at her from under long eyelashes. *Today is my big day.*

"Weren't you supposed to be Dylan's evaluator?" Casey asked.

Jean swiveled in her chair and showed off a walking boot. "Sorry. I tripped in class last week. I'll be in this thing for six weeks."

Ouch.

She lowered her voice. "You two have nothing to worry about. I've seen your scores and they are the highest Roger has ever given." She smiled. "He's always saying Dylan has potential."

He says I look like I belong on a little girl's bed. He says I'm too cute to pass the AKC test. Roger makes me so mad. Dylan thought about growling but that was against the AKC rules. *The AKC has a lot of dumb rules. That makes me mad, too.*

"I've never heard him say that." Casey rolled his eyes. "Why is he always in a bad mood?"

Jean shrugged. "That's Roger's way. I've worked with him for twelve years." Another shrug. "I don't think he knows any other way to be." She leaned forward on her elbows, made sure no one was listening, and whispered, "Underneath it all, Roger has a good heart."

Must be way underneath.

Casey shifted Dylan in his arms and scanned the sea of faces behind him. "Where is Mr. Sunshine anyway?"

"He'll be here." Jean turned her iPad around for Casey. "While we're waiting, please read the Responsible Dog Owner's Pledge out loud and sign here."

"I will be responsible for my dog's safety. I will properly control my dog by providing

fencing where appropriate, not letting my dog run loose, and using a leash in public. I will ensure that my dog has some form of identification, which may include collar tags, tattoos, or microchip ID."

I have a microchip. Dylan whined. *I'll never be lost.*

Casey signed his name. "Okay, Little Buddy. You're one step closer to your vest."

"Look, lady," Roger pushed through the people. He was yelling into a cell phone held in one hand and waving an iPad in the air with the other. "I've told you there is no way your pitiful excuse for a dog is going to graduate from Dream Big K-9 Academy. Not now. Not ever. *Never.* He doesn't have what it takes and neither do you, so get lost."

People standing behind Casey and Dylan went quiet. Jean suddenly found her iPad interesting.

"Oh, yeah," Casey snorted. "A good heart."

I don't think so.

Roger shoved his cell phone into his shorts pocket and came around to Jean's side of the desk. "Next time my sister calls, tell her I'm busy."

Jean sighed. "Will do, Boss."

Dylan rubbed his muzzle against Casey's chin. *Sister? No kidding.*

"Amazing, Little Buddy."

Roger checked Jean's iPad and then scowled at Casey and Dylan. "For cryin' out loud. Why are you still here?"

Why are you still cranky?

"Since we already took the first eight parts of the test with you," Casey smirked, "then you know we only have two parts left."

Roger raked a hand wrapped in a grubby elastic bandage over his face. His fingernails were bitten to the quick. "Suit yourself. You and," he pointed his iPad to Dylan, "have fifteen minutes. One mistake and you're history. Got it?"

"We're not leaving until Dylan gets his vest and AKC patch."

Thanks, Casey.

Roger brought his face close to Casey's. "Don't bet on it. Each test must be done perfect and the first time. You get one shot at it."

"Dylan can do it."

Roger sneered. "I wasn't talking about Dylan."

Behind Roger's back, Jean gave Casey a thumbs up and mouthed, "Good luck."

Casey started to say something, but Roger was already disappearing into the crowd. Casey hugged Dylan to his chest and raced after Roger. They found him standing in front of the two-story storage building at the north end of Dream Big K-9 Academy.

"About time you showed up." Roger dragged his hand across his sweaty forehead. "It's hot out here."

Dylan brought his muzzle up and caught the late afternoon breeze. *Feels good to me.*

"Next time you need to be somewhere," Roger growled, "try moving faster."

"The next time you need us somewhere," Casey put Dylan on the ground, "try telling us where we're going."

Roger ignored Casey. "Only two parts of the AKC Canine Good Citizen Test left. First up, the Reaction to a Distraction, followed by Supervised Separation." He folded his arms across his chest.

Dylan took in the black and blue bruises covering Roger's arms. *Looks like tattoos.*

"The Reaction to a Distraction is my favorite part. You want to know why?" Roger kept his arms folded and tried a grin. Not a good look for him.

Yikes. You look scary.

"Most dogs and handlers can't cut it and flunk out." He wagged his head happily back and forth. "Yup. The sorry pathetic losers are humiliated, disgraced." He jabbed the air between them with his bandaged hand. "They never make it to the last part, Supervised Separation, and I'm betting you won't either."

"Ha!" Casey shot back. "I'm ready. Dylan's ready."

"No talking during the test," Roger snarled.

A shadow fell across the ground. Dylan raised his head up and saw a man standing in the second-story window of the storage building. The next moment, the man heaved a wooden chair out the window. It crashed four feet from where Casey and Dylan were standing.

"Holy, moly, joly!" Casey yelped. He grabbed Dylan and pulled him close. "What was that about, Roger? Dylan could've been hurt."

Dylan whined happily and snuffled Casey's cheek. *Don't tell Roger but I saw it coming.*

Roger scowled and rubbed his upper left arm. "Big deal."

Casey stood up. He started to say something else but stopped when he saw Roger was still rubbing his arm. "What's the matter?"

"What part of no talking don't you understand?"

I bet a dog munched you. That's why your arms are all beaten up. Dylan whined. *Good.*

Ear-splitting music suddenly blasted from somewhere, lasted for five seconds, and then stopped. An explosion boomed behind the storage building, shaking the ground, and sending a mushroom of brown dust high above the building. Moments later a rider on a red Ducati motorcycle tore around the side of the storage building, spitting up debris in its wake.

"Hey," Casey said, shielding his eyes from the dust and dirt with both hands, "is that Jean?"

The rider came closer and idled five feet away from Dylan. She revved the bike's engine before touching her red helmet once in a mock salute and then zooming off.

Roger didn't bother to look up from his iPad. All his efforts were focused on using one finger to type. "Yeah."

"How can Jean ride a bike? Her foot is in a walking

boot."

"Can't keep her off that stupid thing," Roger muttered and stabbed at his screen with his finger.

"Since you're typing," Casey grinned, "that must mean Dylan passed the ninth part—Reaction to a Distraction." Casey's grin got bigger. "Gee, Little Buddy, I wonder what's next? Oh yeah, the last part, Supervised Separation."

Separation? No! Stay with me.

"Shut up, kid." Roger deleted something and tried again. He wiped his sweaty forehead with the back of his hand. "Go to the office and wait by the registration desk."

Dylan pawed Casey's leg. *I don't want to be stuck alone with Roger.*

Casey knelt beside Dylan. "This is the last part, Little Buddy. Wait here for three minutes with grumpy old Roger. Remember, don't move. Don't wander off. Stay put. You can do this."

Roger doesn't like me. Dylan's shoulders slumped. *I need you. We need to stay together.*

Casey brushed Dylan's topknot out of his eyes and whispered, "Whatever you do, don't listen to Roger. He'll try to say something to trick you."

Roger doesn't want me to pass the test. Don't go.

"Keep thinking how great you're going to look in your vest." Casey ruffled Dylan's ears and kissed the top of his head. "Remember, ignore Roger for three minutes."

Okay.

Casey stood up. "Remember, stay here. Don't leave. No matter what. Got it?"

Got it. Dylan watched Casey go and then let a low whine escape. *How long is three minutes?*

"For cryin' out loud."

I'm not turning around. If I turn around, you'll say

something mean to me. Dylan sank to the ground, stretched his front legs out, and waited for three minutes to be over.

"Dylan."

No. Leave me alone. Dylan twitched his nose and put it on his paws. *You want me to flunk.*

Thump!

What was that? Dylan waited but didn't hear anything else. *I'm not going to look.* Dylan let another moment go by and sighed. *I can't help it. I've got to look.* Dylan glanced over his shoulder.

Roger was lying on the ground.

Dylan pulled himself into a sitting position and faced Roger. *I bet this is a mean trick to make me flunk.*

"Go, Dylan, go," Roger's voice rasped out. His right hand struggled to his chest, and he clutched the front of his T-shirt. "Get help. Get Casey." Roger closed his eyes and his hand let go of his shirt.

Dylan padded over and pawed Roger's arm. *When Casey and I were in Basic Skills Class, we saw a dog play dead once. Are you playing dead?* Dylan studied Roger. *Your face is sweaty.* Dylan brought his muzzle close to Roger's mouth. *You're breathing kind of funny.*

I don't know what to do. Dylan sat down. *Casey told me to stay here. The AKC rules say I have to stay here for three minutes. If I leave you, I'll flunk the test.* Dylan nudged Roger's limp hand with his nose. Roger's hand slid off his chest and fell to his side. *If I flunk the test, I'll never get my vest.*

I really, really want my vest.

Roger moaned.

Dylan whined. *This isn't fair. Why should I give up my vest and AKC patch for rotten old Roger? I don't like Roger and Roger doesn't like me.* Sigh.

CHAPTER TEN

"Dylan, help me. Please."

What? Dylan's head jerked back, and he blinked twice. *You said please. Wow.* Dylan brought his face close to Roger's. *Hmm. You don't look so good.*

"Dylan, please," Roger struggled to get each word out. "Get Casey."

This is the AKC Canine Good Citizen test. That means I must be a good citizen. Does being a good citizen mean I must help Roger? Dylan plunked his buns down and scratched his left ear. *I don't remember that part.*

Dylan shook his ears out. *If I leave Roger, the AKC rules say I won't pass the test. If I don't pass the test, Casey can't become a dog trainer.* Dylan's heart began to break. *I can't let Casey down. He's counting on me.* Dylan looked at Roger. *Roger is counting on me, too.*

Dylan thought about the rules, but they didn't make sense. *The AKC rules stink.*

Roger moaned.

Okay, okay. I'll get Casey. He'll know what to do. Dylan blew out a heavy sigh. *It's a good thing you said please.*

Dylan took off running as fast as he could toward the office. His long ears flew away from his face and his paws skimmed the ground.

When Dylan got to the office, it was still packed with handlers and dogs. Dylan began working his way slowly to the front. *Casey where are you?* Dylan craned his neck upward. *All I see are dogs and legs.* Two girls moved aside, and Dylan caught a glimpse of shaggy brown hair and a washed-out T-shirt. *Casey?* Dylan scrunched down low and started checking out everyone's feet. *Tennis shoes. Ugly shoes. Strappy sandals—who wears sandals to run around in an exercise field? That's weird. Boots. More tennis shoes.* His heart skipped. *Beat-up leather flip-flops —yes!*

Dylan still couldn't see Casey, but he knew where Casey was. *I'm coming!*

A large lady with a black and brown Airedale Terrier moved in front of him, blocking his path. Dylan tried tunneling through her thick piano legs but got stuck.

"Help!" the woman shrieked. "I'm being attacked! Help!"

Dylan whined. *Hey! I'm the one that's stuck.*

"Uh." The woman's voice went down a notch when she saw Dylan wedged between her two meaty calves. "Are you a stuffed animal?"

A stuffed animal? Dylan looked down at his fluffy chest, legs, and paws. *Who me?* Dylan shimmied free and started weaving between dog legs and people legs.

"Stop!"

"What's going on here?"

"Dog off leash!"

Hands grabbed for Dylan.

No! Leave me alone. Arf!

"Dylan?" Casey called from somewhere up front. "Is that you, Little Buddy? Come here."

Dylan pushed his way through, ran up to Casey, and planted his front paws on Casey's knees. *Arf! Arf!*

"What are you doing here?" Casey rubbed Dylan's muzzle with both hands and scanned the crowd. "Where's Roger?"

Arf! Arf! You've got to come! Dylan dropped down and shifted from paw to paw. *Now!*

"What's going on?" Jean called from the desk. "Where's Roger?"

Arf! Come see for yourself.

"I don't know. Dylan's excited about something. We need to check."

Jean pushed her chair back from the desk and motioned for a man wearing a Dream Big K-9 Academy shirt to come over. "Louis, take care of registration for me." She slid her iPad over to him. "I'll be back."

"Sure." Louis sat down and cheerfully announced, "Next."

Dylan didn't wait for Casey and Jean to follow him. Instead, he charged ahead to the storage building. Dylan collapsed at Roger's side and nuzzled his hand. *Still sweaty.* Dylan scooted closer and put his paws on Roger's chest. *I brought Casey and Jean.*

Roger griped, "What took you so long?"

Hey, I ran as fast as I could.

Casey gently eased Dylan off Roger. "It's going to be okay, Roger."

"My chest," Roger groaned. "Must be indigestion. Get me up."

"Nah-uh." Casey put a hand on Roger's shoulder.

"9-1-1?" Jean was standing off to the side and talking

into her cell phone. "This is Jean with Dream Big K-9 Academy. We need paramedics right away. Something has happened to Roger Bennett." She listened for a moment and her eyes slid to Roger. "He's conscious, and he's in pain. Come to the storage building on the north side of Dream Big K-9 Academy. There is a parking lot." She talked some more and then went over to Casey and Roger.

Casey looked up. "What did they say?"

"They said to keep him calm." Jean put her cell phone in her pocket and crouched beside Roger. "He's so pale. I've never seen him like this." She tried pushing Roger's damp hair from his forehead, but he slapped her hand away. She ignored him and turned to Casey. "I'm worried."

"Me, too."

Me, three.

A long low siren sounded in the distance and grew louder.

"They asked me if Roger has been sick." Jean gave a small laugh. "I said he was too ornery to get sick." She bit her lip. "I shouldn't have said that." Jean looked at Casey. "Did you notice anything different about him today?"

Casey shrugged. "He was in a rotten mood, like usual."

Roger was rubbing his arm. Tell her his face was sweaty.

Jean gave a thin smile. "That's Roger."

"You know," Roger growled, fighting for breath, "I'm right here. I can hear you."

"Be quiet," Casey and Jean said together.

He's not yelling. He must be sick.

A siren whooped once, and doors slammed in the parking lot. A minute later a paramedic in navy pants and a white shirt appeared. He spotted them and hustled over. Behind him, two attendants bumped a gurney across the uneven ground.

"I'm Brian." The paramedic gave them a quick smile before kneeling beside Roger. "Who called us?"

Jean spoke up. "I did. I'm Jean."

"I'm Casey and this is Dylan." Casey hooked Dylan's leash to his collar and moved aside. "Dylan is in training here."

Arf! I was supposed to get my vest and AKC patch today. Dylan's heart slipped. He could feel it breaking. *Now I never will.*

Brian looked at Jean. "I understand our friend here is Roger Bennett."

"Correct," Jean said and added, "Roger owns Dream Big K-9 Academy. We work together."

"Why was Roger out here?"

"We've been giving the American Kennel Club Canine Good Citizen test since eight o'clock this morning. It's very intense and very few dogs pass the test."

Dylan whined low and turned away. *Thanks for breaking my heart, Jean.*

"The last part is given out here, between evaluator and dog, just Roger and Dylan. Casey and I were waiting in the office. The next thing we knew, Dylan came running in and got us."

"Good work, Dylan. You might've saved Roger's life. You really are a good citizen."

Yup, but without a vest.

"A lot you know about anything." Roger made a face and clutched his chest. "I just had a lousy lunch."

Brian ignored Roger and got to work. "Jean, does Roger have a healthy diet?"

She laughed. "Roger has the eating habits of a coyote."

Yikes. Dylan sidled closer to Casey. *Coyotes munch little dogs.*

"That's going to change." Brian applied a pressure cuff to Roger's arm. "Has Roger had shortness of breath? Dizziness? Chest pains?"

"I don't know."

"For cryin' out loud," Roger complained, "ask me. I'm not dead yet."

"Be quiet, Roger." Jean kept her voice calm. "Let Brian do his job."

Dylan body-bumped Casey. *Tell him Roger was rubbing his arm.* Dylan watched the paramedic put silver tubes in his ears and a round silver thing on Roger's chest.

"Has he been in a bad mood? Short-tempered?"

Always.

"Not me," Roger stated.

"Roger is always crabby." Casey hesitated and looked at Dylan. "Maybe it's nothing but Roger said it was hot out here. His face was sweaty."

Good job, Casey.

"Hmm." Brian searched the blue sky above them filled with fat white clouds. "It's a nice day."

"Before Dylan started the test, I saw Roger rubbing his arm."

"Which arm?"

Casey thought. "I'm pretty sure it was his left. When I asked him about it, he said to keep quiet."

He yelled at us.

"I've had enough." Roger tried to sit up. "Get me out of here."

"That's the plan," Brian said and started to remove the pressure cuff from Roger's arm. "We're taking you to Brea-Olinda Community Hospital."

"That's good," Jean agreed and moved out of the way. "Best place for you."

"For cryin' out loud." Roger jerked his arm away and shook his fist in Brian's face. "Get lost."

Roger is being mean again. He must be feeling better.

"C'mon, Little Buddy." Casey tugged slightly on his leash, and they joined Jean.

Dylan heard a short siren sound from the parking lot and then it blipped once. Moments later Rory jogged in.

"What are you doing here, Uncle Rory?"

"I heard the call come in. I knew you and Dylan were taking the AKC test today, so I thought I'd check it out."

"That was nice of you to come by," Jean said.

Casey snorted. "Mom would've killed him if he didn't."

Rory raised his eyebrows and huffed out a breath. "You've got that right."

That's Mom.

Jean laughed. "I like your sister."

"Me too. Most of the time anyway." Rory laughed. "Colleen's amazing. She always knows everything that's going on. She was like that when we were kids." Rory nodded toward Roger. "How's he doing? What did the paramedic say?"

"Brian, that's the paramedic, hasn't said anything yet. I'm guessing Roger had a mild heart attack during Dylan's test today. Lucky for him, Dylan came and got us. If Dylan hadn't," Jean shuddered, "I hate to think what might've happened."

I like helping people. Even if it is mean old Roger.

Rory crouched down and gave Dylan a chin rub. "Today is your big day. "When do you get your vest?"

Like never. Dylan whined. *I didn't finish the last part of the test.*

Brian motioned to the attendants. "Load him up, guys." Brian waited for the attendants to wheel Roger toward the emergency vehicle before he called over to Jean, "Follow along when you can."

"Okay." Jean turned back to Casey and Dylan, reached down, and petted Dylan's head. "I appreciate everything you did for Roger, even if he doesn't." She straightened up and hooked a thumb over her shoulder. "I want to talk to Roger before he goes. Thanks for coming, Rory."

"Sure." Rory nodded. "Tell him to feel better."

Jean returned the nod and walked away.

"It's funny," Rory folded his arms across his chest and focused on Casey, "how you and the paramedics have been in the same places lately."

"Huh?"

"First at Mrs. Purdue's house and now here with Roger."

Casey kept his face blank. "Must be a coincidence."

Uh-oh. I think Uncle Rory knows something.

"I'm a cop. There's no such thing as coincidences." Rory kept his dark eyes on Casey. "Why didn't you tell me Dylan's Dog Squad was working a case when you showed up at Mrs. Purdue's house?"

"Well," Casey smiled, "we weren't. I mean not really." He shrugged. "Mom told us to drop off the brownies and that's what we were doing. Right, Little Buddy?"

Dylan leaned against Casey and looked up at him. *You're on your own.*

"Uh-huh."

"Anyway, when we got there, you were busy with Mrs. Purdue."

"I guess," Rory said slowly and cocked his head, "I should say congratulations. After all, Dylan's Dog Squad found Bailey and solved its first case."

"Thanks." Casey's smile got bigger. "Must be beginner's luck."

"Did you know," Rory shifted his weight and rested both hands on his gun belt, "since you found Bailey, the Amazon and mail thefts have stopped?"

Casey's eyebrows shot up. "No kidding." Casey jiggled Dylan's leash. "Did you hear that, Little Buddy? Must be a coincidence."

Uncle Rory says there is no such thing as a coincidence. Dylan flicked his ears. *Uncle Rory is a cop. He knows about this stuff. And we know why nothing else has been stolen.*

"Hmm." Rory changed the subject. "Your mom says Dylan's Dog Squad has another case. Something about keeping an eye on Bailey for the ribbon cutting ceremony at the San Diego Zoo."

I'm so excited. I get to go, too. Dylan turned in a circle. *I've never been to a zoo. What is it?*

Casey changed the subject, too. "Cranky Pants is driving Mom crazy. He's got some weird idea about publishing a kids' cookbook."

Rory barked out a laugh. "Good luck with that one."

A book about cooking sounds good to me.

"Exactly. Anyway, somehow Cranky Pants heard about Bailey and the San Diego Zoo thing. Now he's driving her nuts about that. He's probably thinking of a new book."

"I'm glad Cranston Pantswick is your mom's headache. That man is a lot of work."

He's another grumpy guy.

"Lieutenant," Brian called from the back of the emergency vehicle, "Roger wants to speak to Casey and Dylan. Can they come over here?"

Rory raised his hand to Brian, signaling he'd heard.

Then he turned back to Casey. "What do you think that is all about?"

I bet Roger wants to thank us for saving his life.

Casey winked at Dylan. "I bet Roger is going to tell you that you've passed the AKC test."

Really? Dylan remembered all the bad things he'd thought about Roger. *Maybe I should take some of them back.*

Chatter came from Rory's radio. He checked it and clicked off. "Sorry. I've got another call. Got to go."

"Okay." Casey waved goodbye and then let go of Dylan's leash. "Go on, Little Buddy."

Dylan raced over to Roger and put his paws up as high as he could against the gurney and wiggled his butt.

"Hold on." Casey lifted Dylan up and brought him close to Roger's side.

Roger yanked the oxygen mask off his face and pointed his grubby bandaged hand in Dylan's face. "You. Flunked."

What? Dylan's ears drooped. *Say it isn't so.*

"That's right. You're a two-time loser. No AKC Canine Good Citizen certification for you."

"That's stupid." Casey hugged Dylan close to him. "I was with Dylan. He passed."

"Only parts one through nine. Dylan didn't pass Supervised Separation." Roger sneered. "That's the rules, kid. Dog and handler must be separated for three minutes. Dylan took off in the middle of it and went after you. He flunked big time."

"If it weren't for Dylan, you might've died."

He's too mean to die.

"Maybe," Roger tossed out, "but for sure, he flunked the American Kennel Club Canine Good Citizen test."

"You listen to me, Roger Alistair Bennett." Jean hip-bumped Casey and Dylan aside and got in Roger's face. "Dylan passed the AKC test. I have the start time you logged in on the iPad. Dylan arrived at the office eleven minutes later. That means Dylan was with you and separated from Casey for more than three minutes."

"I say Dylan flunks."

"I say," Jean did a rapid finger jab in Roger's chest, "Dylan passes."

I say listen to Jean.

"Ow!" Roger winced and rubbed his chest. "Knock it off."

"Pipe down, you big baby, or I'll tell mom what hospital you're going to. She'll visit you and drive you crazy."

Roger has a mom. No way.

Brian stepped in and put the oxygen mask back on Roger. "Keep this on."

Casey couldn't let this go. "You're Roger's sister? You said you've worked with Roger for twelve years."

"That's right." Jean rolled her eyes. "I felt sorry for Roger. He'd just started Dream Big K-9 Academy but everyone he hired quit after five minutes."

Gee, I wonder why.

Casey looked from Dylan to Jean. "Roger said the woman he was yelling at on the phone was his sister."

"Monica?" Jean put her hands on her hips. "That's right." Jean laughed. "She's even more hardheaded than Roger. They're always yelling at each other."

Roger is always yelling at somebody.

"Sorry to break this up folks," Brian interrupted, "but I need to get Roger to the hospital for tests."

Jean nodded. "Take him away and give him lots of bad-tasting medicine."

"Just for that," Roger had the oxygen mask off again, "I'm cutting you out of my Will."

"So what?" Jean shot back. "I'm in Mom's Will and you're not."

The attendants slid Roger and the gurney inside the emergency vehicle. Brian closed the door and gave it a fist bump before walking around to the driver's side.

"Let's go home, Little Buddy." Casey hugged Dylan. "I'm really sorry you didn't get your vest." He hugged Dylan again and tickled his chin. "The good news is you saved Roger's life. I'm proud of you."

Thanks. I'll remember that when I'm the only dog leaving without a vest today. All the big dogs are going to make fun of me—again.

"I'm proud of you, too, Dylan. Not every dog could've done what you did." Jean ran her hands over Dylan's shoulders and tipped her head to the side. "Hmm. You look like a medium to me."

Medium? No, I'm an American Cocker Spaniel.

"There's a medium vest with the AKC patch in the office, waiting just for you." Jean winked. "I bet it will be a perfect fit."

Really? Dylan gave her a forty-two teeth smile. *I'm finally getting my vest and AKC patch. Wow!*

"Shouldn't we wait for Roger to get out of the hospital?"

Dylan clamped his mouth shut and whipped his face around to Casey's. *Be quiet.*

"Forget Roger. He isn't here." Jean gave them a big smile. "Besides, when he hears Dylan passed the test, it'll give him something new to gripe about."

"Okay, Little Buddy, what do you say?"

Arf! I say let's go show the big dogs my vest and AKC patch.

CHAPTER ELEVEN

"Mom," Casey kicked the back of the driver's seat, "why do we have to visit Roger? All the kids are hanging out at Big Belly's Pizza today. We're going to be late."

Not fair. Dylan's stomach growled. *Casey promised me cheese and mushroom pizza at Big Belly's. It's my favorite.* Dylan's stomach growled again. *I like the pepperoni pizza, too. And the mozzarella and basil pizza. And the Margherita pizza.* Dylan licked his lips and sighed happily. *I like them all.*

"What's the plan, Ms. D?" Sumo shifted in the passenger seat and held up his cell phone. "I can let the kids know when we'll be there."

Mom eased into a parking space at Brea-Olinda Community Hospital. "I told Roger you have plans and I have a meeting with Cranston Pantswick in an hour." Mom met Casey's eyes in the rearview mirror. "Roger was really in a foul mood. He actually sounded mad because Dylan saved his life." Mom shook her head and gritted her teeth. "Anyway, he insisted he had to meet with you, and it had to be today."

"Why, Ms. D?"

"No idea," Mom said and turned off the ignition. "Roger's such a disagreeable, irascible, cantankerous, querulous, fractious Neanderthal."

Whoa! That's a lot of things to be.

Casey kicked the back of her seat again. "Speak English, Mom. We're twelve."

I'm one and a half.

"Sorry." Mom reached for her purse. "I'm not looking forward to facing Roger and Cranston on the same day." She opened her door. "We'll hurry."

Yes! Then pizza!

"Casey, please help Dylan out and carry him to the front door. He just went to the groomer and must stay clean." Mom smiled over her shoulder at Dylan. "You're going to the San Diego Zoo tomorrow for Bailey's ribbon-cutting ceremony. You'll have so much fun."

Staying clean and having fun don't mean the same thing.

Casey came around to Dylan's side of the car. "Dylan's Dog Squad's second case. Pretty exciting, Little Buddy."

Ha! You didn't have to get wet all over. Dylan sat up straight in his car seat and waited while Casey unfastened his harness. *Today I'm wearing my vest with the AKC patch for the first time.*

Casey reached for Dylan. "Ready to show off your vest?"

Arf! This is the best day ever! I want everyone to see it!

At the front doors of the hospital, Sumo said, "Hold on guys." He held his cell phone up and took Casey and Dylan's picture. "Got to keep social media informed."

Dylan wiggled his shoulders. *Did you get a good picture of my vest?*

"No one's going to believe we're visiting Roger." Sumo laughed and checked the picture. "The guy has no friends."

Casey put Dylan down. As they walked across the shiny tile floor to the Information Desk, Dylan raised his snout and sniffed the air. *Smells clean. No fun.*

Behind the desk, a pleasant-looking elderly lady was busy sorting messages. Fat white curls circled her head like frosted donuts.

Mom gave the desk bell a gentle tap. "Good morning."

The woman looked up, put the messages aside, and put on her meet-and-greet face. "Welcome," she warbled in a paper-thin voice, "to Brea-Olinda Community Hospital. May I help you?" The nametag on her flowered pink smock said Tallulah.

"Yes." Mom smiled and put a file on the desk. "I'm Colleen Donovan, this is my son Casey, Dylan, and Casey's friend Sumo Modragon."

Tallulah pursed her Barbie-pink lips. Green eyes flitted from Mom to Casey and then to Sumo. Tallulah went back to Mom and cleared her throat. "I certainly see you Ms. Donovan but I only see two boys."

Arf! Down here.

Tallulah raised up on tiptoes and peered over the desk. "Hello! You're so cute."

Arf! Dylan gave her a happy grin and wagged his stubby tail.

"That's Dylan." Mom opened the file and handed Tallulah three sheets of paper. "We're visiting Roger Bennett in Room 318. This is Dylan's American Kennel Club Canine Good Citizen Certification, Dylan's authorization from Dream Big K-9 Academy giving permission for his visit today, and Dylan's pet insurance allowing him to be on the premises."

"Oh my," Tallulah stammered, and her flabby cheeks flushed the same Barbie-pink as her lips. "I know you, Dylan. You're famous. I follow you on social media." Tallulah pulled her cell phone out of her pocket, scrolled across its screen, and held it up. "See? I'm a member of Dylan's Dog Squad."

Arf!

"May I take your picture, Dylan?" Tallulah was back on her tiptoes and leaning over the counter.

Arf! Dylan got up on his hind legs and pawed Casey's thigh. *I could use a boost.*

"Hold on." Casey picked Dylan up and brought him closer to Tallulah.

Dylan sat up straight in Casey's arms. *See my vest and AKC Canine Good Citizen patch?*

Tallulah took Dylan's picture and beamed. "You look very dapper in your vest."

Dapper? Dylan nuzzled Casey's cheek. *Isn't that what babies wear?*

Casey whispered, "I'll explain later."

"Ms. Donovan, the elevator is at the end of the hall." Tallulah gave them a little finger wave. "Have a good visit."

"Thanks, Tallulah."

Dylan squirmed. Casey put him down and they trailed behind Mom and Sumo.

Along the way, Dylan peeked into the patients' rooms. Some patients sat up in bed. Some were sleeping. *Everyone here wears pajamas. Comfy.*

A nurse passed them pushing a two-tier cart. Covered plates were stacked one on top of each other. He stopped outside the next room and checked his clipboard. He wrote something on the top sheet of paper, took the lid off a plate, and looked it over. Warm food smells filled the air. He put the lid back on the plate and took it into the patient's room.

"Lunchtime," Casey announced.

Good idea! Dylan's snout twitched. *What's for lunch?*

Sumo turned around and made gagging noises. "Smells like cafeteria food."

Dylan sniffed the air. *Cafeteria food doesn't smell like anything Mom makes. Hmm. Does it taste good?* When Casey and Dylan reached the cart, Dylan pounced on the closest covered plate. One nudge with his nose was all it took. The cover flew off, hit the tile floor, and rolled.

"Dylan!"

Dine-and-dash time! Dylan dove in. He gulped down something white and mushy, followed by a dark square covered in brown stuff, and then latched onto a biscuit.

Casey reeled in Dylan's leash, got half the biscuit out of his mouth, and tossed it back onto the plate. Dylan gulped down the other half.

Hey! Dylan pawed the air. *The biscuit was mine.*

"If Mom had seen you do that, Little Buddy," Casey whispered, "we'd both be in trouble. You've got to stay clean for tomorrow." Casey put the lid back on the plate and patted it into place. "There. No one will ever know."

Dylan nudged the plate again. *I want the rest of the biscuit.*

"Hold still." Casey grabbed Dylan's face and tried wiping it with the end of his T-shirt. "You've got gravy on your muzzle."

Dylan jerked his head free and shot a long pink tongue out and around his muzzle. *No, I don't.*

"When you're wearing the AKC Canine Good Citizen vest, you've got to be good. No messing around." Casey brushed Dylan's topknot out of his eyes and stood up. "Hospitals have all kinds of rules about stuff. Especially eating the patients' food."

Dylan's stomach rumbled. *I don't know why. The food wasn't that good.*

They hustled to the elevator where Mom and Sumo were waiting.

Mom turned around and sniffed.

"What Ms. D?"

She laughed. "Strange. I just got a whiff of meatloaf."

"No kidding," Casey said.

No kidding. Dylan looked down at himself. *I don't see any.*

Dylan watched Mom press a button on the wall and the two doors parted. Mom and Sumo went inside.

Dylan stayed put. *I'm not sure about this.*

Casey threw his index finger forward, traced an arc in the air, signing Go.

No. Dylan threw his head back, nearly slipping out of his chain collar. *It looks like the inside of a really big box.*

"Has Dylan ever been in an elevator?" Sumo crouched low with his cell phone to take Dylan's picture.

Scary. Dylan plunked his buns down. *Not getting in.*

"It's okay, Little Buddy." Casey slowly tugged on Dylan's leash. Dylan's paws and furry buns slid across the tile floor and into the elevator. "It's all part of the great adventure."

"Got it, Dylan." Sumo pressed Send and stood up. "This is an awesome day for your fans."

Dylan watched Mom push another button. He felt himself lift and he started to relax. *The elevator is weird but kind of fun.*

When the elevator reached the third floor, it did a little hiccup and stopped. The doors opened and they walked out. A suspended big screen TV was on mute and playing to an empty waiting room. A blinding white hallway stretched left and right. Dozens of doors stood open to the patients' rooms.

"Wow," Sumo said. "This is a big place."

Mom murmured, "I don't see any room numbers on the walls." She checked the time on her cell phone. "It's getting late. I hope we can find Roger."

"*Sorry?*" a man's voice bellowed from the room across from them. "You're unable to fulfill my dietary needs and all you can say is you're *sorry*. What kind of a hospital is this anyway?"

We found Roger!

"Go ahead, Mom." Casey turned around and started toward the elevator. "We'll wait in the car. Right, Sumo?"

Sumo's head bobbed up and down. "Oh, yeah."

Me, too.

"Forget it, Casey." Mom snagged him by his T-shirt and pulled him with her. "Misery loves company."

"Who said that Ms. D?"

"Henry David Thoreau," answered Casey.

Did he know Roger?

They trooped inside Roger's room. Roger was sitting up in bed, holding a partially eaten Jell-O cup. A sea of empty Jell-O cups littered the bed and floor.

Jean sat slumped in a visitor's chair, her arms crossed over her chest and her walking boot propped up on the side of Roger's bed. She gave them a sidelong glance. "Hi. You're just in time."

"For what?" Mom asked.

"The hospital had the misfortune to run out of blueberry Jell-O cups," Jean began. "They only have lemon, cherry, and strawberry." She gave an exaggerated sigh.

"Since Roger doesn't like those flavors, this error on their part is unforgiveable."

Roger dug into his Jell-O cup, scooped out the last of it, and licked the spoon clean. He gave the spoon a toss, narrowly missing a pretty nurse hanging a clear bag on the stainless-steel pole next to his bed. "For cryin' out loud," Roger snarled to the nurse out of blue-stained lips, "how hard is it to find one simple little thing?"

"Mr. Bennett, I promise to search high and low for blue-berry Jell-O cups." She checked the drip on the bag. "If there are any to be found in the known universe, I'll deliver them personally to you."

"Is that sarcasm, Nurse Dragon?" Roger glowered at her. "Where did you get your nursing degree? Correspon-dence school?"

"Now, now, Mr. Bennett. You know my name is Mandy." She adjusted the flow on the bag. "In a few minutes, you'll be feeling much happier. And so will we," she muttered under her breath.

"I'll feel happier when you get out," Roger growled.

"Cut it out, Roger." Jean let her walking boot slide off the side of the bed and drop to the floor. She leaned over and tapped her brother's arm. "Remember, Mom is only a phone call away."

"You're as bad as Nurse Dragon," Roger griped.

"Call someone else if you need anything, Mr. Bennett," Mandy chirped. She gave the room a cheerful smile and a fast exit.

Mom came closer. "I would ask how the patient is, but I'm sure everyone on the third floor knows."

Roger scowled and pulled the bedsheet higher on his chest. "About time you got here."

"Like you have anything better to do," Casey said and slid his eyes to Mom.

"Casey," Mom warned but let it go.

Dylan started walking around the room. *Not much to look at.* Dylan gave up and padded over to Casey. He leaned against him and whined. *Can we go now?*

"Roger," Mom prompted, "you had something important to tell us?"

"Not me." Roger shifted in the hospital bed. "Ask Jean. It was her idea."

"It was *your* idea," Jean insisted. "Why can't you just spit it out?"

"Mom," Casey complained, "it's really getting late. I'm starving."

Me, too.

"Yeah, Ms. D," Sumo agreed. "I told the kids we'd be there by now."

Mom sighed. "I'm sorry but the boys and I have appointments. We need to go."

"No! Don't!" Jean jumped in, her words tumbling out fast. "Roger's doctors say he can only work part-time at Dream Big K-9 Academy for the next month. I need help with classes."

"What does this have to do with us?" Mom asked.

"Since Casey wants to become a dog trainer and have a school like Dream Big K-9 Academy someday, Roger said Casey and Dylan could help me with classes."

"Did not," Roger interrupted.

"Did, too."

"Uh," Casey hesitated, "what's the catch?"

Dylan shifted from Casey to Jean. *Yeah. What's the catch?*

"This isn't a job, kid," Roger growled. "Once I'm back on my feet, you and fluff dog can hit the bricks."

"This is so cool," Sumo said. "Social media will go crazy when it finds out Roger is doing something nice." He had his cell phone out but paused and looked at Casey. "What's the matter? This will be awesome."

"I, I can't believe it." Casey blinked and gave a slight shake of his head. "You're right. It would be awesome."

"Do it, Dude. Dylan's Dog Squad will get a ton of business."

Mom said softly, "It's what you've always wanted."

"Ah, just forget it." Roger threw up his hands. "I must've been crazy to listen to Jean. No way you can do this."

Jean cut him off. "Don't listen to him, Casey." Her eyes filled with tears, and she bit her lower lip. "We need your help. When people hear you and Dylan will be teaching classes, we'll get lots of new students. We need them desperately." She lowered her head. "Dream Big K-9 Academy has money troubles."

"For cryin' out loud, Jean." Roger jabbed the air between them with his finger. "Don't go blabbing our business to everybody!"

"I don't get it." Sumo shook his head. "You've got lots of students."

"Things are better but they're not great." Jean's voice dropped to a whisper. "When Covid-19 happened, the school closed. No school. No classes. No money. It's like the national debt to run a school like ours. When we were closed, we still had to pay the mortgage, taxes, upkeep on the grounds—everything."

"What did you do?" Casey asked.

"Roger borrowed money." Jean's mouth flatlined.

"Did you have to tell them that?" Roger snapped.

Sumo shrugged. "A lot of people borrowed money."

"You don't understand. The bank wouldn't lend us the money," Jean said slowly. "Mr. Lombardi the manager can't stand Roger."

Casey snorted. "What did you do to him, Roger?"

Roger rolled his eyes. "Nothing."

"Mr. Lombardi loves Batman, his miniature Doberman Pinscher," Jean began.

Uh-oh. I know where this is going.

"When they took classes with us, Roger wouldn't call the dog Batman. He kept calling him Ratman." She grimaced. "Anyway, Mr. Lombardi turned us down flat."

"Where did you get the money?" Mom pressed.

Jean took a deep breath. "Theo Sledge."

"Theo Sledge!" Casey barked out. "The guy they call The Sledgehammer? He's a criminal. Uncle Rory says they've been after him for years. Everybody has heard of him."

Not me.

"Yeah, he's a criminal but he has good branding." Sumo nodded to himself and dug his cell phone out of his shorts pocket. "I wonder who does his social media?"

You're not helping.

"Mr. Sledge made Roger sign loan papers and give the school for collateral. Mr. Sledge is charging us fifty percent interest." Jean gave a heavy sigh. "We can't raise the money fast enough."

"That's insane." Casey thought for a moment. "What happens if you don't pay?"

"Mr. Sledge gets the school." Jean's eyes filled with tears. "Dream Big K-9 Academy will close."

"Dude," Sumo said, "you gotta do this."

"It's up to you, Casey," Mom said softly.

"I need to ask Dylan. We're a team." Casey crouched down. "What do you want to do, Little Buddy?"

I want what you want.

"It's kind of scary. I've never taught a class before."

Dylan rubbed against him. *We took classes together.*

"You can start with the beginner's class. They're always small, and I'll be there to help you." Jean swiped at her tears. "Dylan's famous. Everybody loves you and Dylan."

That's us!

"I know it's asking a lot. If you and Dylan help us," she gave them a trembling smile, "I know we'll get enough money to pay Mr. Sledge back."

"Social media will eat this up and," Sumo grinned, "Dylan's Dog Squad will get more cases."

Then we'll always be together.

"No one can know about Mr. Sledge!" Panic flashed across Jean's face. "You've got to promise not to tell anyone."

Casey and Sumo traded looks. "Promise."

Me, too.

Dylan saw Roger leaning forward in his bed, his fingers gripping his bedsheet. *You're pretending not to care.* Dylan whined. *Our friends need our help.*

"What do you say, Little Buddy?"

Dylan pawed Casey's leg. *We can do this.*

CHAPTER TWELVE

"Boys," Mom's voice came through the intercom in Casey's bedroom, "Breakfast of Champions!"

Hooray! Breakfast is the only way to start the day. Dylan pulled himself into a sitting position, shook his ears out, and gave a jaw-cracking yawn. *I love breakfast.* He thought for a moment. *I love lunch.* Dylan snapped his mouth shut and sighed happily. *I love dinner, too.*

Casey came out of his bathroom wearing shorts and dragging a hand through his wet brown hair. "Okay, Little Buddy. We've got five minutes to get downstairs." Casey grabbed his Dylan's Dog Squad T-shirt off a chair, slipped it over his head, and looked around his bedroom. "Help me find my flip-flops."

They're always in the same place. Dylan went to his water dish where Casey's flip-flop was balanced on the edge. Dylan brought it to him and dropped it on his bare foot. *Here.*

"About time you got out of the shower," Sumo grumbled and tossed his graphic novel onto Casey's desk. "You take longer than my mom. She lives in the shower."

Casey slid his foot into the flip-flop. He found his backpack, rummaged around inside, gave up, and emptied everything onto his bed. "Where's the other one?"

Ask me.

Casey put his hands on his hips and looked around his room. "I don't get it. It was right here."

No, it wasn't. Dylan lowered himself onto his front legs and stuck his muzzle under Casey's bed. *Yup, right where it always is.* Dylan got the strap between his teeth, put his buns in reverse, and brought the flip-flop to Casey.

"Thanks." Casey wiggled his foot into his flip-flop. "Hold on, Dylan. You need your Dylan's Dog Squad bandana." Casey put it on him and rubbed him between his ears. "Hungry?"

Arf! Dylan shot out of Casey's bedroom and ran down the hall.

"Mom says no running in the house."

Agh! Dylan took the corner wide. He slipped on the hardwood floors and slid on his buns before skidding to a stop at the top of the stairs. Dylan sucked in a breath and peered down the stairs. *Whew! That was close.*

"Dylan," Mom called, "are you running in the house?"

Not me. Dylan got to his paws and padded down the stairs. Then he remembered it was breakfast time and ran into the kitchen. *Arf!*

"Good morning, Dylan." Mom reached for a spatula and stirred something in a pan. "I hope you're hungry."

Dylan sniffed the air and his heart bounced. *We're having something with cheese. Yum.*

"Hey, Mom." Casey walked in and rubbed his stomach. "We're hungry."

"Smells good, Ms. D." Sumo peeked around Casey to

see what was on the stove. "Thanks for letting me sleep over."

"You're welcome." Mom put on oven mitts and pulled a tray of jumbo banana walnut muffins out of the oven. Steam fogged up the kitchen windows.

I love muffins. Dylan sniffed the air again. *Got cream cheese? Butter?*

Mom emptied the muffins into a bread basket and handed them to Casey. "Breakfast time."

"Seriously?" Casey stared at the basket. "This is breakfast?"

Mom gave him a patient smile and pointed to the omelet pan. "Cheese and veggie omelets." She went back to the stove. "Orange juice is on the table. Go ahead and start. I'll be right in."

Okay, Mom. Dylan danced in a circle and then scampered into the dining room.

Casey and Sumo followed along and got busy with the muffins and juice.

Hey! Dylan pawed Casey's leg. *It's rude to eat in front of me.*

"Sorry, Little Buddy." Casey broke a muffin in half, popped some into his mouth, and offered the rest to Dylan. "It's hot."

Dylan woofed it down. *Not if you eat fast.*

Sumo slathered butter onto his hot muffin. A river of melted butter ran off the muffin and down his arm. Sumo licked the butter off at his elbow. "Your mom is so cool." He shoved a chunk of the muffin into his mouth and wiped his hands on his shorts.

"She's okay."

"No, really." Sumo swallowed. "She's been really cool about Dylan's Dog Squad." He waved his muffin at Casey and crumbs dropped onto the floor. "You were so chicken to tell her you wanted to start a business."

"Yeah." Casey reached for his orange juice and took a swallow. "I still can't believe we're really doing it."

"Your mom's excited for us, too. I can tell." Sumo pointed to his Dylan's Dog Squad T-shirt. "Just think, two cases in one week. Pretty soon you'll be doing dog training classes. I've got social media covered, so Dream Big K-9 Academy will get more students. They'll make lots of money and be able to pay back The Sledgehammer."

"I hope so."

Me, too.

"Yeah." Sumo went for the cream cheese and loaded up his muffin. The muffin crumbled and cream cheese landed on the front of his shirt. Sumo scraped it off with his finger leaving a white streak. "We're officially in business. I like it."

Dylan pawed at Casey's knee. *I like being together.*

"Here you go, Little Buddy." Casey held out more muffin. "You've got to keep your strength up. We have a busy day."

Mom came in with plates for Casey and Sumo and set them down.

Hey.

"Dylan, yours is coming." A minute later she was back with a placemat and a bowl of fluffy scrambled eggs. "Be careful. The cheese is hot."

Dylan attacked the bowl and was licking it clean when Mom came in with her breakfast. Dylan bumped his empty bowl with his snout and gave Mom a low whine. *Seconds?*

"Nice try." Mom tickled the top of his head and slid into her chair. "That's enough for now."

That's what you think. Dylan moseyed over to Sumo's

chair and licked up the crumbs on the floor. *Gotta love Sumo. The kid is a slob.*

"Thanks, Ms. D." Sumo was hunched over his plate and his omelet was disappearing fast. "This is great."

Dylan sat on his rump, leaned his head back, and watched the yellow mound travel from Sumo's plate to his mouth. Just as Sumo opened wide his fork wobbled. *Yes!* The egg tumbled off his fork and landed on the floor. Dylan pounced on the egg. He gave it one flick of his tongue and the egg was on its way to his stomach. *Thanks, Sumo.*

Sumo gave Dylan and the floor a glance and shoveled up more omelet.

Mom put her napkin on her lap. "Frank—Mayor Matias —called while you boys were getting ready. As you know, Jonah is covering the ribbon-cutting ceremony story for the *Orange County Register* and Anna will be our photographer. They're meeting with Rachel to arrange the schedule for today."

"What about us," Casey looked across the table to Sumo. "Are we still going?"

"Absolutely." Mom took a sip of orange juice. "This is exciting. Frank has arranged for a limousine to take us to John Wayne, Orange County Airport. Holly and Bailey are riding with us." She checked her cell phone for the time. "The limousine will be here in forty-five minutes."

"Limo!" Casey and Sumo said together.

Arf! What's a limo?

Casey picked up his fork but put it down again. "If we're taking a plane, what about Dylan and Bailey? They can't ride on the plane."

What? Dylan's heart hitched. *No limo? No plane? No zoo? We're Dylan's Dog Squad!* Dylan scrabbled around to

Casey, stood on his hind legs, and pawed Casey's thigh. *Don't go without me. We're a team.*

"I wanted this to be a surprise but," Mom started to smile but giggled instead, "we're taking a private plane, a Gulfstream G550. When we land at San Diego International Airport, another limousine will meet us and take us to the San Diego Zoo."

"Oh man. The Gulfstream is so awesome." Sumo forgot his omelet and attacked his cell phone. "Get out!" He showed them the screen. "The plane costs something like sixty-two million brand new." His head went down again, and his thumbs went crazy. "But," he paused and nodded to himself, "they're only about fifteen million used."

"Definitely a bargain," Mom agreed.

Casey and Dylan did a high-four and then a down low. "We're going in style, Little Buddy!"

As long as I get to go.

"How did Mayor Matias swing a Gulfstream, Mom?"

"He didn't." Her smile got bigger. "Cranston Pantswick arranged it."

"Old Cranky Pants?" Casey and Sumo chorused.

Mom gave them The Look but laughed. "I was surprised, too, but I'm sure Cranston has some idea for a new book." She shrugged. "I'm okay with it."

Casey pulled Dylan onto his lap and hugged him. "This is going to be the best day ever. You get a limo ride, *and* you get to fly in a plane. What do you think?"

Dylan snuffled Casey's cheek. *I think I want a window seat.*

CHAPTER THIRTEEN

"Mom," Casey yelled from their front door, "it's here. Hurry up!"

Casey and Sumo ran outside to get a better look.

Wait for me, guys.

At the top of the brick driveway, Casey and Sumo shot their arms straight up in the air and shouted, "Stretch!"

Okay. Dylan stopped in his tracks, stretched his body forward, and looked up at Casey. *Now what?*

"Not you, Little Buddy." Casey laughed and pointed. "That."

Dylan studied the long shiny black car parked on the street. A man in black pants and a white shirt was leaning against the driver's door. When he saw them, he raised a hand in greeting and hustled to open the passenger's door. *His name is Stretch?*

"The car is called a stretch limo, Dylan." Casey laughed again. "That's because they took a car and stretched it out."

Got it but I don't get why you're laughing. It's not that funny.

"Let's go." Sumo didn't wait. He just took off down the driveway.

Mom walked over to Casey. "Rachel just emailed our security passes. I need to print them out. It will only take a few minutes."

"Okay."

"Please carry Dylan down the driveway. He's got to stay clean."

Casey made a face but scooped Dylan up. "He's going to get dirty at the zoo anyway."

"Yes," Mom dragged the word out and smiled, "but he'll be clean when he gets there."

Dylan gave Mom a forty-two teeth grin. *I get to have fun today.*

Casey and Dylan went down the driveway and over to the man. "I'm Casey and this is Dylan." Casey tipped his head toward the house. "My mom is coming."

"I'm Gibson." He ruffled Dylan's ears. "What's up, little guy?" He smiled and opened the door of the limo. "Your friend couldn't wait to get in and play with the gadgets."

Casey held Dylan tight, hunched over, and climbed into the limo. "Wait until you see this, Little Buddy."

Dylan blinked up at the ceiling. *Wow! Fairy lights are dancing above me.*

"Have you ever seen a sunroof?" Casey tipped Dylan back a bit so he could see. "It opens and closes."

There's a window in the ceiling. No way!

"Too bad Mom is going with us. If she wasn't, we could stand up and stick our heads out the sunroof all the way to the airport."

Not me. I'm too short.

Dylan spotted the big wraparound couch. *This isn't a car. This is like a big living room.*

"Hi, Holly."

"Yeah, yeah, yeah." Holly was sitting cross-legged in one corner of the couch, nibbling on a hangnail. She spit something out and said, "Let's get this show on the road."

Casey whispered in Dylan's ear, "She looks mad."

She always looks mad.

Bailey was sitting by himself in the opposite corner of the couch. Bailey's little black eyes locked onto Dylan, and his two big hands patted the couch.

Casey whispered again, "Want to sit next to Bailey?"

Are you nuts? No way.

Sumo called from the center of the couch. "Check this out." Sumo palmed M&Ms into his mouth and pressed a button on a burlwood panel. A flat-screen TV slowly eased down from the ceiling. Sumo leaned forward, got a bag of Cheetos from a goodie basket on the coffee table, and tossed it to Casey. "The mini fridge is over there." He raised a can of soda and grinned. "I'm thinking about moving in."

"This is so cool, Little Buddy." Casey settled Dylan next to him on the long couch. "We can really stretch out." He laughed. "Get it? Stretch out in the stretch limo."

Got it. And it still isn't that funny. Dylan lay on his side and straightened out his back legs. *Feels good.* Dylan rolled around, rubbing himself and his muzzle up and down the soft leather couch. When he sat up his topknot was sticking straight up and his skin tingled.

"Hold on." Casey used both hands to smooth Dylan's topknot down.

Hey! Dylan jerked away when he felt a little shock. *What was that all about?*

"Static cling, Little Buddy."

Huh?

"It's like some kind of electricity."

I don't like it.

Sumo waved his cell phone. "I've already sent photos of our ride to social media. Got to let everyone know Dylan's Dog Squad is traveling in style to our second job."

"That's great, Sumo."

"About twenty of Dylan's Dog Squad volunteers are going to be at the zoo today." He put his cell phone away. "Everyone wants to see Bailey at the ribbon-cutting ceremony."

"Dominick is coming."

"Yeah, he said he would meet us."

Casey leaned back and ran his hands over the pale grey leather seat. "Wow, Holly. It was so awesome of your grandfather to get us this limo."

"Anything for Bailey," Holly said flatly and rolled her eyes. "Here's the kicker." She sat up and showed off her black T-shirt with gigantic gold letters. "Rachel's idea. She thinks it's cute."

What? Dylan put his muzzle on Casey's lap and whined. *I can't read.*

Casey leaned down to Dylan. "It says, I'm With Bailey."

Yikes! Holly doesn't like Bailey.

"Oh man," Sumo cracked up and pointed. "You've got to wear that stupid shirt all day. I can read it from here."

"Listen up, Smart Mouth," Holly leaned forward and jabbed the air between them with her gnawed finger. "If you ever say what's on this shirt, you're dead. If you ever tell anyone what's on this shirt, you're dead." She narrowed her eyes. "If you ever even *think* about what's on this shirt, you're dead. Believe me, I'll know it and," she paused and nodded, "you'll be dead."

Whoa! Dylan pawed Casey's bare leg. *That's a lot of dead.*

"Yup." Holly sat back and rolled her eyes. "Just when I think my life can't get any suckier."

Sumo ignored Holly. "Hey, Bailey, show us your shirt."

Bailey's buns bounced on the couch. He followed this by treating everyone with a thin-lipped smile and beating both hands on his chest.

Dylan nuzzled Casey's arm. *What does his shirt say?*

"His shirt says, Bailey and there's a huge gold star dotting the i."

Nice.

Sumo popped more M&Ms into his mouth, kicked back, and put his feet up on the coffee table. "When Bailey smiled, he didn't show his teeth. That means he likes his shirt." Sumo munched the candy. "Tell him you like it, too."

Casey gave Bailey a thumbs up. "Nice shirt, Bailey."

"Sure, take his side," Holly muttered and turned to stare out the window. "Everybody does."

Holly is one unhappy kid. Dylan whined.

Bailey's head swiveled at the sound of Dylan's whine. He leaned forward in his seat and zeroed in on Dylan's bandana. Bailey pointed, gibbered, and sent quick, closed-mouth smiles to Dylan.

What?

"Bailey," Casey turned Dylan's Dog Squad bandana around, "see?"

Bailey did. He took that as an invitation to be best friends and hopped off the couch. The limo protested by dipping once when he landed. Bailey's two flat feet pounded the floor between them. In a heartbeat, he was on the couch sitting next to Dylan.

Uh, Casey.

Bailey's hairy fingers lightly touched Dylan's vest and he let out a string of sounds.

You talk funny. Dylan scooted closer to Casey. *Save me.*

"It's okay, Little Buddy." Casey put his arm around Dylan's shoulders. "You have a fan."

No, I don't. Dylan kicked out with his back paw. *A fan is something on the ceiling and it keeps you cool.*

Bailey's fingers spider-walked over Dylan's shoulders and stopped at his bandana. Bailey tugged on it.

Casey, I could use your help here.

"Dylan," Casey turned Dylan's muzzle up, so he had to look at him. "Bailey is asking you for your bandana."

No! Dylan jerked his face back. *It's mine.*

"You have more Dylan's Dog Squad bandanas at home. Besides," Casey hugged him, "you'll have to wear your American Kennel Club Canine Good Citizen vest while you're working at the zoo. It's hot today. C'mon. Let Bailey wear your bandana."

No.

Bailey made crooning noises and patted Dylan's bandana.

"Dylan," Casey glanced at Holly. She had her back to them and was staring out the limo window. "This is going to be a long day." Casey put his right hand on his chest with his thumb sticking out and his fingers extended. He moved his hand clockwise two times, signing Please.

Dylan turned his face away from Casey and Bailey flashed him a tight-lipped smile. *Oh brother.*

"If you let Bailey wear your bandana," Casey tapped Dylan on his shoulder, "we can get vanilla ice cream after the ribbon-cutting ceremony."

Okay, okay. Dylan turned back to Casey and sighed. *I*

want a full scoop of ice cream. No stingy half-scoop of ice cream.

Casey untied Dylan's bandana and put it on Bailey.

Bailey looked down at the bandana. Slowly one hairy finger traced the Dylan's Dog Squad logo. When he looked up, he smiled quickly and wrapped his long arms around Dylan's neck, and squeezed. Hard.

Ugh, Casey. Dylan's eyes bulged and his butt wiggled backward to get free. *Help!*

"Okay, Bailey." Casey peeled Bailey's arms away. "Dylan's glad you like the bandana."

No, I'm not.

Casey pulled Dylan close to him. "You made a new friend, Little Buddy. That's good, right?"

Nuh-uh. Dylan rotated his neck and opened and shut his mouth a few times. *Still works.* He looked up at Casey. *You can be Bailey's new friend.*

Mom poked her head inside the limo and waved some papers in the air. "Sorry. This took longer than expected." She spotted Holly curled up in the corner, staring out the window. "Is everything all right?"

"Oh, yeah," Holly tossed over her shoulder, "just peachy."

CHAPTER FOURTEEN

Dylan was in the middle of a world-class snooze when he felt the limo make a wide turn. He rolled over onto his stomach and yawned. *This limo is one comfy ride. It's even more comfy than my bike trailer.*

"Ms. Donovan," Gibson said over the intercom, "the Gulfstream is ready and waiting for you."

Casey and Sumo high-fived. "Yay!"

Dylan watched Casey and Sumo do the down low. *You're really excited.*

"Thank you." Mom gathered up the papers she was working on and put them into her computer case. "Kids, make sure you have everything." She zipped up the case and looked around her. The floor of the limo was littered with candy wrappers, soda cans, and empty chip bags. The goodie basket was empty. "Sumo, you can put it away."

"Thanks, Ms. D." Sumo smiled and wiped his face with the hem of his Dylan's Dog Squad T-shirt.

Mom smiled, too. "No, I mean you *really* can put it away." She gestured at the messy floor. "Please pick all this up. We need to leave the limousine as we found it."

Sumo got busy and Casey pitched in.

Sumo's a skinny kid but he can eat a lot of junk food. All I got were a few measly Cheetos. Mom says junk food isn't good for me. I bet if I lived at Sumo's house, I'd get to eat junk food all the time. Dylan sighed. *I really like junk food.*

But... Mom makes Breakfast of Champions for me every day. Mom's fluffy eggs and muffins are the best. Dylan's stomach growled. *Pretty soon it will be lunchtime. I really like the grilled cheese sandwiches Mom makes but my favorite is the French dip sandwiches.* Dylan's stomach growled again. *I hope we get home in time for dinner. Mom always grills a steak for me.*

Dylan scooted forward on the couch and hooked his paws over its edge. *I'd really miss Mom's great cooking if I lived at Sumo's house.* Dylan flicked his ears and put his muzzle on his front paws. *Maybe Casey and I could just hang out at Sumo's house between meals.*

Casey tossed the last empty bag into the trash and flopped onto the couch. "Done."

Sumo was already going out the door. "Hurry up."

"Finished," Mom corrected and changed the subject. "Holly, do you have the leash I gave you for Bailey?"

Holly nodded.

Mom waited but Holly didn't move off the couch. "Please bring Bailey with you to the Gulfstream."

"That's Dylan's Dog Squad's job. They're the ones getting paid the big bucks." Holly stood up and tossed Bailey's leash to Casey. "I'm outta here."

Mom closed her eyes and rubbed her forehead with both hands. "This is going to be a long day."

Dylan and Casey exchanged looks. *Oh yeah.*

Mom's cell phone vibrated, and she checked its screen.

"Oh no. It's Cranston. I'll take this outside." She hesitated. "Are you okay here?"

"We got this." Casey hooked Bailey's leash onto his collar.

Dylan pulled himself into a sitting position and swiveled around to look out the limo window. The sleek airplane sat on the runway ready for takeoff. Fingers of dazzling California sunlight shot out from its gleaming hull. Dylan began to tremble. *Whine.*

"Hey." Casey put his arms around Dylan's shoulders. "You're shaking. How come?"

Dylan dropped down, turned into Casey, and rubbed his muzzle against his bare arm.

Casey opened his left hand with his fingers separated. Then he pointed to the center of his palm with his right index finger, signing Show Me.

Dylan got up on his hind legs again and scratched at the window. Then he slid down onto his buns and faced Casey. *That.*

Casey looked over Dylan's head and out the window. After a moment he stroked Dylan's back. "Do you remember when you lived with my brother in South Korea?"

Dylan's ears drooped. *I loved Aiden.*

Casey petted Dylan's ears. "Do you remember when Aiden sent you to me?"

Aiden said he didn't want me anymore. He put me on a plane and sent me to live with you in America.

"Do you remember the plane trip?"

Whine. I was in cargo hold. It was dark and cold. Then it got really hot. My crate was too small. I tried to move but I scraped my shoulders and knocked over my water bottle. I was so thirsty and so scared.

Dylan let out a ragged breath and nuzzled Casey's arm again. *I don't want to ride in cargo hold today. Whine.*

Casey stroked Dylan's ears. "I'm guessing that's a lot to remember but remember this. You're the best gift my brother ever gave me." Casey pulled Dylan onto his lap. "You're my little buddy." He turned Dylan's muzzle up. "Dylan's Dog Squad has a job to do today. Can't do it without you."

You mean it?

"Don't forget," Casey laughed, "we're getting ice cream later."

Dylan slurped a kiss on Casey's cheek. *Awesome!*

Bailey clapped his hairy hands together, gibbered, and slid off the couch.

"Hold on, Bailey. Wait for us."

Bailey kept going but Casey grabbed his leash with his right hand. He jiggled Dylan's leash with his left hand. "Let's go, Dylan."

Yes! Dylan jumped off the couch and started to scamper, but Casey held him back. *Oh yeah.* Dylan moved around to Casey's left side and looked up. *Sometimes I forget about this whole walking on the leash thing.*

Bailey didn't care about walking on the left side or the right side of Casey but lumbered straight ahead.

Outside Dylan cocked his snout in the air. Summer sun warmed the top of his head, and a gentle breeze fluffed his ears. *California is so much better than South Korea.*

Mom was still talking on her cell phone, but she waved them over. "That's a fabulous idea, Cranston." She raised her eyebrows at Casey and smiled. "Yes, yes. I'll contact Jonah and Anna right away. Talk to you later."

Mom dropped her cell phone into her purse. "The stairs

to the plane are steep. If you can carry Dylan, I can take Bailey."

Casey handed Bailey's leash over. "Thanks."

Bailey sidled up to Mom. He reached for her hand and gave her a tight-lipped smile.

"Well," Mom said taking his hand but still holding onto his leash, "this is, uh, cute." They walked to the plane, Bailey gibbering all the way. "I hope you can climb the stairs, Bailey. I can't carry you."

Dylan studied the back of Bailey's thick shape. He looked at Mom's slender arms and small waist. *Bailey could carry you.*

When they reached the stairs, Bailey didn't skip a beat. Keeping his right hand in Mom's, Bailey grabbed the railing with his left hand. His two big hairy feet plodded their way up the stairs.

Dylan wiggled in Casey's arms. *Mom can be Bailey's new friend.*

At the top of the stairs, Casey and Dylan paused in the doorway of the plane. Casey swiveled so Dylan could get a good look at the cabin. "Check this out, Little Buddy."

Whoa! This is even better than the limo!

Four white leather chairs were grouped around a small glass and chrome table at the farthest end of the plane. Holly was sitting cross-legged in one of the chairs and clutching a cell phone. She had earbuds in, and her eyes were closed.

Sumo had already made himself at home on the couch and had kicked off his flip-flops. He was shuffling his bare feet back and forth on the thick white carpet. "Forget the limo. I'm moving in here."

"Amazing!" Mom said. "I've never seen anything like

this." Mom's gaze swept around the interior of the cabin. "White leather furniture and white carpet." She shook her head. "Very optimistic."

"You're blond, Little Buddy. That's almost white."

Dylan looked down at his fluffy curls. *How about that? We almost match.*

"You're not going to believe this," Sumo piped up. "We have two pilots and there's room in here for seventeen people."

"Get out," Casey said.

No! We just got here.

"We'll be flying at about eleven thousand feet." Sumo hooked a thumb over his shoulder and tapped the window behind him. "The pilots said it's a clear day, so we'll follow the coast. We'll see Dana Point, Oceanside, Carlsbad, and Del Mar." He reached for his cell phone. "Social media will never believe this." He smiled to himself and got busy. "This is like the best day ever."

"Since you two are enjoying this so much, you'll have to send Cranston a thank you note."

"Aw, Mom."

"Do we have to, Ms. D?"

Mom gave them The Look and guided Bailey to the couch across from Sumo. "Here you go."

Bailey climbed up, sat, and wiggled his toes. Then he patted the spot next to him and reached for Mom.

"Uh, sure." Mom sat, put her purse on the couch between them, and opened her computer case. "Sumo, did the Captain say how long we'd be in the air?"

"About fifty minutes."

"Not much time. One moment," Mom said when Casey and Dylan started to sit next to Sumo. She took a stack of papers out of her case. "This is the schedule for today. Let's join Holly at the back of the cabin. We can spread everything out on the table and talk about what we need to do."

What about me?

Mom stood up and looked from Dylan to Bailey. "We don't have enough chairs for you two."

Bailey scissor-kicked his legs and bared his teeth.

"Uh, Ms. D," Sumo said, "that means Bailey is upset."

"Okay." Mom hesitated and then gave Dylan a sweet smile. "Dylan, you can keep an eye on Bailey for me."

Why me? He's your new friend.

"Bailey likes to watch TV," Casey suggested. "Holly said *Animal Planet* is his favorite show."

"Really? I didn't know chimpanzees could see color." Mom looked to Sumo who was already logged into Google.

"Dogs can only see blue, yellow, green and shades mixed together. But chimpanzees," Sumo read out loud, "have good color vision and depth perception."

Bailey clapped his hands together and sent Dylan a tight-lipped smile.

Grr. Dylan looked away. *Show off.*

"I don't think I can get Animal Planet but," Mom pulled her laptop out of her bag and set it up on the chrome and glass coffee table in front of Bailey, "I have a documentary on surfing."

Casey made a face. "Why would you have that?"

"Teri is writing a new Hieronymus the Hamster book. Priscilla and Gina are doing the illustrations. It's about surfing."

"Isn't this like Hieronymus's eight hundredth book, Ms. D?"

"Fifty-second." Mom laughed. "Who knew kids would

fall in love with a hamster who travels all around the world just to paint the perfect picture?"

That dumb old hamster is always painting something, Dylan huffed out a breath. *Kids aren't too smart.*

Mom sighed happily. "I think the series could go on forever."

Good grief. How long do hamsters live anyway? Dylan flicked his ears. *Even a cat only has nine lives.*

"Where is Hieronymus going this time, Mom?"

"Hieronymus," Mom angled the screen, "wants to paint the perfect wave. Since Australia is known for surfing, he's going there."

That's really dumb. Casey and I go to Laguna Beach all the time and watch the surfers. Casey said we can rent a board and go out in the ocean. Dylan wagged his stubby tail. *How can I wear board shorts like Casey?*

Mom gave Sumo a stack of papers. "Please take these to the table for me. I'll be right there."

"Okay."

Mom pressed a few keys on the laptop, angled the screen again, and motioned for Dylan to scoot closer. "You can watch this with Bailey."

Big wow.

"Thanks, Dylan. I appreciate your help." She kissed him on his topknot. "We have a lot to go over, and we'll need every minute. Coming, Casey?"

"Yeah." Casey waited a moment, bent down to Dylan, and whispered, "This is important. You watch Bailey while I'm with Mom. There's a bunch of stuff in here. Don't let Bailey get into anything. Don't let him take anything. Remember all that stuff he had in his tree house?"

I remember all that stuff he stole. Dylan pawed Casey's leg. *We could put Bailey in cargo hold.*

"Look after Bailey, Little Buddy." Casey scratched Dylan on his head and followed Mom and Sumo to the back of the cabin.

CHAPTER FIFTEEN

Dylan saw words flash across the computer screen and then he saw a crowded beach. A girl paddled out on her board and waited for the wave. On shore, people cheered. In an instant, she was up, her arms outstretched for balance, and she was heading for shore. *Wow!* Dylan wiggled his butt. *This is exciting.*

Bailey wasn't interested in surfing and leaned back against the couch. He spread his arms out to his sides and ten hairy fingers tapped, tapped, tapped the white leather couch.

Dylan shot Bailey a look. *You're annoying. Stop that.*

Bailey's little black eyes darted to the back of the plane.

Dylan returned to the screen. The beach crowd was going wild. They were shouting the surfer's name and jumping up and down in the sand.

Bailey leaned closer to Dylan and gibbered softly.

Be quiet. Dylan ignored Bailey and kept his eyes glued to the surfer. *This is the good part.*

Bailey sat back. He slid his shiny round eyes Dylan's way and waited. Still watching Dylan, he slowly hooked the strap of Mom's purse with one finger and dragged it onto his lap.

Dylan held his breath for the girl and inched himself closer to the screen. *You're doing great! You're almost to shore.*

Suddenly her knees wobbled. She arched her back, and her arms went over her head. *Oh no! Don't fall.* Dylan swiveled his muzzle toward Bailey. *Did you see that?*

Bailey stuck his big hand into Mom's purse and felt around.

Hey! That's not yours. Dylan lunged for Mom's purse. *Grr.*

Bailey jerked Mom's purse away from Dylan and peeked inside. He found her lipstick and saw himself in its shiny lipstick case. Bailey smiled from ear to ear at his reflection.

You grin too much. It's creepy.

Bailey slid the case off and studied the lipstick.

Put it back!

Bailey hummed softly, gave Dylan a sly glance, and took a big bite of lipstick.

Oh, this is bad. Dylan panicked. He looked over his shoulder and saw Mom, Casey, Sumo, and Holly huddled around the table. *Hey! Over here. Whine.*

Bailey smeared what was left of the lipstick over his big lips and smacked them four times before giving the lipstick tube the heave-ho. The lipstick blazed a pink trail across the white couch cushion and landed on the white carpet.

Arf! Casey!

Casey looked up and gave Dylan a quick wave. "I'm right here, Little Buddy."

Exactly! Arf! Arf! I could use some help here.

"Listen to that," Mom nudged Casey. "Dylan's really enjoying the documentary."

"I promised I'd take him out on a board the next time we go to Laguna Beach."

"Hey," Sumo said, "let's go next week."

"I have a meeting in San Clemente on Tuesday. I could take you then," Mom offered.

"Great. Thanks, Mom."

"What about you, Holly?" Mom asked. "Would you like to go?"

Holly hitched a shoulder. "Maybe."

Dylan sat up straight. *Mom, look over here.*

Instead, Mom unfolded a map of the San Diego Zoo and uncapped a highlighter. "When we get inside the zoo, we're going to Treetops Way." Mom circled the location. "That's where we're meeting Rachel, Jonah, and Anna."

Sumo and Holly nodded.

Casey tapped a spot on the map. "Isn't the new primate habitat here?"

"Yes, but since Jonah's covering the story for the *Orange County Register,* he wants to do a short interview with Rachel first. Besides Anna needs to get some photos." Mom capped the highlighter and put it away. "The new habitat is only a five-minute walk."

"Okay."

"Here are your security passes." Mom slipped a security pass on a lanyard around her neck and waited while Casey, Sumo, and Holly put theirs on. "This is the program for today." She handed each of them a small booklet. "We need to go over it."

You need to look over here, Mom!

Dylan turned back to Bailey just as Bailey did an underhanded wind-up. He sent Mom's cell phone whizzing past Dylan's ear, and it disappeared under the couch.

Hey! Dylan scooted back on the couch. *Watch it!*

Bailey was having a great time. He scouted around inside Mom's purse again and found Mom's car key. He dangled it in front of Dylan.

Mom needs that!

One flick of Bailey's wrist was all it took, and the car key was airborne. The key made a soft plopping sound before getting lost in the thick carpet.

Stop! Dylan lunged for Bailey.

Bailey hugged Mom's purse to his chest and kicked out with both feet. One hairy foot landed on Dylan's shoulder.

Ouch! Dylan put it in reverse.

Mom's wallet was next. Bailey emptied it onto his lap. He bit down on a credit card, ground his teeth on another credit card, and sent them both sailing over his shoulder. Bailey found the cash. Gibbering to Dylan, he wadded up the bills and pitched them toward the door of the cabin.

That does it! Dylan jumped off the couch and ran to Casey. *Arf! Come quick.*

"What's up, Little Buddy?" Casey reached for Dylan. "We're almost done."

Mom's purse is done for.

"Finished," Mom said automatically and glanced up. She saw the mess and shrieked. "Bailey!"

Bailey wrapped the strap of Mom's purse around his neck. Clamping his hands behind his head, Bailey leaned back against the couch and crossed one hairy leg over the other. He gave quick, thin-lipped smiles to everybody.

"Oh man," Sumo had his cell phone up, but he was laughing so hard, he couldn't take the picture. "Social media has to see this."

"Gimme!" Holly pounced on Sumo. She grabbed his cell phone and took pictures of Bailey and the mess. Holly tapped the screen. "I just sent this to Rachel. She's going to freak out." She tossed the cell phone back to Sumo and gave him a wicked grin. "Do your social media thing."

Sumo's head went down, and his fingers danced across the keys with lightning speed.

"What happened, Little Buddy?" Casey tossed his hands out to his side. "I told you to look after Bailey!"

Dylan rolled his big brown eyes up to Casey and heaved out a colossal sigh. *I told you to put Bailey in cargo hold.*

CHAPTER SIXTEEN

"Where's our ride?" Casey complained and shifted Dylan in his arms. "It's hot out here."

You think? Dylan panted hard, letting doggie spit drop onto Casey's bare arm. *Try wearing a fur coat and a vest.*

"Yeah, but today is the greatest." Sumo grinned. "This is like the life of a rock star."

Casey wiped the dog slobber off his arm. "When our ride gets here, Little Buddy, we can have some water."

Dylan brought his muzzle close to Casey's face and coughed. *I want lots of water.*

"I hope it gets here soon." Mom adjusted her sunglasses. "I'm beginning to melt."

Sumo checked the weather app on his cell phone. "It's already ninety-two degrees. Just wait until we get to the primate habitat." Sumo dragged the back of his hand across his forehead. "It's like totally in the sun. Only the chimpanzees get to be in the shade."

"This is so like Rachel," Holly snorted. "She couldn't be interested in penguins. Nope. Had to be interested in dumb old chimpanzees."

Bailey fidgeted at the end of his leash, puffed out his lips, and gibbered up at Mom.

"Don't listen to her, Bailey." Mom smiled down at him. Not all the pink lipstick had come off. "You know Holly likes you."

Bailey bared his teeth and screeched.

"Okay. Maybe not." Mom offered her hand, and Bailey took it.

An open-air Electric Hummer painted in brown and tan camouflage cruised into view and slowed to a stop in front of them.

"Oh man." Sumo stared open-mouthed. "I'm definitely living the life of a rock star."

"Shotgun!" Holly announced and sprinted past everyone. She yanked open the passenger's door of the Hummer, jumped inside, and slammed the door shut.

Casey, Dylan, Mom, Bailey, and Sumo just stared.

"Holly is one weird kid," Sumo said under his breath.

"Oh yeah," Casey agreed.

"Boys!" Mom's voice was sharp, but she didn't disagree.

Dylan leaned against Casey and whined. *Holly is a lonely kid.*

A young guy with sun-bleached hair, a golden tan, and wearing a safari shirt and shorts hopped out of the car. "Ms. Donovan? I'm Rocco." He flashed a dazzling white smile before running around to open her door. "Right this way."

"Thanks," Mom said and helped Bailey inside. She pulled her cell phone out of her purse and tapped the screen. Without looking up she said, "Casey, please watch Bailey. I need to let Jonah know we're on our way. Then I need to text Cranston."

Rocco waited for everyone to get settled before putting

the Hummer in gear. "There's a cooler with bottled water and a tote bag back there with some snacks. Help yourself."

"What did I tell you?" Sumo was already raiding the cooler. "This is the life of a rock star."

"You're really hung up on this rock star thing," Casey laughed. "Pretty weird since you're the one who gave me grief about being a chimp's bodyguard."

"Yeah, well that was before I knew the job came with a limo, a Gulfstream, and this cool Hummer."

Sumo is making some excellent points but, Dylan panted harder, *does the job come with water?*

Casey settled Dylan on the seat next to Bailey. "Hold on." Casey smoothed Dylan's damp topknot away from his face. "Water is coming."

Sumo tossed a bottle of water to Casey.

"Thanks."

Without looking back Holly snapped her fingers once and stuck out her hand.

Sumo handed a bottle of water over.

Holly didn't say thank you, just unscrewed the cap and chucked it out the open window. Tipping back her head, she glugged the water down and then sent the bottle flying out the window.

Dylan pawed Casey's arm. *Grr!*

Casey interrupted Dylan by putting his index finger to his lips, signing Quiet. Casey whispered, "Mom didn't see. Let's keep it that way."

Sumo got another bottle of water and held it out. "Ms. D, do you want one? They're really cold."

"Please." She took the bottle with her left hand and kept texting with her right. Instead of uncapping the bottle, she rolled it across her forehead. "Ah, much better."

"Good idea." Casey held the bottle of water to Dylan's forehead. "Like that?"

Dylan pressed his forehead against the cold bottle. *Oh yeah.*

Bailey reached over Dylan and held out his hand to Casey.

"Okay, Bailey." Casey uncapped his bottle of water and gave it to him. "Sumo, give me two more."

Sumo tossed him the bottles. He kicked off his flip-flops, leaned back, and propped both feet on the back of Holly's headrest.

"Yeck." Holly turned around and pushed his feet off. "Your feet stink."

"Sumo!" Mom stopped texting and gave him The Look. "You're not at home."

"Sorry, Ms. D."

Casey got Dylan's collapsible water dish out of his backpack and filled it to the brim.

Dylan dove his muzzle into the bowl and drank until the water disappeared. Dylan looked up and shook out his muzzle. *More?*

"Sure." Casey filled the bowl again.

"Did you know the San Diego Zoo is like the largest zoo in the world?" Sumo pulled the Hummer's tote bag onto his lap, pushed snacks around, and tossed Casey a package of peanut butter cookies.

Casey caught the cookies one-handed. "How do you know this stuff?" Casey tore the package open and gave half a cookie to Dylan. He shoved the other half into his mouth. "Have you been reading again?"

Sumo ripped open a bag of trail mix with his teeth. "Try it some time."

"Nah." Casey rubbed Dylan's shoulders. "That's your

job."

"The zoo was built in 1916." Sumo tipped his head back, letting trail mix slide into his mouth. "That was over a hundred years ago. It has like four thousand animals and about eight hundred species."

Mom hit Send and beamed at Sumo. "I'm glad you like to read."

"Yeah," Casey smirked. "Me, too. That gets me off the hook."

Fifteen minutes later Rocco brought the Hummer around to the security entrance of the zoo. He tapped the Hummer's horn and waved to a young woman seated at a table. "Security check-in won't take long."

A perky young woman wearing a perky smile and a perkier ponytail bounced to her feet and beelined toward the Hummer. Her nametag said Cricket.

Rocco handed her a sheet of paper. "Ms. Donovan and Dylan's Dog Squad are here to attend the ribbon-cutting ceremony for the new primate habitat."

"Super!" Cricket chirped and checked the paper against her iPad. When she scanned the faces of the people in the Hummer she frowned. "There are six of you." She checked her iPad again. "I show Ms. Donovan, Dylan's Dog Squad—Casey Donovan, Dylan Donovan, Sumo Modragon—and Bailey. That would be five."

"Listen up, Bug Girl," Holly groused from the front seat. "You've only got five names on your dumb old list because Rachel *forgot* to mention me." Holly gritted her teeth and said to herself, "This is so typical." She let out a long-suffering sigh. "I'm *just* her daughter."

"Uh," Cricket's perky smile became a puzzled look, "I didn't know Ms. Langdon had a daughter."

"Nobody does." Holly jumped to her feet and faced

Cricket. "See this?" Holly pointed to her I'm With Bailey shirt and snarled, "Like anyone else would be caught dead wearing this stupid shirt."

Dylan nose-bumped Casey's arm. *She's talking about dead again.*

Casey put his index finger to his lips, signing Quiet.

Dylan bumped Casey's arm again. *Holly is making some excellent points.*

Holly collapsed into her seat and folded her arms across her chest.

Mom jumped in. "This is Holly Langdon, Rachel Langdon's daughter." She gave Cricket her best smile. "I'm sure Ms. Langdon just assumed you knew."

Casey snickered. "Nice save, Mom."

Mom gave him The Look.

"Well, uh, of course." Cricket made a quick recovery and gushed, "Welcome to the San Diego Zoo." Cricket tucked her iPad under her arm, stood on tiptoe, and looked inside the Hummer. "Hello, Bailey." She gave him a huge smile. "I'm a big fan!"

"Yeah, yeah. You and everybody else," Holly said and kicked the glove compartment with her foot.

Bailey clapped his hairy hands together, crooned, and wrapped his long arms around Dylan.

"Oh my gosh!" Cricket covered her mouth with both hands and squealed, "You're Dylan! You're the little dog that saved Bailey from drowning."

Dylan's chest puffed with pride. *It was nothing.*

She looked closer. "Is that an American Canine Good Citizen patch you're wearing on your vest? My, you really are a good citizen."

Dylan sat up straighter. *Thank you.*

Bailey touched his wrinkled fingers to Dylan's vest and patted Dylan's back.

"Today is a special day at the zoo! We have two celebrities. May I take your picture?" Cricket already had her cell phone up. "Everybody, say zoo!"

"Say goodbye," Holly muttered.

"See you later at the ceremony, Bailey and Dylan!" Cricket stepped back and gave an energetic wave. "Have a wonderful day!"

CHAPTER SEVENTEEN

Rocco put the Hummer in gear, and they crept along Front Street. Visitors filled the street, looking at maps, eating junk food, slurping smoothies, taking pictures, and walking wherever they pleased.

Dylan lifted his snout and inhaled the yummy scents of pizza, nachos, hamburgers, and sugar. *This is a great place.*

A mom and dad pushing a baby stroller made a sudden left turn in front of the Hummer and Rocco slammed on the brakes. Dylan slid forward and his ears flopped over his face. Bailey made a grab for Dylan's vest but got his ear instead.

Yip!

Rocco's eyes went to the rearview mirror. "Sorry, Ms. Donovan. People like to wander here. They aren't used to seeing vehicles on the road." He smiled. "We could walk but Treetops Way is a hard, thirty-minute hike up a very steep hill. Ms. Langdon thought the car would be easier on Dylan and Bailey."

"Thank you." Mom brushed her hair out of her eyes. "That was very thoughtful of her."

"Oh, yeah," Holly agreed. "Rachel's always thinking of Bailey."

"This place is so much fun." Casey smoothed Dylan's topknot away from his face and pulled him onto his lap so he could see better.

Awesome. Dylan leaned against Casey's chest. *Now I won't miss a thing.*

"The zoo is sold out," Rocco explained. "You should've seen the parking lot at seven this morning."

Bailey pointed at something.

Mom followed his point. "What is it?"

Bailey made mewling sounds and grabbed Mom's hand. His round black eyes locked onto hers.

"Mom, over there." Casey shifted Dylan around so he could look too. "Bailey sees the gift shop. Check out the window, Little Buddy. All kinds of woobies."

Wow! Dylan wiggled his buns and leaned closer. The window was filled with stuffed giraffes, leopards, monkeys, elephants, birds, and snakes. *That's a lot of woobies.*

Bailey tipped his head up to Mom and gibbered.

"After the ceremony," Mom asked, "would you like to pick out a woobie?"

Bailey gave several quick closed-mouthed smiles and clapped his big hands.

Arf! What about me?

Mom laughed. "You, too, Dylan."

Okay.

"Look, Dylan, there's the ice cream shop."

Dylan nuzzled Casey's cheek. *Tell Mom you promised me ice cream.*

"Check it out!" Sumo leaned back in his seat to get a better look at the Skyfari Tram Ride. "It's my favorite."

Casey gently raised Dylan's muzzle up. "That's Skyfari."

Hmm. The people look like they're riding in gigantic white eggs. Dylan cocked his head at Casey. *Do people get scrambled if they fall out?*

"Visitors catch a gondola over there," Casey turned Dylan toward the platform, "and ride to the other side of the park." He turned Dylan again, showing him the trees on the hill. "Kind of cool to watch the gondolas cruise along those thick wires."

Bailey tapped Dylan on his vest. He raised his right arm up high, letting a wrinkled finger follow a gondola as it inched across the sky. He turned back to Dylan and waited.

What?

"I think Bailey is excited about the tram, Dylan."

"A tram ride would be more fun than swinging through the trees," Sumo laughed.

Bailey didn't. He bared his teeth at Sumo.

"Amazing," Mom said. "Bailey understood you."

"Bailey has a three hundred word and phrase vocabulary," Holly said flatly. "Rachel writes about it in her books."

That's a lot.

Casey scratched Dylan's ear. "Yeah, but we know American Sign Language. Right, Little Buddy?"

Arf!

"So does Bailey." Holly rolled her eyes and added under her breath, "Rachel taught it to him, not to me."

Bailey swung his hairy head from Holly to Casey and nodded.

Casey wadded up his empty cookie wrapper and tossed it at Sumo. "Want to go on the tram after the ceremony?"

Sumo sat up straight. "You bet."

Bailey grunted happily.

"Great." Casey ruffled Dylan's ears. "It's all set."

Nobody asked me. Dylan studied the white things gently swinging in the air way above him. *The tram is really, really high up.* Dylan looked away and his shoulders slumped. *I could never get on that. I'd be too scared.*

"Don't worry, Little Buddy." Casey hugged him. "You know they're safe because people ride them all the time."

What about little dogs?

When Rocco turned onto Treetops Way, Dylan scooted closer to the open window, hung his head out, and caught the summer breeze. *There's a lot of trees here and it's really shady.* He closed his eyes, listening to the leaves rustle above him. *Time for a world-class snooze.*

Shrill sounds suddenly erupted. *Yikes!* Dylan's eyes flew open. He sat up and craned his neck as far back as it would go. *What was that?* Dylan moved his buns in a circle on Casey's lap until he spotted large black birds with red faces. They screamed to each other, spread their wings, and flew away. *They're really noisy.*

"What are those birds," Mom asked. "They look familiar."

"California Condors." Sumo brought out his cell phone. "They were almost extinct but they're doing okay now." He went to Google and showed everyone their picture.

Not very pretty.

"California Condors are one of the largest flying birds," Sumo read out loud. "They can fly at fifteen thousand feet and fifty-five miles an hour."

"The Gulfstream flew at eleven thousand feet today, Dylan. The California Condors can fly four thousand feet higher than that," Mom explained. "Cars go fifty-five miles an hour."

That's very high and very fast. Dylan stuck his face out

the window again. *I'd never want to be that far off the ground. I'd rather ride in a car.*

Treetops Way wound around, steadily climbing up the steep hill. When they reached the last bend, people stood shoulder-to-shoulder blocking the road. Rocco hit the brakes and gave a gentle toot of the horn.

"Casey, look!" Sumo leaned out the Hummer's window. "Dylan's Dog Squad volunteers are here."

Dylan wagged his little tail. *They're all wearing Dylan's Dog Squad T-shirts.* Dylan licked Casey's cheek. *We have lots of friends.*

Casey found Dominick in the crowd. "Hey! You made it."

Dominick shouted back, "Told you I'd be here!"

Rocco put the Hummer in Park, grabbed the top of the windshield with both hands, and hoisted himself up. "Folks," he tried motioning them to the side, "we need to get through."

People turned and gave a friendly wave. Then they spotted Bailey and went crazy.

"Hey, look!"

"Oh, my gosh!"

"It's Bailey!"

Bailey kicked out his hairy legs and gave a big hairy hand wave to the crowd.

"Who is that cute little dog with Bailey?"

"That's Dylan," a Dylan's Dog Squad volunteer said. "He saved Bailey from drowning." She showed off her Dylan's Dog Squad T-shirt. "I know Dylan personally."

The crowd charged the Hummer, muscling forward with cell phones held high. Getting a selfie with Bailey and Dylan was a must. From out of nowhere zoo employees dressed in beige safari shirts and shorts stepped in and formed a human wall around the Hummer.

"Ladies and gentlemen," a tall man gave a short blast on his whistle and ordered, "please step away from the Hummer." The man caught Rocco's eye and jutted his chin to the left. "We've got this. Go to the clearing in front of the large tent and park. Ms. Langdon will be right out."

"Thanks, Larry." Rocco dropped down into his seat, put the Hummer in gear, and did what he was told.

Outside the big tent, Dylan saw Jonah and Anna huddled together around an outdoor table covered with camera equipment. They looked up, waved, and went back to work.

Arf! Today is getting exciting.

A small woman burst out of the tent. She ran toward the Hummer, her black hair flying about her face. "You're here!"

"That's Rachel Langdon," Casey whispered to Dylan. "Holly looks just like her."

Dylan watched the pretty woman with the friendly smile come closer. *No way. Rachel looks happy.*

"Ms. Donovan, I'll be here waiting for you after the event today." Rocco took a business card out of his pocket and gave it to her. "Text me if you need anything."

"Thanks." Mom waited for Sumo, Bailey, Casey, and Dylan to get out. She followed and opened Holly's door. "We're here."

"Yeah, yeah." Holly climbed out and back kicked her door shut, leaving a shoe print on the brown and tan door.

Rachel grimaced when she saw the footprint but let it go. She smiled at everyone else. "Welcome! Thanks for coming, Colleen."

"My pleasure." Mom smiled back. "This is my son Casey, Dylan, and their best friend Sumo."

"Oh yes." Rachel nodded. "So nice to meet the famous Dylan's Dog Squad." She beamed at Dylan. "Congratulations on getting your American Kennel Club Canine Good Citizen vest."

Dylan sat on his rump and two-pawed the air. *Thanks!*

"Boys, I know you're working today but," Rachel leaned close, "I hope you're having some fun, too."

"Are you serious? This is like," Sumo began.

"The life of a rock star," Casey finished for him.

"Nah." Sumo made a face and punched him in the arm. "This is like the best day of my life."

Bailey lumbered over to Rachel. He opened the fingers on his hand and brought his thumb to his chin, signing Mom.

"Bailey!" Rachel squealed, spread her arms wide, and hugged him close. "I've missed you so much!"

Bailey broke away, gibbered, and held up his pinkie, his index finger, and his thumb, signing I Love You.

Dylan body-bumped Casey. *We sign I Love You, too.*

Rachel's eyes misted. She wiped them with the back of her hand before signing I Love You. She pulled Bailey into another hug, and they rocked back and forth.

"I hate to break up this Hallmark moment." Holly stood off to the side, her hip cocked and chewing on her thumbnail. "Did you forget about *me*, Rachel?"

Rachel tipped her head but kept her left arm around Bailey. "Of course not." She held her right arm out to Holly.

Holly didn't budge.

Pink flashed across Rachel's face. She patted Bailey

once on his back, took a step closer to Holly, and dropped her voice, "What's your problem?"

"*My* problem?" Holly's voice went up an octave and she backed away. "I'm spending my *birthday* with *Bailey* at the *zoo*."

Casey and Sumo elbowed each other and mouthed, "Birthday?"

Dylan's heart hurt for Holly. *No wonder you're so sad. And really grumpy.*

"Oh no," Mom murmured.

Rachel gave Holly a patient smile. "You and Bailey always spend your birthdays together. You love Bailey."

"No! *You* love Bailey!"

Patience turned to parent power. "We're not having this conversation again." Rachel's mouth flatlined and she held up her index finger, "Just once, I wish...."

Holly cut her off. "Here's what I wish." Holly whipped a pamphlet out of her back pocket and shoved it into Rachel's hands. "I wish I could go to boarding school in Wyoming."

Rachel's eyebrows shot up. "Wyoming? There's nothing in Wyoming."

"You got that right." Holly's black eyes flashed, and her small fist jabbed the air. "It's the only state in America that doesn't have a zoo."

No kidding.

"Actually," Sumo broke in, "Wyoming has the Kindness Ranch Sanctuary." He went on, "It's kind of like a zoo. They have an adoption program for animals they've rescued from research labs. If the animals are too old to get adopted, they care for them for like forever." He smiled happily.

Mom, Casey, and Rachel stared open-mouthed at Sumo.

Dylan pawed Sumo's leg. *You're not helping.*

"Shut up," Casey whispered out of the corner of his mouth. "That's too weird for even you to know."

"Sorry," Sumo shrugged but kept his smile. "Zoos are cool. Someday I'm going to visit every zoo in the United States."

"Well, *Mom.* Do I get to go?" Holly put her hands on her hips and tapped her right foot. "That's my birthday wish."

"Oh, Holly." Rachel's voice softened. "You've got this all wrong." She cupped Holly's face in her hands. "I love you more than anything. Bailey is," Rachel searched for words, "my work."

Holly glared at Rachel.

Rachel dropped both hands onto Holly's shoulders and gave them a gentle shake. "You're my daughter. Bailey is a chimp."

Bailey bared his teeth, whipped his Bailey T-shirt off, and stomped on it. Screeching loudly, he dropped to all fours and took off across the clearing.

"Oh no! Bailey," Rachel yelled, "come back!" She whirled around to Casey, Dylan, and Sumo. "Do something! The ribbon-cutting ceremony is in an hour!"

"Go on, boys," Mom urged and pulled Rocco's business card from her purse. "I'll text Rocco. Maybe he can help."

"Dylan." Casey closed both hands into fists in front of him, then tapped his right fist on top of his left fist in the wrist area twice, signing Work. "Get Bailey, Dylan."

Arf! Dylan left the clearing and shot down the road after Bailey, his paws kicking up dirt and leaves. *Arf! Arf!*

"C'mon, Casey." Sumo started after Dylan and Bailey.

"Wait." Casey grabbed Sumo's arm. "Text Dominick. He's with the Dylan's Dog Squad volunteers. Tell him

Bailey is headed their way. They can catch Bailey and hold him."

Sumo busted up laughing. "Not going to happen. Chimpanzees are four times stronger than humans."

"Do it!" Casey shouted.

"Okay, okay." Sumo's fingers tapped rapidly on his cell phone. "Then what?"

"Then follow me." Casey was already sprinting after Dylan. "I'm coming, Little Buddy."

Dylan ran as fast as he could after Bailey, trying to close the gap between them. *Bailey, you can really move.* When Dylan saw Larry and the zoo employees up ahead, he got excited. *It's over, Bailey. You can't get away.*

Bailey had other ideas. He made it past Larry and crashed into a woman eating from a bag of popcorn. She choked on the popcorn and kernels went flying.

"Bailey," Larry put one hand out in front of him like a traffic cop and blew his whistle, "cease and desist!"

Dylan skidded to a halt beside Bailey and looked quickly to Larry. *Cease and what?*

Bailey whipped his head around, covered his ears with both hands, and showed Larry his yellow teeth.

Uh-oh. Cease and desist aren't favorite words in Bailey's three-hundred-word vocabulary.

Bailey stomped over to Larry and yanked the whistle away from him.

"Hey! You can't do that."

Bailey gave Larry a one-handed shove to the chest that sent him flying back on his butt. Bailey flashed Dylan a quick grin, tossed the whistle over his shoulder, and took off.

Arf! Arf! Come back here, Bailey.

Dylan turned around and saw Casey and Sumo

running down the hill. *Hurry up guys, Bailey is getting away.*

"Go on, Dylan!" Casey called, holding a hand to his side. "We're right behind you."

Arf! Dylan sucked in a deep breath, hurdled over Larry, and followed Bailey down Treetops Way. *Slow down Bailey, I'm getting tired.* Dylan came around a bend just as Bailey disappeared around the next bend. *Whew! This is a really long way.* When Dylan and Bailey broke through the last of the trees, they were blasted with sunshine and the happy sounds of people.

Hey! This is Front Street. There's the woobie shop. The ice cream shop is over there. Dylan gulped in air and looked over his shoulder to Treetops Way. Casey, Sumo, and the others were way behind him and had stopped running. Everyone was bent over at the waist, gasping for air. *You're tired?* Dylan's heart was still banging in his chest. *You only have two feet. You should try running on four paws.*

Casey cupped his hands around his mouth and shouted, "Get Bailey."

I did! See? Dylan turned back around. *No Bailey.* Only visitors were milling about on Front Street. *That does it.* Dylan shook his ears out and plunked his buns down. *This is nuts. I'm tired and my paws hurt. And for what? Some dumb chimp that takes off all the time.* Dylan scratched his left ear with his back paw and then stretched out on his stomach. *I quit. Bailey can just stay gone.*

"Dylan," Casey called. "You've got to find Bailey."

No, I don't.

"There can't be a ribbon-cutting ceremony with Bailey if there's no Bailey."

Fine by me. Dylan looked down at his naked chest. *I'm still mad at you. You gave Bailey my bandana. Grr.*

"Please."

Dylan blew out a sigh. *It's a good thing you didn't give Bailey my vest. Otherwise, you'd be on your own.* Dylan heaved to his paws and headed for Front Street. *I'd better be getting a really big scoop of vanilla ice cream after this.*

CHAPTER EIGHTEEN

Dylan sniffed the air for Bailey. *No chimp smells.* His nose twitched. *French fries? Barbecue? My favorites.* Dylan's stomach growled but he put one tired paw in front of the other and worked his way along Front Street. When he got to the souvenir shop, he raised his head up for a better look. *People, people, people.* A woman eating a popsicle bumped into him. *Yip! I'm walking here!* Dylan tried dodging two little kids wearing backpacks. One backpack bopped Dylan in the face. *Hey!* Dylan tried scrunching down low. *Legs, legs, legs. Why are there so many people here? Doesn't anybody work?*

Dylan shook his sweaty topknot out of his eyes and sniffed the air again for Bailey. *Zip.* Dylan plodded along, the hot pavement burning his sore paws. *This is dumb.* Dylan looked behind him but there was no sign of Casey and Sumo. *What's taking you so long?* He searched the crowd for Bailey and panted. *Where's Bailey?*

"Help!" A woman's scream arrowed through the air. "Somebody, help! There's a thief in my shop!"

Dylan spun around and saw Bailey's bulky body filling

the doorway of the souvenir shop. *Found you!* Dylan shoulder-bumped his way through the crowd. Bailey had two large shopping bags filled with stuffed giraffes, elephants, flamingos, rhinos, lions, and zebras. His black eyes darted up and down Front Street.

"Stop him," the woman yelled. "Stop the thief!"

Grr, Bailey! You and your sticky fingers are at it again! Dylan shook his ears. *Stealing is so low. No matter what, I'd never, ever take anything that wasn't mine. You're bad, bad, bad.*

Bailey made a break for it and barreled through the crowd, knocking people aside left and right like a halfback running with the football.

"Hey!"

"Is that King Kong?"

"That beast made me drop my cotton candy!"

The crowd parted. On the sidelines, parents hugged their children close. The curious held their cell phones up, videos were rolling. Social media would never be the same.

Dylan raced after Bailey. *You shouldn't take things that don't belong to you. Uncle Rory says it's against the law and only bad people steal.* Dylan thought about that. *Bad chimps, too.*

Bailey stumbled and a black-and-white woobie bounced out of his bag, landing at Dylan's paws.

Oh, wow! I've always wanted a panda bear! Dylan waited a moment, looked left and right, but no one came running to claim it. *Hmm.* Dylan's heart bubbled with happiness. He clamped his jaws on the woobie and gave it a happy shake. *Mine, I think!* Dylan scampered after Bailey.

Bailey zipped past the fast-food restaurants. When he came to Skyfari Tram Ride, he made a sharp left and bounded up the ramp.

I'm right behind you. Dylan scanned the long line of visitors waiting their turn. *Got you now, Bailey. You can't go on the ride by yourself. You have to wait for Casey.*

Dylan slowed to a trot and watched a gondola glide closer to the platform. The attendant grabbed it and held it while the riders got out. *Bailey, the line is too long. It will take forever for your turn.*

Bailey didn't believe in standing in line. He headed to the first gondola and flashed his big teeth at the mom and little girl waiting for the ride. The little girl screamed, and the mom gathered her up and ran in the other direction.

Stop Bailey! Dylan wove his way between the legs of the people standing in line. *Cutting in line is cheating.*

Bailey leaped into the gondola with both shopping bags and plopped down on the bench. The gondola bounced and the crowd gasped.

"Henry," the attendant let go of the gondola and fumbled for the walkie-talkie on his belt. "We have a situation here." The gondola started creeping along the long platform and toward the open air. The attendant tried again, "Henry! Stop Skyfari! Now!"

Bailey leaned back against the seat and crossed one hairy leg over the other. He spotted Dylan on the platform and gave him a big wave.

I've had it with you. You're not getting away. Dylan circled around the attendant, raced up to the gondola, and jumped.

Dylan's chest hit the floor of the gondola, knocking the air out of him. *Agh!*

Dylan's two front paws and eight nails scrabbled for a grip on the metal floor. *Uh.*

Dylan's head flew back, and he saw fat white clouds

above him in a blue sky. *Help!* Dylan's back legs started pistoning in the air.

"Dylan!"

Dylan spotted Casey standing on the platform. *What took you so long?*

Mom, Sumo, Dominick, and Dylan's Dog Squad volunteers stood behind Casey, looking up. Jonah was working his iPad and Anna was taking photographs. A crowd had gathered around, pointing fingers and cell phones in Dylan's direction.

"Look at that little dog!"

"He's going to fall!"

"Someone call 9-1-1!"

The gondola swung away from the platform and into the air.

Casey shoved past the others and raced down the platform. "Kick harder, Dylan!"

Dylan kicked out with his back paws, sending his front half into the gondola. *Good!* He wiggled forward. He felt his vest catch on something and then heard his vest tear. *Not good.* When Dylan tried to check out his vest, the panda bear he was holding in his mouth got in the way and he could only see blue sky. *How did I get way up here? Where did the ground go?* Dylan gave a low whine. *Definitely not good.* He leaned to the right, wiggled his bottom, and tried to hook a back paw onto the gondola. *Nope!*

"That's it, Little Buddy!" Casey cupped his hands around his mouth and yelled, "You've got this!"

Got what? Give me a clue. Dylan's heart started beating like a jackhammer. *I don't want to be up high. I'm a ground dog, not a gondola dog. Help me, Casey. I'm scared.*

A flock of California Condors flew close to Dylan and screamed.

Arf! No! Dylan tried taking back his bark, but it was too late. Sadly, he watched his panda bear drift down, down, down. *Whine.*

"Kick, Dylan!"

Dylan took a deep breath and kicked out again.

Rip!

Dylan's vest broke loose from the gondola, and he tumbled backward into blue sky.

CHAPTER NINETEEN

N-o-o-o!

Dylan squeezed his eyes shut. *If I can't see, I can't be falling.* Suddenly his head snapped back. *Ow!*

He felt himself jerked straight up by his vest. *Hey!*

Dylan kicked out a little and pawed the air a lot. The wind whistled around him and blew his ears over his eyes. He shook them away. *Much better.*

Slam! Dylan's muzzle kissed the floor of the gondola. *Maybe not.*

Dylan stuck his long pink tongue out and waggled it. *I bith my thongue.* He blinked twice.

Two hairy feet.

Two hairy bowed legs.

One homely Bailey face staring down at me.

Yikes! Dylan pushed up from the floor with his front paws and sat back on his rump. *What did you do that for?*

Bailey crouched in front of Dylan. He patted Dylan's topknot and smoothed the tear in Dylan's vest.

Uh, thanks.

Bailey cocked his head. He pointed his index finger at

Dylan, withdrew his index finger, held up his thumb, and moved it in two quick circles, signing Are You Okay.

Dylan held up a furry paw and sighed. *I only know American Sign Language. I can't sign.*

Bailey signed again.

Hmm. This time Dylan gave Bailey an open-mouthed grin.

Bailey grunted and patted Dylan's topknot again.

Okay. You can stop that now.

Bailey reached out and dragged over one of the bags of woobies he'd shoplifted from the souvenir store. One by one he put a woobie on the floor next to Dylan.

For me?

Bailey clutched the other souvenir bag to his chest and climbed onto the bench across from Dylan. He rummaged inside and pulled out a green and black snake. Bailey held it up for Dylan to see.

Nice.

Bailey agreed. He wrapped the toy snake around his neck and pointed to the stuffed animals around Dylan.

Dylan nuzzled through the woobies on the floor. *This is a tough choice. I like them all. Giraffe or lion? Hmm.* He used his teeth to pick up a fluffy lion. *You do steal really good stuff.*

Bailey scooted over and patted the bench next to him. Dylan jumped onto the bench and dropped the lion between them.

Bailey took the stuffed snake from around his neck and put it around Dylan's neck.

Thanks.

Bailey reached down and stroked the lion's mane.

Your fingers are wrinkly. You should use lotion on your hands. Mom does.

Bailey tipped his head and made a soft sound low in his throat.

I like this woobie. Dylan covered the lion with his paw. *You gave it to me.*

Bailey wiggled his toes.

All right, already. Dylan licked the lion once before tossing it onto Bailey's lap.

Bailey hugged the woobie, crooned, and gave Dylan several quick closed-mouthed grins.

Dylan sighed and put his muzzle on his front paws. *This has been a really long day.*

CHAPTER TWENTY

Dylan felt the gondola slow and do a lazy swing. *What's happening?*

Bailey scrunched up his nose and swiveled on his seat beside Dylan. He let out a string of quick sounds and clamped a hairy hand on Dylan's vest, rocking him back and forth.

Stop that! Dylan shook Bailey off. *I need to see.* Dylan got to his paws just as the gondola lurched forward on its thick wire. *Agh!* Dylan spread his legs to steady himself. The wire vibrated and the gondola hiccupped. Dylan toppled off the bench and landed flat on the floor of the gondola.

Dylan raised his head and shook his ears out of his eyes. *I bith my thongue again.* He stuck it out of his mouth anyway and lifted it up and down, trying to see the end of it. *Thish hurths.*

Bailey clapped his hands together, rocked back and forth, and gibbered loudly.

Not funny.

"Little Buddy!"

Casey! Dylan scrambled to his paws. The gondola was at the end of the line, and Casey was waiting for him. Dylan leaped into Casey's arms and covered his face with canine kisses. *I knew you would come for me.*

"Hey," Casey hugged him. "It's okay." He hugged him again and then wiped the dog slobber off his face. "You're safe."

I was up high. I hate being up high. I was with Bailey. I hate, Dylan began but thought some. *I guess I don't really hate Bailey.*

"Dylan!" Mom rushed over and put her arms around Dylan and Casey. "I was so scared when you jumped into the gondola. You were so brave."

Thanks, Mom. Dylan slurped a doggie kiss on her cheek.

Mom laughed. She ran her hands over his shoulders and her hand caught on the jagged material of his vest. "What's this?"

I tore my vest. Dylan hung his head. *Now I can't be an American Kennel Club Canine Good Citizen.*

"Not to worry." She kissed Dylan on his topknot. "I can fix it."

Suddenly Dylan's day was as bright as candy. *Thanks, Mom.*

"Bailey," Mom called, "it's time for the ribbon-cutting ceremony."

Bailey didn't budge from the gondola's bench. Instead, he flashed a toothy smile her way and crossed his arms over his chest.

"Uh-oh, Ms. D," Sumo whispered. "That means Bailey is still upset."

"Rachel was afraid of that," Mom whispered back. "She wanted to come but the press conference is still going on."

Mom's voice turned cheerful, and she rooted around in her purse. "I have something for you, Bailey."

Bailey kept his arms crossed over his chest, but his black eyes tracked her movements.

"You have Bailey's attention, Mom."

"That's good," Mom said softly through a half smile. She showed Bailey a plastic bag filled with something like green balls cut in half. The insides were reddish-purple. "Yum."

Dylan leaned away from Casey and stretched closer to the bag. *Looks weird.* His nose twitched. *Smells weird.*

"What's that, Mom?"

Sumo held his cell phone up. "Figs. Right, Ms. D?" He waved the picture at Casey and read, "Figs make up half of a chimpanzee's diet. They are honey-like sweet and taste like a berry."

"Eww." Casey and Dylan backed up. "Don't even think about making me eat them."

Or me.

Sumo shrugged. "They're not bad if you like getting purple teeth and a lot of seeds."

Mom smiled at Bailey and shook the bag. "Rachel says figs are Bailey's favorite snack."

They were. Bailey climbed out of the gondola, ambled over to Mom, and reached for the bag.

Mom gave it to him and blew out a breath. "That went well."

Arf! Dylan pawed Casey's arm. *Aren't you forgetting something?*

"Sure." Casey put Dylan on the ground, slipped off his backpack, and pulled out a bag of butter cookies. He shoved one between his teeth, broke one in half for Dylan, and tossed the bag to Sumo.

Sumo helped himself to a cookie. "We'd better be getting lunch after the ribbon-cutting thing, Ms. D. I'm starving."

Me, too. Dylan gulped down the cookie, licked his muzzle, and wagged his tail.

Casey gave Dylan the other half of the cookie.

Dylan chomped the last of the cookie open-mouthed, raised his face up to Casey, and coughed.

"Hold on, Little Buddy." Casey got out Dylan's collapsible dish and a bottle of water. He filled the dish to the brim. "I bet you're thirsty."

No kidding. Dylan nudged Casey's hand aside and drank deep. *You try chasing a chimp for a mile and then flying in a gigantic egg way up high.*

Bailey grunted, flashed a purple smile, and held out his hand. Casey dug another bottle of water out of his backpack and tossed it to Bailey.

Bailey caught it, drained the bottle, and smacked his purple lips.

"Ready, Bailey?" Mom held out her hand to him. "We need to meet Rachel."

Bailey gave her the empty treat bag and slipped his hand into hers. They started walking toward the Hummer, but Bailey stopped. Letting go of Mom's hand, he raced back to the gondola.

"No, Bailey," Mom wailed. "Not again. Come back."

Listen to Mom. Dylan plunked his buns down. *No way am I chasing you.*

Bailey ignored her. He gave a two-flatfooted jump into the gondola, scooped up the stolen woobies, and jammed them into the shopping bags. Grunting happily Bailey hopped out of the gondola and hotfooted it back to Mom.

"Bailey, where did you get these?" Mom showed the bags to Casey and Sumo.

You don't want to know.

Bailey turned his face away from Mom.

"Okay," Mom said and handed the bags to Sumo. "We'll worry about this later. Right now, we need to hurry." She took Bailey's hand and lead him to the Hummer.

Sumo raced ahead. "Shotgun!" Sumo tossed the shopping bags into the back of the Hummer and climbed in front. "This was so cool of Rocco to let us use the Hummer."

"It was," Mom agreed. "He said to meet him at the security entrance after the ceremony and he'll drive us back to the Gulfstream."

Casey opened the back door, put Dylan on the seat, and slid in next to him. "The Hummer is cool. We should get one."

"Oh yes." Mom laughed and helped Bailey inside. "This behemoth would be so much fun in rush hour traffic on the 5 Freeway."

Be moth? Dylan rubbed his muzzle on Casey's arm. *Isn't that a little bug that flies around?*

"I think it means big," Casey whispered.

Why didn't Mom say so?

When they approached the new primate habitat, a young woman wearing a safari shirt and shorts waved them over. "Hi, Ms. Donovan. I'm Amber." She turned away and clicked on her walkie-talkie. "Ms. Donovan has arrived." She listened and clicked off. "Please park over there," she gestured to a clearing where a man was waiting. "Thomas will take you to the dedication area. We'll be starting soon." She stepped back from the Hummer. "Have fun today!"

Mom guided the Hummer to the dirt lot where Thomas was waiting.

"Welcome." Thomas opened her door. "Right this way, everybody."

They trooped along behind Thomas to the new primate habitat where Rachel was talking with Jonah. Behind them, a wide red ribbon had been strung between two trees. Holly stood off to the side, her small hands scrunching the hem of her I'm With Bailey T-shirt. Anna was moving through the people taking photos. She saw them and waved.

"There's got to be a hundred people here," Sumo murmured. "Dominick is with Dylan's Dog Squad volunteers over there."

Bailey delighted the crowd by giving out thin-lipped smiles and big waves. His fans waved back, calling his name, and taking pictures like crazy. No one mentioned his purple teeth.

"Bailey could be a politician." Casey picked up Dylan. "Now you can see everything."

Dylan snuggled close. *Thanks!*

Jonah broke away from Rachel and came over. "This place is unbelievable." He hooked his thumb over his shoulder. "Rachel is incredible. I can't believe how much work she has done for the primates."

Mom nodded. "I can't wait to read your story about her."

Jonah smiled and rubbed his hands together. "There's more to come." Jonah gave her a wink. "Just wait."

CHAPTER TWENTY-ONE

Anna slipped through the crowd and worked her way over. Bailey put an open hand to his forehead and quickly pulled it away, signing Hi.

"You're one clever chimp," Anna laughed and signed Hi.

Dylan rubbed Casey's chin with his muzzle. *We know Hi, too.*

Anna put something silver on her camera, checked something else, then started taking pictures of Bailey.

Bailey wiggled his buns, dipped his chin to his chest, and peeked up at Anna through long, spiky eyelashes.

"Bailey, you're such a flirt." Anna brought the camera closer and snapped away.

"It's time, Bailey." Jonah held his hand out. "Let's go see Rachel."

Bailey hung back and waited for Mom.

"It's okay, Bailey." She gave him a hug. "Go with Jonah."

Sumo got his cell phone out and aimed it at the stage. "This is so cool. Social media will eat this up, Ms. D."

"This is a big day for the zoo. Rachel worked hard to make this happen. Everyone who meets her says she's amazing."

"Everyone but Holly," Casey said.

Mom nodded. "You should've heard Holly go on and on when Bailey took off."

Casey laughed. "She was mad?"

"More like, she was mad Dylan brought him back," Sumo said.

I was just doing my job.

Mom held up her hand and whispered, "Quiet. The ribbon cutting ceremony is starting."

Rachel stepped forward and addressed the people. "Welcome! Your support means so much to me and to everyone who has spent so many hours making this new primate habitat a reality. I wish I could hug every one of you." Her eyes filled with tears, and she crossed her arms over her heart.

Not to be left out, Bailey gave everyone several quick thin-lipped smiles and crossed his long hairy arms over his heart.

"Ohhh!" the crowd cooed and sighed.

Holly rolled her eyes, shook her head, and kicked the dirt with the toe of her sneaker.

"Bailey," Rachel handed a pair of oversized scissors to Bailey. "Are you ready?"

Good thing she didn't give the scissors to Holly.

The crowd went wild when Bailey took the scissors and neatly cut the red ribbon.

"Yay, Bailey!"

"Good job!"

"Look this way!"

People pushed forward holding their cell phones high.

"Wow," Casey said. "Bailey can use scissors."

"You should check out the chimpanzee websites." Sumo tapped his cell phone. "Chimps can do pretty much anything we can do."

"They have opposing thumbs," Mom explained, "just like humans."

Dylan shoulder-bumped Casey's chest. *What's that?*

Casey shifted Dylan in his arms, held up his right hand, and bent his thumb back and forth.

Dylan studied his fluffy paws. *I don't have those. Not fair.*

"The new primate habit is large enough for thirty more primates." Rachel smiled brightly at the audience and drew Bailey close to her. "That means," she paused, "Bailey and I are leaving for Central Africa next week."

Jonah turned to Mom, Casey, and Sumo and gave a thumbs up.

"Oh no," The three of them moaned.

"Poor Holly," Mom said.

"Ms. Langdon," Dominick called out, "what will you do there?"

"I'm so glad you asked." Rachel's smile got bigger. "I'll be working with my team to locate chimpanzees in danger of human predators. We're going south of the Congo River and north of the Kasai River. We'll be gone all summer."

A female reporter stepped up and shoved a microphone in Holly's face. "Are you going too?"

"No way." Holly held her hands up in surrender and she gave a huge grin. "I'm going to Environmental Camp and save the world."

Casey cracked up. "Environmental Camp?"

That litterbug?

"What happened to Wyoming?" Sumo wondered.

"Who knows?" Mom got the Hummer keys out of her purse. "Anyway, there is nothing so satisfying as a job well done."

"Who said that, Mom?"

"Me." She laughed. "I'm glad Dylan's Dog Squad's job is finished. Rachel, Holly, and Bailey are on their own now." She checked the time. "We have an hour before we're supposed to meet Rocco. Just enough time for lunch."

"Yes!" Casey and Sumo high-fived.

Dylan rubbed Casey's cheek with his muzzle. *Don't forget the vanilla ice cream—large scoop.*

They hurried away, leaving Rachel to answer the flood of questions.

"Ms. D," Dominick called and loped up to them. "I'm glad I caught you." He held out a stuffed panda bear. "Dylan dropped this when he jumped into the gondola."

My bear! Dylan wiggled happily and pushed forward in Casey's arms.

Dominick tried wiping a smudge of dirt from the panda's white cheek. It stayed put. "Can't have Dylan leaving without his toy."

Mom shook her head. "This isn't Dylan's."

Oh yeah. Dylan whined. *Bailey stole it.*

"Maybe it's Bailey's." Sumo pointed to the back seat. "He had two shopping bags of woobies."

Mom took the bear from Dominick and held it out to Dylan. "Do you know something about this?"

No. Dylan flicked his ear and looked away. *Maybe.*

"Thanks, Dominick. We'll take care of it." Mom tilted her head toward the Hummer. "Want to go to lunch?"

"Thanks, but Ms. Langdon is giving a small party after this, and I'm invited." Dominick started walking backward toward the people still crowded around

Rachel. He blushed. "I've never had so much fun. This is the best day." He waved around him with both hands and grinned. "This is like the life of a rock star."

Sumo snorted. "Who'd say anything so dumb?"

You.

"You," Casey snorted back. "You're such a geek."

"Am not."

"Are, too."

You both are. Whine.

Mom beeped the Hummer open. She waited for Casey, Dylan, and Sumo to pile in before going around to the back of the Hummer. Mom started to put the panda bear in one of the shopping bags but stopped. "The logo on these bags says, 'Safari Souvenir Shop.'"

Casey, Sumo, and Dylan said nothing.

"Boys, do you know how Bailey got these woobies?"

"Dylan was chasing Bailey, Mom. We were way behind them."

"Dylan?"

Hey, don't look at me. I was busy chasing the criminal chimp.

"By the time we caught up Bailey and Dylan were already at the gondola, Ms. D. I didn't see any bags."

"Me neither. Bailey must have gone shopping earlier. Right, Little Buddy?"

Dylan turned his big brown eyes to Casey. *Sort of.*

"Shopping?" Mom's eyebrows went up. "Hmm. Rory said mail and personal property were stolen when Bailey went missing from Holly's house." She waited.

Sticky-fingered chimp.

"Omission is the most powerful form of lie," Mom reminded Casey.

"Quoting George Orwell?" Casey made a face. "It's just a coincidence."

Uncle Rory says there's no such thing as a coincidence.

Mom gave him The Look and then gently put the panda bear into a bag. "Right."

CHAPTER TWENTY-TWO

Dylan hung his head out the Hummer's open window and let the wind blow his ears away from his face. *It's been forever since breakfast.* His stomach rumbled. *There are lots of people at the zoo today. I hope the ice cream shop hasn't run out of vanilla ice cream.*

Front Street was busy, but Mom lucked out and found a parking space in front of Safari Souvenir Shop.

Mom! Why are we stopping here? Dylan swiveled on Casey's lap and whined in his ear. *Do something.*

"We want lunch," Casey grumbled. "Can't this wait?"

Mom turned off the ignition and grabbed her purse. "This will only take a minute. Sumo, please get the shopping bags."

"Okay."

"Casey, please carry Dylan. The sidewalk is too hot for him to walk."

"Good news, Little Buddy." Casey brushed Dylan's topknot out of his eyes and smoothed down his ears. "Now you can check out the store."

Dylan gave a happy yip when Mom pushed the door to Safari Souvenir Shop open. *I've never seen so many woobies in one place.*

"This place is huge," Sumo whispered to Casey. "I'm surprised Bailey left with only two bags of stuff."

No joke.

Mom scanned the store bursting with people and souvenirs. When she spotted a middle-aged sales associate in a safari shirt and shorts chatting with two teenage girls she said, "This way, boys."

"We'll take these T-shirts," said one girl, as she handed the sales associate her money.

"They're cute," the sales associate bubbled. "You'll love them."

Mom, Casey, Dylan, and Sumo waited until the sales associate gave the girl her receipt before stepping up to the cash register.

"May I help you?" The sales associate gave Mom a sunny smile.

"Yes." Mom gave her a sunnier smile.

The sales associate's sunny smile turned suspicious when she spotted the two shopping bags Sumo was carrying.

Mom took the shopping bags from Sumo and held them out. "We found these and thought they might belong to you. Perhaps a guest forgot to pay for them."

"That wasn't a guest. It was Bailey. His picture is on display right outside my door."

"I'm sure it was a mistake," Mom began.

Stealing is a mistake.

The sales associate went from suspicious to surly. "That chimp ripped me off! He had some nerve coming in here and helping himself."

"Please lower your voice," Mom urged but it was too late. Customers were already gathering behind them and starting to talk.

"Did you hear that? The sales associate called Bailey a thief."

"Not true! Bailey dedicated the new primate habitat today."

"That sales associate is wrong. It had to be some other chimp."

"Mom!" a little boy wailed. "She's saying mean things about Bailey."

"She's mistaken, Timmy. Bailey would never steal." The mom cast a look to the other shoppers. "Right?"

Their vote was unanimous. "Right!"

"I bet animals get loose at the zoo all the time." A man with a sunburn glared at the sales associate. "It couldn't have been Bailey."

Arf! Dylan pawed Casey's arm. *It was Bailey.*

"Not now, Little Buddy."

"Hey, everybody," the man with the sunburn announced. "That's the dog!"

What dog? Dylan looked around the store. *Where?*

"We saw that little blond dog this morning," the man said to the people around him. He touched his wife's arm. "Remember? The dog risked his life running after the chimp with the shopping bags!"

"Yeah," a teenage boy chimed in. "They ran right past me. I got a good look at the chimp, too. It wasn't Bailey."

"I've got it on video." The man's wife showed her cell phone to the other customers. "You should've seen this little guy run down Front Street. He's fast!"

I am.

Shoppers forgot about buying souvenirs they couldn't

live without. Heads were down. Cell phones were out of pockets. Fingers were scrolling across the screens. Strangers were sharing pictures.

"Look. This is when the chimp ran to the gondolas."

"See? This little dog chased him all the way."

"Then the little dog jumped into the gondola after the chimp."

"Wow! I can't believe he made it. He's like some kind of super dog."

That's me.

A burly man wearing a pink flamingo muscle shirt stepped up. His forearms were covered in tattoos. The arm with a tattoo of a yellow flag and a coiled snake pointed first at Dylan and then at the sales associate. "This little dog," he growled, "risked his life to save your merchandise."

Dylan stared at the snake tattoo. *Scary.* He pressed himself against Casey. *I like Bailey's snake better.*

The sales associate's surly face went stony. "That's ridiculous."

"I wouldn't mess with that guy," Sumo warned. "That's a Gadsden flag tattoo on his arm and it says, 'Don't tread on me'. You know what that means?"

"Not now, Sumo," Mom and Casey hissed.

The sales associate's stony face sneered. "It was Bailey, I tell you. Bailey and this dog are in cahoots." She jabbed a finger in the air toward Dylan. "The cute one is always the ringleader."

I'm cute? Aw, thanks. Dylan looked up at Casey. *What's cahoots? What's a ringleader?*

"Dylan saw your thief and chased him." Casey came closer to the sales associate. "Look at his paws. They're filthy."

I'm filthy? Dylan wiggled his fluffy feet caked with dirt. *That's not a very nice thing to say.*

"Dylan's very brave." Casey hugged Dylan. "He's a hero."

True. Dylan shifted so the sales associate could see the tear in his AKC Canine Good Citizen vest. *I risked my life for that crazy chimp.*

"Thanks to Dylan," Sumo took the shopping bags from Mom and put them on the counter, "you're getting your stuff back."

The sales associate sniffed and peeked into the first bag. "It seems to be all here. Fine. You may go."

"That's it? You've got nothing else to say?" Burly Man With Snake Tattoo turned to the crowd. "Who thinks Dylan deserves a reward?"

"We do!"

"Yes!"

Okay. Dylan looked up at Casey. *What's a reward? Can I eat it?*

"Who says," Burly Man With Snake Tattoo raised his voice, encouraging the others, "Dylan should pick out something from the shop. After all, he's a hero."

Well, since you put it that way.

"Let the little dog get what he wants!"

"It's the least the store can do!"

Casey ruffled Dylan's topknot and moved the shopping bags closer to Dylan. "What do you like?"

Dylan stretched forward and licked the panda bear. *Mine!*

"Great." Casey held the panda bear up so everyone could see.

The shoppers cheered.

"That'll be $24.95," the sales associate declared.

The shoppers gasped.

"You gotta be kidding me," Sumo snatched the panda bear from Casey and held it up for everyone to see. "It's dirty. That means it's used."

"Boo!"

"Give the pup a new bear!"

"What a cheapskate!"

"Take it or leave it," the sales associate insisted and snatched the panda bear back.

She took my panda bear. Whine.

The two girls who had bought the T-shirts marched up to the cash register. One girl took the shirts out of the bag and flung them onto the counter. "We want our money back."

The other girl picked up the empty bag and put a dollar in it. "Hey everybody. What do you say? Let's chip in for Dylan." She held out the bag to a lady wearing a straw hat.

"Absolutely." The woman dropped a dollar into the bag and announced, "I'll never buy anything here."

"Uh," the sales associate stuttered and waved the panda bear in the air, "I was just kidding."

"No, you weren't," Casey argued.

Wallets were opened and dollar bills were put into the bag. When the money had been collected, the girl counted it out. "Perfect." She handed the money to the red-faced sales associate and gave Dylan the panda bear.

Dylan licked its face. *Thank you.*

The crowd went wild.

Dylan flashed a happy grin to the shoppers in the store. *I love my panda bear.*

"Thank you, everyone." Mom said and smiled at Casey,

Sumo, and Dylan. "I told you this wouldn't take long." She checked the time. "Let's get lunch."

"What do you say, Little Buddy?"

Dylan slurped a sloppy kiss on Casey's cheek. *I say let's get ice cream first.*

CHAPTER TWENTY-THREE

Casey and Sumo sat down cross-legged on Casey's bedroom floor. Dylan dropped to his stomach, wiggled in between them, laid his muzzle across Casey's lap, and yawned.

"Okay," Casey scratched Dylan's ear, "here's the plan."

Uh-oh. Dylan snapped his muzzle shut and rolled his dark brown eyes up at Casey. *Whenever you say that we end up in trouble.*

"We've got to get out of here while Mom is still on her Zoom conference with Cranky Pants."

"Why?"

"If she's busy with Cranky Pants she won't ask too many questions. You know Mom. She'll want to tag along to Dream Big K-9 Academy and watch us teach our first class. We don't want that. Mom will hang around and take a bunch of pictures."

Sumo frowned. "So what? I do that."

"You're supposed to. You're in charge of social media for Dylan's Dog Squad. Mom is," Casey blew out a sigh, "Mom."

"Your mom is cool."

"Yeah."

Sumo wishes he had a mom like ours.

Sumo checked his cell phone. "It's getting late. What's the other reason?"

"I'm only saying we're going to Dream Big K-9 Academy. That's it. Otherwise, she'll ask a lot of questions and we don't want that."

"We're meeting Jake, Tanya, Tabitha, and Tori afterward." Sumo put his cell phone in his shorts pocket. "Your mom likes them. What's the big deal?"

"Are you nuts? We're meeting them at Big Belly's."

This is an excellent day. We're teaching our first class and we're getting pizza. Dylan stretched out his front paws. *Big Belly's extra cheese and mushroom pizza is the best.*

"If I tell her we're going to Big Belly's, she'll say pizza is loaded with fat. She'll say it's not good to have too much fat."

Yes, it is.

Casey shook his head. "Her idea of pizza is cauliflower crust with organic marinara sauce and low-fat mozzarella cheese."

"Yeah but," Sumo laughed, "your mom's cool."

"She's okay." Casey got to his feet. "Where's your Dream Big bandana, Little Buddy?"

Dylan got up and used his teeth to tease his bandana off Casey's desk chair. He brought it to Casey and waited, holding it in his mouth. *Don't wrinkle it.*

"Thanks." Casey knelt and tied Dylan's bandana around his neck. "Hold on." Casey sat back on his heels, smoothed Dylan's topknot, and then fluffed out his ears. "You look sharp."

Arf! Dylan raced down the hallway, his furry paws slipping on the hardwood floors. When he reached the turn in the hallway, his four paws slid out from underneath him, and he side slammed into the wall. *Agh!* Dylan wobbled to his feet.

"You've got to remember not to run in the house, Dylan!"

He shook his ears out and padded down the hall. *We've got to get carpet in the house.*

Outside Mom's office, Casey caught up to Dylan. He put his index finger to his lips, signing Quiet. Casey turned around to Sumo and whispered, "Be quiet."

"What?" Sumo said in a loud voice.

"Sumo!"

Sumo should learn sign language. Dylan trotted into Mom's office and pawed her leg. She reached down and put him in the chair beside her.

Dylan sniffed the air and checked out the plate next to Mom's laptop. *Hmm. Blueberry bagel and cream cheese.* Dylan hooked his paws over the edge of the chair and scooted forward. A lick later that glop of cream cheese was his. *Yeck, yeck, yeck.* Dylan spit it out. *Low-fat.*

Mom moved the plate farther back.

"Colleen," Cranston's paper-thin voice came out loud and clear. "You simply must budget your time better."

"Cranston," Mom's voice was firm, "you know I've been at the San Diego Zoo. I didn't get home until late last night." She attempted a pretty smile. "However, as always, you are my number one priority."

"Then why don't you have any ideas for my children's cookbook?" he snapped. "It's summer!"

Mom slid her eyes to Casey and Sumo, rolled them, and returned to her computer screen. "Pray tell, what does summer have to do with a children's cookbook?"

He tossed his bony hands into the air. "Isn't it obvious?"

Mom lost her smile and muttered, "Apparently it isn't."

"What?"

Her smile was back. "I'm listening."

Cranky Pants brought his lined face close to the screen. "One," he held up his bony thumb, "this is summer." A wrinkled index finger shot up. "Two, I want a children's cookbook. Three," a third digit went up, "and—therefore obviously—the cookbook must have a summer theme." Two bushy white eyebrows came together like a fluffy pipe cleaner. "Now do you understand?"

"Perfectly. Summer theme. My favorite." She tapped the calendar app on her cell phone. "Let's talk again in two days."

Cranky Pants's mouth flatlined and he drummed his gnarly fingers on his mahogany desk. "Fine." He waited a moment. "Are you going to tell me about the San Diego Zoo event, or must I do all the talking?"

Mom brightened. "Since you asked," she reached for the stack of newspapers on her desk, "Jonah sent these over this morning. All the major papers picked up his story of Bailey at the ribbon cutting ceremony."

"Ridiculous," he grumbled. "All that hoopla over some chimp."

Exactly. Dylan whined. *Make that some criminal chimp.*

Mom patted the papers. "Jonah also wrote a public interest story for the *Orange County Register*. Anna did the photos for that, too. It's quite the spread." She opened the paper and held it up so Cranston could see. "It's about Casey, Dylan, and Sumo starting Dylan's Dog Squad. Jonah included background on Dylan. Jonah writes, "Dylan knows American Sign Language, graduated from Agility Class, works for Children's Hospital, performs search and rescue, and has recently received his American Kennel Club Canine Good Citizen vest."

That's me.

Cranky Pants began tapping his pen on his desk, a sign he was losing interest. None of this was about him.

Mom continued, "When Cranston Pantswick, owner of the largest children's book publishing company in North America, published his bestselling children's book about Scotch Tape, his beloved childhood dog, he personally chose Dylan to portray Scotch Tape on the cover of his book."

Arf! I'm a star.

"Scotch Tape." The old man's chin quivered. "My little dog."

"Jonah went into great detail about your generosity in providing the Gulfstream for our use." She scanned the article and read out loud, "Cranston Pantswick has long been recognized for his compassion and his humanitarian contributions."

Cranky Pants's flabby face broke into a smile.

Yikes! Dylan wiggled backward in the chair. *Don't do that.*

"My pleasure, Colleen. I've always been a friend to animals." He winked. "Anything for Dylan." He leaned closer to the screen and warbled, "Does Dylan want to visit his Uncle Cranston soon?"

No.

"He'd be delighted." Mom hugged Dylan and went back to business. "In the meantime, I'll come up with some ideas for you."

Cranky Pants gave a limp wristed handwave and warbled to Dylan, "Goodbye-e-e."

Mom hit End Meeting and swiveled in her chair. "Two

days to come up with something brilliant," she raised both eyebrows, "about a kid's cookbook." She wagged her head back and forth. "No problem. I've had harder projects, right?"

You made that dumb hamster Hieronymus famous. A cookbook should be easy.

"You can do it," Casey said cheerfully. He hooked a thumb over his shoulder. "Gotta go. See you later."

"Thanks for letting me stay over, Ms. D."

"Any time, Sumo."

Sumo is here all the time.

Mom stacked the newspapers and put them aside. "Any news from your mom?"

Sumo gave a lazy shrug. "Nah. She and Melvin are still in Paso Robles."

"Michael," Mom corrected.

"Whatever."

Casey punched Sumo in the arm. "You should remember his name."

"Why?" Sumo made a face. "My mom never stays married very long."

Good point.

"Anyway, Mom's all excited. Melvin's winery is having a big party and she's planning it. The governor will be there."

"Very impressive." Mom let it go. "What are you boys doing after Dream Big K-9 Academy?"

Whine. Dylan stood up and pawed the air at Casey. *Mom's getting snoopy. Time to skedaddle.*

Casey reached for Dylan and put him on the ground. "You know, hang out. The usual."

"Hmm." Mom shifted her gaze. "Sumo?"

"Uh, yeah, Ms. D. Do stuff."

"Well," she nodded, "when you see Tanya, Tabitha, and Tori at Big Belly's, please remind them to be home by two o'clock."

"Uh," Casey tried looking vague, "Big Belly's?"

"You know about that, Ms. D?" Sumo blurted out.

Casey glared at Sumo.

Mom knows everything.

"Their mom called earlier." She finger-tapped her cell phone. "She was worried the girls would be having too much fun and forget their grandmother arrives from Boston today."

"Uh, yeah, sure, Mom."

"I was hoping to see you teach your first class but," Mom's shoulders slumped, "I'm swamped."

"No problem! Dylan and I know the cookbook is really, really important." Casey's mouth twitched and he winked at Dylan. "We understand totally. Right, Little Buddy?"

Arf! I understand you lucked out.

Casey made fists with both hands, held out both arms, then tapped his right fist on top of his left fist twice in the wrist area, signing Work. "Let's go to work, Little Buddy."

Arf! Dylan flew out of the office and down the stairs. At their front door, he plunked his butt down. *We can't be late.*

"Hold on." Casey gently nudged Dylan aside with his knee and opened the front door.

Dylan stuck his snout out the door, wagged his short tail, and then muscled past Casey. Dylan raced down the front walk. When he reached Casey's bike he hopped up and planted two front paws on his bike trailer. *Hurry up. We're burning daylight.*

"You're excited about class." Casey reached down, unzipped the front of Dylan's bike trailer, and waited for

Dylan to jump in. Casey leaned closer and whispered in Dylan's ear, "Don't tell Sumo but I'm kind of nervous."

We'll be great. Dylan slurped a sloppy kiss on Casey's hand. *We're a team.*

"What if I bomb?"

No way. Dylan snuffled Casey's arm with his nose. *You've got me.*

Sumo reached for his bike helmet. "I've been sending out social media blasts all week." He put his helmet on and started laughing. "Nobody can believe you're teaching a class today. You don't even like school."

You're not helping, Sumo.

Casey unhooked his bike helmet from the handlebars. "I hope Roger isn't there."

He's not a happy guy.

"Are you nuts?" Sumo smirked. "That would be the best part."

"Huh?"

"Don't you get it?" Sumo swung his leg over his bike. "Roger has never been nice to you and Dylan. Then you and Dylan went and saved his life. Now he owes a big bag of money to The Sledgehammer. Roger needs your help again or else he'll lose Dream Big K-9 Academy. That's gotta sting."

"Yeah?"

Sumo grinned. "Yeah."

Casey high-fived Sumo and grinned. "Yeah."

Oh yeahhhhh. Dylan turned around twice on his fluffy cushion and flopped down. *Serves Roger right for saying mean things to me. He says I'm short and look like a stuffed animal.* Dylan put his muzzle on his fluffy front paws and got ready for a snooze. *Roger says he only likes working with big dogs.* Dylan sniffed. *Not fair. Little dogs can do anything big dogs can do.*

Ten minutes later, Dylan felt Casey's bike make a turn and then bounce along the gravel driveway to Dream Big K-9 Academy. Dylan sat up, stretched, and yawned. *Not a world class snooze but not bad.*

Dylan pushed his nose against the side screen of his trailer. Smells of fresh mowed grass and summer came back to him. Dylan's ears picked up happy yips and barks. He hunkered low, searching the grounds until he spotted the exercise field. *My favorite place.* Dylan saw a black and white Great Dane going over the jumps. *I remember when the jumps were hard for me.* A Belgian Malinois puppy slipped and fell off the teeter-totter. *Yikes.* A young woman ran up to him and hugged him. The dog shook himself all over but backed away when she tried to get him on it again. *Don't give up! I used to fall off all the time.*

Casey's bike turned slowly, and Dylan leaned with it. When the bike came to a stop Dylan's paws danced on his cushion. *Hurry up! Hurry up!* Casey unzipped the screen on the bike trailer and Dylan hopped out. *Show time!*

"Jean just texted. We're to meet her at the registration office," Sumo said, his fingers working the screen on his cell phone.

"Yeah, sure."

Sumo's fingers paused midair, and he looked up. "What's the matter?"

"What if no one comes?" Casey ran his hands through his shaggy hair. "What if no one wants to be in a class taught by a kid and a dog?"

"Look, you're not just any kid and Dylan isn't just any dog."

Dylan swung his head from Casey to Sumo. *Thanks, Sumo.*

"Remember," Sumo grinned, "I've been sending out social media blasts." He held up his cell phone. "You've got this."

Casey shrugged into his backpack and hooked Dylan's leash to his collar. "Okay."

Today will be great. Dylan body-bumped Casey and tugged at his leash. *You'll see.*

"Hold on, Little Buddy. You know the rules." Casey waited until Dylan moved to his left. "No tugging on the leash. You've got to set a good example."

You sound like Mom.

Dylan, Casey, and Sumo set off across the parking lot. When they rounded the corner to the registration office, they stopped cold.

"Whoa!" Sumo dropped his cell phone.

"Uh." Casey reined in Dylan's leash.

Gulp.

CHAPTER TWENTY-FOUR

A sea of kids and little dogs were waiting outside the registration office.

"There's gotta be like thirty kids here with their dogs." Sumo had his cell phone up and video rolling.

Casey shook his head. "Yeah."

I've never seen so many little dogs. Looks like all the kids are wearing furry slippers. Dylan swiveled his head left and right. *Yorkies, Maltese, Chihuahuas, Bichons, Pugs, Beagles, Jack Russell Terriers, Pomeranians, Dachshunds, Shih Tzus, Pekingese, Lhasa Apsos, and Toy Poodles are everywhere.* Dylan's mood took a bounce, and he pranced in place. *How about that? I'm the big dog.*

Kid voices came their way. "Casey!"

"Sumo!"

"It's Dylan!"

Every kid had their cell phone out. Kids and little dogs rushed toward Casey, Dylan, and Sumo. A black and tan pug collided face-first with Dylan.

Agh!

The pug snorted, huffed, and puffed. Snot dribbled out

his nose. The pug shot out a pink tongue and licked the snot away. He huffed again and tried to lick Dylan's face. Dylan scrambled away and hid behind Casey's leg. *Help!*

"I've got you." Casey picked Dylan up.

Thanks. Dylan peered down at the fuzzy faces. *Whine.*

That was all the little dogs needed to hear. Together they started yipping and yapping and jumping and pawing. An eager Jack Russell Terrier sprang the highest and landed on an apricot Toy Poodle. The Toy Poodle nipped the Jack Russell Terrier on its rump. The Jack Russell Terrier ignored the attack and launched himself again.

Jean came out of the registration office and hurried over to them. "What do you think of your class, Casey?"

I think it's big.

"I think I'm going to need help." Casey looked at Sumo.

Sumo backed up. "Uh-uh. I'm social media."

"I put our two beginner's classes together," Jean pointed to her walking boot, "so we'll help each other. We're only covering the basics today."

"Hey! Stop that!"

Dylan hooked his chin over Casey's shoulder and followed the noise.

A young girl dragged her Yorkie away from a Chihuahua and got into an older boy's face. "Your dog peed on Princess. Her bow is ruined."

Princess confirmed this by shaking her head. The pink bow holding her topknot together dripped pee into her eyes.

"Bad dog, Diesel," the boy began and then busted up. "You gotta stop doing that."

"Not funny," the girl insisted. Princess whined and her five-pound body trembled.

Jean sighed. "Sometimes we're more referee than

teacher in the beginner's class." Jean clapped her hands together and got the attention of the kids. "Please take your dog to the field," she pointed, "and line up. We'll start in a few minutes."

Kids and dogs trooped off.

"Are you ready, Dylan?" Jean brought her face close to his and rubbed his ears. "Remember when you had your first class?"

Arf!

Sumo searched the fields. "Where's Roger?"

"Sumo!"

"Somebody had to ask."

Why?

Jean tucked her iPad under her arm and motioned for Casey, Dylan, and Sumo to follow her. "He'll be here soon. His doctor has him on light duty." She took a deep breath and beamed. "Let's enjoy the quiet, shall we?"

When they reached the field, Sumo went off to the side. Casey, Dylan, and Jean walked to the middle of the field and faced the kids and dogs.

"I'm Jean and this is Casey and Dylan," she began. "We'll be your teachers. Does everyone have a bag of dog treats?"

Faces nodded. Tails wagged.

"Great." Jean smiled. "We're a large class. Half of you will be with me and the other half will be with Casey and Dylan."

"No!" The kids rebelled and dogs barked.

"I want to be in Dylan's group."

"Me, too."

"Dylan's group!"

"Okay, okay," Jean laughed. "You can take turns being with Dylan." She started down the row of kids until she got halfway. "You'll stay here. The rest of you take your dog and make a line over there."

Casey put Dylan on the ground and straightened his bandana.

Show time!

Jean moved Casey and Dylan aside. "You take this group," she gestured to the other group, "and I'll take that one."

"What do we do?"

She smiled. "I'll use you and Dylan to demonstrate each skill. Then you can work with your group."

Arf!

"Class, we'll begin with greeting a stranger. Watch me."

They did.

Jean turned to Casey. "May I pet your dog?"

"Sure."

Jean reached down and gave Dylan a pet.

And?

She gave Dylan a treat.

Dylan gave her a big grin. *I like this class already.*

"Okay, Casey and Dylan. Good luck." Jean walked over to her group.

Casey and Dylan went to the first boy. A small furry dog sat very still at his feet.

"Hi. Can I pet your dog?"

The boy looked confused. "Why?"

"Uh," Casey looked to Jean, but she was already petting the third dog in her group.

Casey reached down to pet the dog. The dog lunged forward, black eyes shining, and lips curled back showing sharp, pointy teeth.

Hey! Dylan danced away.

Casey pointed to the dog. "No treat for you!"

You tell him, Casey.

"Not fair," the kid griped.

"Tough," Casey shot back.

"You're not supposed to fight with the kids!" Sumo called from the sidelines and then cracked up. "You're as grumpy as Roger."

Casey glared at Sumo and went to a little girl holding a Pomeranian.

"Hi. If you want me to pet your dog, you've got to put it down."

The girl heaved a sigh. She gave the dog a bone-crushing hug and a smoochy kiss. As soon as she put the dog on the ground it dropped to its stomach and put its paws over its head. A little black nose stuck out.

"This was easier when Jean did it," Casey complained.

Show her what to do. Dylan pawed Casey's leg. *Hint, hint.*

Casey got the treat bag out of his shorts pocket.

Dylan plunked his butt on the ground.

"Dylan, can I pet you?"

Dylan kept his eyes glued to the treat bag. *Can you give me a treat?*

Casey petted Dylan.

Well?

Casey gave him a treat.

Dylan munched it loudly. *Thanks.*

Casey and Dylan moved down the line. A sturdy boy in a striped T-shirt and clutching a red leash was next. The leash was hooked to the collar of a chubby Boston Terrier licking its paws.

"Hi," Casey began.

The boy dropped the leash, pounced on Dylan, and grabbed an ear with each hand. "I want to pet Dylan."

Dylan's eyes bulged out and he flung his head back. *Casey!*

The kid squealed happily, and his grip tightened.

"No!" Casey peeled the kid's fingers away from Dylan's ears. "You don't get to talk. That's my job."

"This is great," Sumo called. He was holding onto his sides and laughing loudly. "You're turning into Roger."

"Shut up, Sumo."

This is harder than it looks.

The boy's happy face pouted. "I'm gonna tell."

"So what? I'm the teacher." Casey ignored the boy and pulled Dylan close. "Okay, Little Buddy?"

No. Sumo's laughing at us. Dylan sighed. *A treat would help.*

Casey gave him a treat. "Hold on." He smoothed Dylan's Dream Big bandana and checked out the rest of the line. "This line is like a mile long."

What's a mile? Dylan licked the crumbs off his muzzle and looked for himself. *Seven more kids to go.*

A boy with a brown Dachshund was next. "This is Herman."

Herman quivered from nose to tail when he heard his name. He dropped to the ground, rolled over onto his back, and waved all four paws in the air. His skinny muzzle opened, and a long pink tongue fell out. Two anxious black eyes darted from Casey to Dylan.

"That's Herman's favorite trick," the boy bragged.

Herman panted. Four tiny paws went wild in the air.

"Cool." Casey asked, "What else does he know?"

The boy stammered, "That's it."

"It can't be his favorite trick if it's the only trick he knows."

That's why it's his favorite trick. Dylan body-bumped Casey's leg. *Just pet Herman. I want to go to Big Belly's.*

"Whatever." The kid brought out the treat bag and Herman got to his paws. "Pet him so I can give him a treat."

Dylan studied Herman's short legs. *You're the same size standing up or lying down.*

Casey gave Herman's smooth head a pat and pointed to the bag. "Give him a treat."

Dylan glanced over his shoulder. *Jean is already finished. Dylan tugged on his leash and dragged Casey to a little girl with a Maltese.*

After they finished with the kids and dogs, Casey and Dylan went over to Jean. "What's next?"

"Sit."

Okay. Dylan sat.

"Show-off," Jean laughed.

What's so funny? You said Sit, so I sat. Dylan got to his paws and shook himself out.

Jean clapped her hands and waited for the kids to look at her. "Next, we'll work on Sit." Jean took a treat from the bag. "This is very easy for your dog to learn. Show your dog the treat." She brought the treat close to Dylan's nose.

Dylan wagged his butt. *Bring it closer.*

"When your dog is watching you, slowly pass the treat over his head."

I'm watching. Dylan kept his eyes on the treat. When Jean passed the treat over his head, Dylan's head tipped up and his body leaned back.

"Sit," Jean said the moment Dylan's rump hit the ground. "Class, when your dog is watching the treat and you pass the treat over your dog's head, your dog will natu-rally sit. As soon as he sits, say Sit." Jean gave Dylan's head a pat. "Class, give it a try."

Dylan pawed the air. *Give me a treat.*

Casey, Jean, and Dylan took turns with the students. After they worked through Stay and Heel, class was over.

Whew! I'm really hungry now. Teaching is hungry business.

Sumo ran over to them. "I sent out a bunch of pictures and videos. You've already gotten like a hundred hits on this stuff. People are asking if they can sign up for classes."

They already did. Check out the crowd.

Kids and little dogs covered the lawn outside the registration office. When they saw Dylan, hands went up and shouts went out.

"We want to sign up."

"I was here first."

"We know Dylan!"

The door of the registration office banged open. Roger charged out, cell phone held to one ear and angry voice at full volume. "I told you I'd pay by the end of the week. What do you want? Blood?" He glowered at Jean and kept walking.

"Is Roger talking to The Sledgehammer?" Casey asked.

Jean's lower lip trembled. "He wants his money."

Oh no.

CHAPTER TWENTY-FIVE

"Roger owes a ton of money. We've got to do something, Sumo."

You bet! Dylan danced between Sumo and Casey. *What are we waiting for? We need to get going!*

"No way. The Sledgehammer is one scary dude."

Oh, yeah. Dylan stopped so fast he tripped over his own paws. *Now what?*

"I've been thinking." Casey glanced around the patio area at Big Belly's. "Right now, we need a table. Jake and the girls will be here soon."

"Here's one."

"Okay." Casey pulled Dylan's blanket out of his backpack and spread it smoothly on the ground. "Here you go, Little Buddy."

Dylan hopped onto his blanket and pawed at it until the blanket was in a heap. *Nice and comfy.* Dylan plopped down. *Just the way I like it.*

"We need a plan," Casey insisted. "Dream Big K-9 Academy can't close."

No way. Dylan looked down at his Dream Big bandana.

No school. No bandana. Dylan got on his hind legs, put his front paws on the table, and looked from Sumo to Casey. *I love my bandana. Think, guys.*

"Hi!" Tanya, Tabitha, and Tori came up and took chairs. "How was class, Dylan?"

Dylan kept his paws on the table and side-shuffled closer to the girls so they could pet him. *Triplets are funny. You look the same. You talk the same. You even pet me the same.* Dylan shifted and they took turns rubbing his other shoulder. *Ah. Nice.*

Casey looked beyond them. "Where's Jake?"

"He's coming," Tanya or Tori, or Tabitha said.

"He'd better get here soon." Sumo rubbed his stomach. "I'm dying of hunger."

"Me, too," said Casey.

Me, three.

"Hi, guys!" Jake strolled up and pulled out a chair. He reached over and stroked Dylan's back. "Did you have fun in class?"

Arf! Now I'm starving.

"The stuff Sumo posted was pretty funny." Jake started laughing. "What did you do to that little brown dog, Casey?"

Herman.

"He was so-o-o cute," Tabitha, Tanya, and Tori crooned.

"It cracked me up when he did this." Jake leaned back, let his tongue hang out, and waved both hands in the air.

Weird. Dylan couldn't watch. *People always imitate dogs, but dogs never imitate people.*

Jake wiped the drool off his chin. "The dog looked like he'd been electrocuted."

"It was the only trick he knew." Casey gently eased Dylan's paws off the table and flicked a glance to Sumo.

"Aw," Tanya, Tori, and Tabitha sighed.

Jake caught the look between Casey and Sumo. "What, guys? What happened?"

Dylan popped back up between Casey and Sumo. He leaned against Casey. *Tell them.*

Casey put his index finger to his lips, signing Quiet.

"Roger borrowed a bunch of money from Theo Sledge and now he can't pay it back," Sumo blurted out.

Tabitha, Tanya, and Tori yelped, "The Sledgehammer!"

"Oh man," Jake's eyes bugged out. "Is Roger crazy?"

"Sumo! Jean said not to tell anyone."

"I didn't." Sumo made a face. "They're not anyone. They're our friends. Maybe they can help."

"You know my dad's accounting firm specializes in real estate." Jake leaned in close and dropped his voice to a whisper. "A few years ago, some of his clients had him look over an investment plan from Theo Sledge. Dad said the whole thing was fake. The only person who was going to get rich was Sledge."

"Uncle Rory says the police know The Sledgehammer is crooked, but they can't catch him on anything."

"Bad guys always get other people to do their dirty work," Tanya or Tori or Tabitha said.

"Probably hires muscle from out of town," Sumo agreed. "Spine crackers with no fingerprints and no ID."

You watch too much TV, Sumo.

"We need fuel food if we're going to come up with an idea." Casey dug money out of his pocket and handed it to Sumo. "Pizza with extra cheese and mushrooms. And a large, iced tea."

Sumo picked up the money. "Okay."

Jake, Tanya, Tabitha, and Tori stood up. "We'll go with you."

Casey waited for them to leave before leaning down to Dylan. "This is bad for Jean and Roger, Little Buddy. Really bad." He reached for his backpack and pulled out Dylan's collapsible dish and a bottle of water. "What if we can't help them?"

We will. Dylan waited for Casey to fill his dish and then dove in. *They're our friends.* Dylan shook his muzzle out, sending a spray of water everywhere. *Even grumpy old Roger.*

When Jake, Tanya, Tabitha, and Tori came back, Jake was carrying a large tray loaded with their drinks.

"Pizza won't be long," Tabitha or Tanya, or Tori said. She handed an iced tea to Casey.

"Thanks, Tori." Casey reached for a straw and unwrapped it.

Dylan searched Tori for something that was different from her sisters. *Nope. I think Casey guessed.*

Jake reached for his drink. "When does Roger have to pay the money?"

"By the end of the week," Casey said.

"Wow. That's quick," Tanya or Tabitha gasped. "How much does Roger owe? Maybe we can raise the money." She looked at her sisters. "Let's have a car wash." Their two identical heads bobbed up and down.

"A hundred grand. Plus," Sumo stirred his drink, "The Sledgehammer is charging fifty percent interest."

That's a lot of cars to wash.

"American money?" Jake slumped in his chair. "Forget it. Roger can't do it. Nobody could get that kind of money in a few days."

Six kids slurped their drinks.

Dylan got up on his hind legs and put his paws on the table again. *We can't give up now. Whine.*

"I've got a plan." Casey kicked back in his chair. "Dream Big K-9 Academy is doing better." He pointed to Sumo. "We'll go talk to The Sledgehammer. Ask him to give Roger more time."

That's a lousy plan. Whine.

Sumo's mouth dropped open. "Talk. To. The. Sledgehammer? Are you insane? The guy's a criminal."

Dylan nuzzled Casey's arm. *Sumo is making some excellent points.*

"If you don't ask, the answer is always no. Right, Little Buddy?"

Whine.

Sumo snorted. "Is that one of your Mom's quotes?"

"Nora Roberts." Casey blushed. "But Mom says it a lot."

Mom never says she's going to talk to The Sledgehammer.

Big Belly's doors opened, and Samantha came out carrying four personal-size pizza boxes and one extra-large pizza box. "Okay, I've got The Works."

"Right here."

She set it down in front of Jake.

"Extra cheese and mushrooms for Casey and Dylan." She put it in front of Dylan.

Arf! Thanks, Samantha. Dylan tried opening the box with his nose. *Stuck.* He pawed at it. *Casey?*

Casey got ahold of the tab on the cardboard box and flipped the lid up. He gave Dylan a nibble of pizza. "Not too much. You had a lot of treats during class."

So what? Dylan chewed open-mouthed and pawed the box for more. *I'm a working dog.*

Casey eased Dylan back onto his blanket before helping himself. "If you get sick, Mom will kill me."

I won't tell. Dylan watched Casey take a big bite. *It's rude to eat in front of me.*

"Canadian bacon with beef jerky, pepperoni, jalapeno peppers, sausage, black olives, and pineapple?"

Sumo's hand went up and Samantha set it on the table. "You're one brave kid, Sumo."

Sumo already had the box open and was digging in. "It's good."

"Tanya, here are yours. One pepperoni and one large veggie to go."

"Great. Our grandmother is visiting us from Boston. She loves your pizza."

"That's always nice to hear." Samantha handed the boxes over and wiped her hands on her apron. "Your table is too small. Want me to hold onto the veggie until you leave?"

"No, thanks." Tanya set the box on the ground near her chair. "This is fine."

"Okay. Let me know if you need anything."

"Okay," they mumbled through mouthfuls of pizza.

Arf! I'm still here.

Casey tore off some crust with marinara sauce and cheese. He held it out.

Dylan stretched up and inhaled. *Where are the mushrooms?* He woofed it down anyway.

Casey scratched Dylan's head but kept eating.

Thanks a bunch. Dylan slid down to the ground. He nosed around Sumo's chair and found some pineapple. *Yeck!* He ate it anyway. He checked out the floor around Jake's chair. *Zip. But wait. Tanya's take-out pizza is on the ground.*

Dylan padded over and sniffed at the box. *Veggies. Yum.* He raised his muzzle up and looked through the glass tabletop. *Everybody's eating. No one's sharing with me.* Dylan flicked his ear. *So mean.*

Back to the box. Dylan dropped to his stomach. He found the tab on the cardboard box and grabbed it with his front teeth. The box lifted off the ground but wouldn't open. *Hmm.* Dylan got a paw on either side of the box lid and hugged it tight. *Good.* He grabbed the tab again with his front teeth and raised his muzzle up. The box opened a little. *Hey, it's working.* Dylan kept his teeth locked onto the tab, wiggled his butt, and flung his head back. *Good!*

Dylan teased a slice out of the box, but the cheese and veggie toppings slid off. *Bummer.* Dylan got down low on his front legs and licked it up. Some dirt and leaves came with the toppings. *Not so good.*

There must be a better way. Dylan gave up and ate right out of the box. *Kind of messy.* The chopped tomatoes got in his ears. He shook his ears out, but the tomatoes stayed. *Flavor saver for later.* The last slice was stuck to the bottom of the box. *What's with that?* Dylan sank his teeth into the crust and pulled up. The slice stayed where it was. *Forget it. I'm getting full.* Dylan burped and pizza fumes came back to him. *Whew! That stinks.* His stomach rumbled. *Uh-oh.*

"Is that Dylan?" Sumo peered through the glass tabletop.

Dylan burped again and his stomach gurgled. Pizza shot out from his muzzle and landed splat in the open box. *Agh.* Dylan jumped back.

"Eww!" Tanya, Tabitha, and Tori squealed. "What's that smell?"

Casey pushed his chair back and reached for Dylan. "Geez, Little Buddy."

"Casey!" The girls shrieked. "Dylan!"

"Good one, Dylan." Jake looked under the table and started laughing. "No one will want that pizza now."

"That pizza was for our grandmother," Tanya wailed. "We don't have any more money. What are we going to do?"

What's the matter? Dylan swung his head from Tanya to Casey. Bits of tomato flew off. *I left one slice in the box. She can have that.*

"That was awesome." Casey pulled Dylan onto his lap and wiped his face with a napkin. "Your barf landed in the box. Good job!"

It was nothing.

Tanya, Tabitha, and Tori wadded up their napkins and pelted Casey and Dylan with them. "Not funny."

"Dylan's sorry he ate your pizza." Casey tried a serious face but couldn't pull it off. He turned Dylan to him. "Aren't you, Little Buddy?"

Not really.

Jake and Sumo were holding their sides and laughing.

Three identical girl faces started to crumple.

"Okay, Sumo and Jake, knock it off." Casey shifted Dylan on his lap and pulled some money out of his pocket. "We're sorry. Get another pizza." He gave them a cheerful smile. "Dylan's buying."

Dylan sat up straight and pawed the air. *Do I get some?*

"Thanks, Casey," Tori sniffled. "C'mon Tanya and Tabitha."

Jake and Sumo were still laughing.

"Oh man. That was so funny," Sumo kicked back in his chair. "I wish I'd gotten that on video."

Casey waited until the girls walked away. "Listen up. I have an idea. First, we've got to get rid of the girls, and then we've got to go to Sumo's."

Jake stopped laughing. "Are we going to get into trouble?"

"Us?" Casey rounded his eyes. "Trouble? No way."

Oh no.

Sumo frowned. "Why my house?"

"You'll see. I've got this all worked out."

Dylan leaned against Casey. *I don't think so.*

CHAPTER TWENTY-SIX

Casey and Jake dropped cross-legged onto Sumo's bedroom floor.

"Let me get my laptop," Sumo said.

Dylan stretched out on his stomach, put his muzzle on Casey's lap, and sniffed the air. *No Cheetos. No Doritos. No nothing. Sumo's room is too clean. Disappointing.*

"I have an idea," Casey began when Sumo sat down.

No! Dylan slapped a paw on Casey's thigh. *Whenever you say that we get into trouble.*

"Forget it," Sumo snorted. "Your last idea was dumb."

It was.

"Nuh-uh." Casey stretched his long legs out. "It just needed a little work."

A lot of work.

"What's your idea?" Jake asked.

Sumo leaned forward and put his elbows on his knees. "I'm not getting arrested."

Yip! Me either.

"I can't get arrested," Jake insisted. "I have to be home in time for dinner."

Me, too. Dylan sighed and then whined. *Don't worry. It doesn't take long for Casey to get us into trouble.*

Casey pointed to Sumo's laptop. "Can you find out where The Sledgehammer lives?"

"Yeah."

Uh-oh.

Sumo checked out a few websites. "Now what?"

Now we should think of another idea.

"What's it called," Casey snapped his fingers quickly, "when you find out what a house looks like inside?"

Snooping?

"Looking at blueprints?" Jake guessed.

"Yeah." Casey waved his hand at Sumo's computer, "Can you find the blueprints for The Sledgehammer's house?"

Sumo sat up straight and blinked. "Hacking is a crime."

"Really?" Casey's eyebrows shot up and then he shrugged. "Not if you're a kid. I think."

Think again.

Sumo snorted, hunched over his laptop, and got to work.

This isn't good.

Sumo stayed glued to the screen and tapped some keys. "Hold on." He tapped a few more keys. "Okay. I'm in. The Sledgehammer built his house four years ago. It's six thousand square feet. The blueprints show all the rooms in the house."

Casey leaned over Dylan to get a better look. "Where's his office?"

"Everything is labeled." Sumo scanned the computer screen. "This is the front of the house. This is the foyer. That's the living room," Sumo pointed, "and this is a hallway. I see a game room, a library, a gym, and a music room.

Hey, he has an indoor swimming pool. Nice." Sumo looked closer. "Office. Fourth door on the right."

"Great." Casey leaned back on his hands. "We're going to visit The Sledgehammer."

"Uh-uh." Jake raised both hands in surrender. "The guy's a criminal."

"Jake's right," Sumo agreed. "I bet he eats kids for lunch."

What about little dogs?

Casey grinned. "Relax, The Sledgehammer won't be home."

Jake wasn't so sure. "How do you know?"

Yeah, Casey.

Casey gave a half laugh. "What criminal works from home?"

"Okay," Sumo chewed on his lower lip. "So?"

"So, here's the plan. Jake and Dylan will wait outside. Hide behind a tree or something. We'll go to the front door. Somebody will answer and I'll say I lost my dog."

I don't want to be lost.

Sumo dropped his head into his hands and moaned, "Oh, brother."

"They'll say they haven't found a dog. Dylan, that's when you run inside the house."

I don't like this.

"Sumo is going to chase after you," Casey tapped Dylan on his shoulder, "and you're going to run really fast."

I'm going to run home.

"I don't get it," Jake interrupted.

"I'll run after Dylan and Sumo. Sumo will keep chasing Dylan. When no one's looking I'll go into The Sledgehammer's office."

Sumo lifted his head up and squinted. "Where is the plan part?"

Yeah.

Casey heaved out a sigh. "Jean said The Sledgehammer made Roger sign loan papers. That means The Sledgehammer will have the papers in his office."

"So what?" Sumo tossed his hands into the air. "What makes you think you can find them?"

Yeah, Casey.

"I *will* find the papers and take them. If The Sledgehammer doesn't have proof Roger owes the money, Roger won't have to pay him. Get it?"

"We're going to get caught." Sumo shook his head.

You'd better listen. Dylan pawed Casey's knee.

"No way. Look, Dylan's Dog Squad finds stuff all the time," Casey reasoned. "This time we're finding something for a friend."

Sumo's voice went up. "What happens if they call the cops?"

We'll end up in the slammer.

"Not going to happen. We're just some kids looking for a dog. If anything happens Jake can call us." Casey grinned happily at Jake and rubbed his hands together. "You get to be our lookout."

Get out while you can, Jake.

CHAPTER TWENTY-SEVEN

Casey slowed his bike to a stop in front of a big brick house with white shutters. "We're here."

Dylan peeked out the side screen of his bike trailer. *Pretty house.*

"This can't be The Sledgehammer's house." Jake pointed to the front yard littered with garden gnomes. "Gnomes are an old person's thing."

Gnomes? Dylan tipped his head to get a better look at the little plastic men with pointy hats and long beards. *Creepy. Only Santa should have a beard.*

"This doesn't look like a criminal's house." Sumo got off his bike and checked his GPS app. "Where are the electric gates?" He searched the quiet yard. "This place should be crawling with no-neck goons wearing pinstriped suits."

I don't see any goons. Dylan pressed his snout closer to the screen. *What are goons?* Dylan stretched his neck up and down. *Why don't goons have necks?*

"You've been watching too many crime shows," Casey laughed. "This is Brea. Criminals blend in."

Jake parked his bike. "Where do you want me and Dylan?"

Casey waved a hand toward the house. "Hide by the big bush next to the front door. When someone opens the front door, count to ten and then let Dylan loose."

"Okay."

Casey unzipped the front screen of Dylan's bike trailer and waited for him to step out before he crouched down. "Remember you're going to wait with Jake. When you get my signal run up the front steps. Don't stop. Run into the house."

Dylan whined. *I should run home.*

"When you get into the house," Casey straightened Dylan's bandana and fluffed out his ears, "run down the hall. Let Sumo chase you all over the place. Make lots of noise." He brushed Dylan's topknot out of his eyes. "I'm going into The Sledgehammer's office. As soon as I get the loan papers, I'll call for you."

Whine.

"Got that?"

What came after waiting with Jake?

Casey sat back on his heels. "This is a great idea."

Dylan dropped his buns on the ground. *Taking stuff that doesn't belong to you is a bad idea.*

"We have to do this. It's called helping a friend."

Dylan flicked his ears and looked away. *Uncle Rory calls it breaking the law.*

Casey turned Dylan around and raised his muzzle up, so Dylan had to look at him. "It's not nice to judge."

It's not nice to get your friends into trouble.

"What could go wrong?" Casey grinned. "My idea is foolproof."

Grr. Fool is more like it.

Casey stood up. "Ready Sumo?"

Ready for the slammer?

"Remember, if anything goes wrong," Sumo said to Jake, "call us. Then we can get out of there."

Jake gave them a thumbs up. "Got you covered."

"We've gotta be nuts to do this," Sumo muttered. "C'mon."

Dylan started to hunker down with Jake behind the bush but popped back up. He peeked around the bush and watched Casey ring the doorbell.

Nothing.

No one is home. Great! We can go now.

The heavy wooden front door creaked open and a girl about nine stared at Casey and Sumo. "My dad's not here."

Casey sent Sumo a face-splitting grin and whispered out of the corner of his mouth, "Told you." Turning back to the girl he said in a loud voice, "That's okay. We're here because my very little, very cute dog ran this way." Casey looked over his shoulder and gave Dylan the hurry-up sign.

All right, already. Dylan started toward Casey.

Casey turned back to the girl. "He's probably so scared. I've got to find him." Casey let his bottom lip quiver. "Before he gets lost for good."

"Yeah." Sumo brought his hand down to his knee. "He's about this big."

"His name is Dylan," Casey added and held up Dylan's leash. "I was putting his leash on him, and he took off. I think the garden gnomes spooked him."

The girl rolled her eyes. "They're plastic."

Dylan sprinted up the front steps alongside Casey and Sumo. Without slowing down, he went into the house. *Hurry up, guys.*

"Hey, that's him," Sumo said and took off after Dylan.

"Yeah." Casey brushed by the girl and ran into the house. "That's him."

"You can't come in," the girl called after them. "I don't know you."

"I'm Casey and this is Sumo!"

Dylan found the hallway and paused. *Whoa! This is a big house. How far do I go?*

"Keep going," Casey called and detoured into The Sledgehammer's office.

Dylan saw an open doorway. *Did Casey say to go into the rooms?*

Dylan looked back. Sumo was far behind him. The hall stretched far in front of him. *Okay.* Dylan took off down the hall again. *Run, Sumo.*

Dylan went past one open door after another and glanced into the last one. Bookcases lined three walls. He couldn't help himself and stopped for a look. *This room has more books than the Brea Library.* Dylan padded inside and craned his neck up. *Mom would like it here. The bookcases go all the way to the ceiling.* He sniffed at a few books on the bottom shelf. *Casey wouldn't like it here. He hates to read.*

Sumo jogged into the library and panted, "We'll wait here until Casey calls us."

Fine by me. Dylan plopped down and settled his muzzle on his front paws. *I've had enough.*

Sumo wandered over to the bookshelves. "There are a million books here." He ran his hand over the titles. "We could read something while we wait for Casey."

Dylan glanced up at him. *Any books about dogs?*

Sumo's cell phone vibrated, and he pulled it out of his pocket. "Hey, Jake. What's up?"

Police sirens suddenly sliced through the air, coming closer and sounding louder.

"Get out, Jake," Sumo shouted into his cell phone. "Save yourself!"

Dylan jumped to his paws. *Us, too.*

"Oh man, oh man." Sumo ran over to the window and croaked, "It's the cops, Dylan. We're busted." Sumo's eyes darted around the library. "There's no way out. Oh man, oh man." He ran back to Dylan and grabbed him by his shoulders. "We're dead. We're really dead."

You sound like Holly.

"We gotta get outta here."

We've got to get Casey.

Outside the sirens blipped twice and went silent. Doors slammed.

Moments later Dylan heard heavy footsteps pounding down the sidewalk and up to the front door. Dylan pawed Sumo's leg. *We need to find Casey.*

"We'll get Casey and get out of here."

Arf! What a good idea.

Dylan and Sumo ran out of the library but stopped in their tracks.

Up ahead an officer with dark hair and a grim face had Casey by the elbow and was leading him down the hall.

"I'm looking for my little dog," Casey protested and tried turning to face the officer. "He ran in here. He's lost. This is all a mistake, Officer."

"Yes, it is, and you made it." The officer tightened his grip, and they kept walking.

Sumo knelt close to Dylan and whispered, "Stay. They haven't seen us."

Dylan body-bumped Sumo. *Casey needs our help.*

Another officer stepped out of The Sledgehammer's office and zeroed in on Sumo. "Hey, kid!" He dropped his hand to his gun belt and ordered, "Yeah, you. Hands against the wall."

Sumo straightened up and put his hands flat against the wall. "Uh," he squeaked, "what seems to be the trouble, Officer?"

You've gotta be kidding, Sumo. Dylan vibrated with fear. *I can't stand this.* He broke away and ran up to Casey.

"It's okay, Little Buddy." Casey gave him a thin smile.

No, it's not. Arf! You're handcuffed. Dylan got up on his hind legs and pawed Casey's thigh. *Arf! Arf!*

Casey tried again. "See officer? This is my dog, Dylan. I told you he ran in here."

Arf! Listen to Casey! Arf! Arf! Arf!

"Quiet." The dark-haired officer brushed Dylan's paws away from Casey. "Both of you."

The second officer stepped up behind Sumo and grabbed his wrists. Quickly he brought them behind Sumo's back and handcuffed him. "You and your friend are under arrest. California Penal Code 459, Burglary."

"What about the dog?" the dark-haired officer asked.

"We'll bring him in. He's an accomplice."

I'm not an accomplice. I'm an American Cocker Spaniel.

"Okay, Sergeant."

Dylan plunked his butt down, hung his head, and raised both paws up to the grim-faced officer. *Cuff me.*

CHAPTER TWENTY-EIGHT

Dylan's heart skipped when Captain Rizzoli walked into her office. *You always stop to pet me.* When she strode past him without stopping, Dylan's heart dipped. He watched her sit down behind her scarred wooden desk. *We must be in trouble.*

Captain Rizzoli turned her cop eyes on Casey, Dylan, and Sumo. She picked up a pencil and began to slowly tap it on her desk. Tap, tap, tap.

Yup. Big trouble. Dylan squirmed on the hard wooden chair. His furry paws slipped, and he whacked his muzzle on the armrest. *Ow!*

Casey pulled Dylan onto his lap and brushed his topknot out of his eyes.

Tap, tap, tap. Captain Rizzoli pointed the pencil at Casey and Sumo. "I'm not surprised to see you two here but Dylan," she shook her head, "you should've known better."

Dylan's shoulders slumped and he turned his brown eyes away. *I'm a loser.*

She tossed the pencil aside, leaned back in her chair, and swiveled. "Your mother's coming, Casey."

Yikes! Dylan buried his face in Casey's chest. *We're done for.*

Casey hugged Dylan. "Uh, thanks."

"I called your house, Sumo, but there was no answer."

"It's Ingrid's day off. Mom and Maxim are still in Paso Robles."

Captain Rizzoli frowned. "I thought his name was Michael."

"Whatever."

Whatever is right. Dylan let out a huge sigh. *I give up. I don't care what the guy's name is.*

Cadet Chen rapped once on the door jamb and stuck her face in. "Captain, Ms. Donovan is here."

"Thanks, Lisa," Mom said and came in. "Thank you for calling me, Captain. I was in a meeting with Cranston Pantswick in Beverly Hills. I came as soon as I could."

Casey perked up and gave Mom a big smile. "How did your meeting go? Does Cranky Pants still want to do his kids' cookbook? I bet you came up with a great idea."

"Yes, he does. And no, I didn't." Mom slipped into the empty chair next to Casey but didn't return his smile. "I had to leave early because you, Dylan, and Sumo got arrested."

Sorry, Mom.

Mom ruffled Dylan's topknot. "Honestly, what were you thinking? You know better than this."

Dylan blinked at Mom. *You know I'm a dog, right?*

Captain Rizzoli opened the police report. "This is serious, Colleen. The boys have been charged with burglary."

Mom held up her cell phone. "I tried calling Rory, but it went straight to voicemail."

Captain Rizzoli looked to Cadet Chen. "Any word from Lieutenant Kellan?"

"He's still in the field, Captain."

"Thanks. That's all." Captain Rizzoli waited until the door closed. "I'm sorry, Colleen. It's out of my hands. The boys were arrested at the scene, and they'll have to appear in juvenile court in a few weeks."

"I understood from the arresting officers," Mom cleared her throat, "Mr. Sledge isn't pressing charges. Surely that helps."

"No, it doesn't." Captain Rizzoli hitched one shoulder. "Burglary is a crime against society. The boys must be held accountable."

Mom folded her hands in her lap. "What happens to them now?"

"Juveniles are released to their parents until the court hearing."

Mom huffed out a breath. "Well, that's something at least."

"What about me? My mom isn't here!" Sumo swung around to Casey. "You said we wouldn't get into trouble. Now I'm going to be locked up in the slammer with murderers, shifty-eyed con artists, and drug dealers."

Captain Rizzoli interrupted. "I can arrange for you to be released into Ms. Donovan's custody until we locate Ingrid."

"Thanks," Sumo mumbled. "I can't believe this. I'm a criminal. I've got a rap sheet."

Me, too. What's a rap sheet?

Sumo covered his eyes with both hands and rolled his head from side to side. "I'll never get into Harvard."

"Who needs Harvard," Casey snorted, "when you do social media for Dylan's Dog Squad?"

"Shut up."

Captain Rizzoli held up both hands. "Enough, you two. Let's focus on what's next."

"Yes," Mom agreed. "What will happen at the court hearing?"

"The boys had a clean record until today. I'm guessing they'll get probation and be ordered to perform community service."

"I'm gonna wear an orange jumpsuit, pick up trash on the side of the road in the blazing hot sun and use a tin cup to drink from a pail of filthy water with other criminals?" cried Sumo.

What about me? I don't like the hot sun. What's a jumpsuit?

Captain Rizzoli almost smiled. "You watch too much TV."

"Dylan and I volunteer in the Read To Me Program at the Brea Library," Casey said. "Does that count? Maybe Sumo can do it, too."

"I can recommend it." Captain Rizzoli let her words hang in the air. "But it will be up to the judge."

"Okay." Mom sighed. "We'll worry about that later. Let's get back to today. Start talking, Casey."

Casey gave a half laugh. "This is really kind of funny."

No, it's not.

"Forget funny, Casey. Try the truth." Mom wasn't smiling. "Why were you at Mr. Sledge's house?"

"Huh?"

"I've already heard the wild story you told the officers about Dylan. How he just happened to get off his leash and run into a house that just happens to be owned by a notorious criminal. A criminal that Roger Bennett just happens to owe a lot of money to."

Mom's pretty smart. Dylan nudged Casey. *You'd better come clean.*

Mom and Captain Rizzoli looked to Casey. Sumo looked ready to faint.

"Okay." Casey sat up straight and told the whole story. When he finished, he shook his head. "How did the police show up so fast? We just got there."

Captain Rizzoli opened her iPad. "Mr. Sledge has cameras everywhere. He sent over the footage." She studied the screen. "Did Jake make it home all right?"

"Jake?" Sumo chirped and his eyes jumped to Casey and Dylan.

Don't look at me.

Captain Rizzoli turned the screen around so they could see. "I had no idea Jake could run that fast."

Dylan leaned forward and studied the screen. *Me, neither.*

"Mr. Sledge's team in the security room spotted you the moment you parked your bikes in front of the house."

"Security room," Casey echoed and punched Sumo on the arm. "Why didn't you say The Sledgehammer had a security room?"

Sumo punched him back. "You only asked where his office was."

It would've been good to know.

"Focus, boys," Captain Rizzoli reminded them.

"Okay, so we messed up." Casey held onto Dylan and turned to Mom. "But Dream Big K-9 Academy is in trouble. We had to do something to help. They're our friends."

"Burglary is against the law," Mom began and then softened her voice. "It's a hard lesson but Roger borrowed money from Mr. Sledge and now he must pay it back."

"Nobody can pay back that much money," Casey argued.

Dylan's stomach growled. *Can we worry about this after dinner?*

Casey shook his head. "There's got to be a way to help."

"We could still do a carwash," Sumo offered, "but we'd never get that much money."

Dylan studied his furry paws. *I could wash cars.*

"I've heard Rory talk about Mr. Sledge for years," Mom pressed. "Everybody knows he's a criminal. Why isn't he behind bars?"

"We've been watching him but," Captain Rizzoli patted a thick file on her desk, "he's been able to hide behind his businesses."

Sumo was searching Google. "Like what?"

"He's into real estate development big time. Also, he owns three restaurants, a gym, two bakeries, a dry cleaner, and a mobile pet grooming business called Royal Treatment."

"I've seen it," Casey said. "It's a pink van and has a picture on the side of a Poodle wearing a crown."

I've always wanted a crown. Dylan tipped his head from side to side. *How does it stay on?*

"For a criminal, he sounds like an ordinary man," Mom mused.

"You've probably seen him around Brea." Captain Rizzoli opened the folder and took out his picture.

Mom, Casey, Dylan, and Sumo leaned closer for a better look.

Dylan saw a sandy-haired man with a smiling face. *You could be anyone's dad.* He remembered the little girl who answered the front door. *Does she know you're a criminal?*

"Blending in is a good quality for a criminal to have," Captain Rizzoli confirmed.

"Told you," Casey snickered to Sumo. "This is Brea. Criminals blend in."

"Thank you for everything, Captain." Mom stood up. "It's too hot to cook, boys. We'll grill something for dinner."

Yes! Dylan's stomach growl filled the room.

Captain Rizzoli laughed. "You've got Dylan's vote."

"Grillin' with Dylan." Casey started laughing but stopped. "Hey! Grillin' with Dylan," he repeated slowly and turned Dylan to face him. "You gave me a great idea, Little Buddy!"

"No!" they shouted.

"Hold on." He turned his best smile on everyone. "You're going to thank me for this."

Mom, Sumo, and Captain Rizzoli looked doubtful.

Dylan's muzzle rubbed Casey's cheek. *Don't bet on it.*

"I know how we can do the community service. The only problem is," Casey hesitated, "we'd be doing it before we go to court. Is that okay?"

"Depends." Captain Rizzoli raised her eyebrows. "What do you have in mind?"

"Mom, Cranky Pants wants you to come up with an idea for some dumb kids' cookbook. So." He waited for them to fill in the rest.

"So what?" they prompted.

"So, we'll have a 'Grillin' With Dylan and Friends' contest at Dream Big K-9 Academy. Any kid who comes with their own grilling recipe for steak will get in free. We'll charge everyone else admission."

Sumo snorted. "How many ways can you grill steak?"

This is a very good question. Dylan looked from Sumo to Casey. *I want to know.*

"We're about to find out." Casey grinned. "Every kid in Brea will want to enter the contest."

"We could have fifty winners." Sumo was catching on. "The winners get their recipes printed in Cranky Pants's cookbook."

Mom was nodding her head. "It would be excellent publicity for Cranston's book but how does this help Roger?"

"Ask Cranky Pants to rent Dream Big K-9 Academy from Roger for the day. That would put a big dent in the hundred grand Roger owes, right?" Casey was getting excited. "Cranky Pants can donate all the steak that will be grilled."

"Would Cranky Pants do that, Ms. D? That's a lot of dough."

"Sure." Mom shrugged. "Cranston would pay more than that in publicity for his book. We'll need a buffet table for potato salad, corn on the cob, and watermelon. Cranston will take care of that, too."

Dylan started to drool. *All my favorites.*

She pulled out her cell phone to make notes. "I'll ask Jonah to cover the story for the *Orange County Register*. Anna can do the photos. I'll ask Mayor Matias to give out the prizes to the winners." She sighed happily. "Cranston will love this. Thanks, Casey."

Sumo touched the screen on his cell phone. "I'll get started on social media."

"See? You don't need Harvard," Casey said cheerfully. "You've already got a job."

Sumo glared at him.

Captain Rizzoli wasn't so sure. "I can't have kids grilling steak without adult supervision. That's a big risk."

"No problem." Sumo waved his cell phone. "Dylan's Dog Squad volunteers can help. Lots of them are adults."

Dylan whined happily. *We're on a roll, guys.*

"This is good," Mom looked over her notes, "but we need more."

Casey bounced Dylan once in his arms. "Ice cream goes great with grilled steak. Right, Little Buddy?"

Ice cream goes great with everything.

Mom went back to her notes. "I'll ask Crystal if Brea's Ice Cream will do an ice cream station with all the fixings. Cranston will pay for that, too."

"Since this will be at Dream Big K-9 Academy," Captain Rizzoli began, "talk to Jean. The handlers could put on a show with their dogs."

Mom nodded. "Perfect."

Sumo chimed in. "People will see what the dogs can do and sign up for classes. Especially when they hear Casey and Dylan are teaching the beginner's class. I'll play it up big on social media."

"We could give Dream Big bandanas away, Mom. People like free stuff."

Mom made a note. "Cranston will pay for that, too."

"Excellent, Ms. D."

Casey hugged Dylan. "We could have photo ops with Dylan."

"Anna can take care of that." Mom added it to her list.

Sumo nodded. "Roger is going to make big bucks."

"The sooner Roger is free of Mr. Sledge, the better," Captain Rizzoli added.

"Can we get a celebrity, Mom?"

Dylan wiggled against Casey. *Bailey could come.*

"Dude, great idea." Sumo high-fived Casey. "Can we, Ms. D? That would be so cool."

"Sorry, boys. That would cost a bundle." Mom shook her head. "Cranston would never go for that."

Dylan whined. *Bailey.*

"Mom, you've gotta know someone who'd do it for free."

Dylan waved a paw in the air. *Bailey.*

"Sorry, boys."

Dylan turned in Casey's arms and quickly pawed his chest. *Bailey! Arf!*

"Ow." Casey put a hand over Dylan's paws. "Hey, wait a minute. What about your friend Bailey?"

Dylan whined and collapsed against Casey's chest. *Took you long enough.*

"Great! I'll contact Rachel." Mom nodded, "Then it really will be Grillin' With Dylan and Friends."

Thanks, Mom.

CHAPTER TWENTY-NINE

I'm bored. Dylan wandered around the top of their driveway, sniffing, and checking out stuff. He stopped to watch a lizard catching rays on the brick planter. The lizard did a pushup, swished its tail, and scurried off. A road-runner streaked by Dylan, its skinny legs pistoning. It looked left and right before continuing down their drive-way. Dylan went back to Casey and panted. *It's hot. Let's go.*

A delivery truck from Brea's Office Supply pulled up in front of their house and cut its engine. A young guy hopped out and carried four large paper bags up the driveway. "Delivery for Ms. Donovan."

"Thanks." Casey took the paper bags and put them on the ground. "Mom," he called, "they're here."

Mom hurried out their front door. "Wait until you see this." She slipped a poster from the first bag and held it up. "I had a hundred printed. What do you think?"

Dylan looked at the Grillin' With Dylan and Friends poster Mom was holding. *Why am I wearing a gigantic marshmallow on my head?*

"How did you get the chef's hat to stay on Dylan's head, Ms. D?"

"The wonders of photoshop."

Casey grinned at Dylan. "You look just like one of those chefs on TV."

I look stupid.

Sumo pointed to Bailey's picture at the bottom of the poster and read out loud, "Special appearance by Dylan's Best Friend Bailey." He dug his cell phone out of his pocket and took a picture of the poster. "Social media is going to eat this up. I bet we sell out."

Mom smiled. "Now I need to deliver the posters. Mayor Matias, Dream Big K-9 Academy, Brea PD, and Brea's Ice Cream all promised to put them up right away."

"That's great, Mom."

"Oh no." She checked her watch. "I can deliver all the posters except the ones for Brea's Ice Cream." Her happiness faded. "They're on the other side of town. They'll have to wait until I finish my Zoom meeting with Cranston."

Ice cream? Dylan pawed Casey's leg, stuck out his tongue, and panted.

Casey gave Dylan a casual look. "We could take the posters to Brea's Ice Cream, right Little Buddy?"

Dylan plunked his butt down. *Yes!*

"Are you sure you can manage them on your bike?" Mom took a deep breath. "They were really expensive."

Casey put a bag on top of Dylan's bike trailer. "I'll use a bungee cord to hold it on."

Sumo clapped his hands together. "Problem solved, Ms. D."

"Okay, boys." Mom heaved a big sigh. "That's wonderful!"

Casey and Sumo waited until Mom went into the house before shouting, "Ice cream!"

Arf! Ice cream! I'm liking today.

Casey unzipped the front of Dylan's bike trailer and waited for him to hop in. "I'll be right back." A few minutes later he returned with a bungee cord.

Dylan watched Casey wrap the cord around the paper bag and the bike trailer. *Seriously?*

"The bungee cord is too long."

"Nah." Casey grabbed a corner of the bag and wiggled it. The bag slid all over the place. "Close enough."

Listen to Sumo.

Casey swung a leg over his bike and put on his helmet. "We'll ride really slow. Anyway, we're stopping by Jake's house on the way to Brea's Ice Cream."

"Jake texted me last night. He's grounded. What if his mom is home?"

"I talked to him this morning. She's at the dentist."

Dylan settled back and put his muzzle on his paws. *Plenty of time for a world class snooze.*

They made it down the driveway but when Casey turned onto the street Dylan heard a strange sound. He looked up and saw the paper bag sliding slowly across the roof of his bike trailer. *Casey! The bag is moving. Arf!*

Dylan sat up and scratched at the front screen. *You need to stop. Arf!* Dylan pressed himself against the side of the bike trailer keeping his eyes glued to the bag.

Casey made a turn at the streetlight.

Oh no! The bag inched toward the edge of the roof. *Pedal faster, Casey.*

Casey made another turn and familiar smells drifted Dylan's way. He scrunched down and brought his face close to the side screen. *Jake lives on this street.* Dylan let out a slow breath. *We're going to make it. Whew.*

Casey took a speed bump. Bike and bike trailer bounced. The poster bag hiccupped and moved closer to the edge.

Dylan shot up and sat straight back. *Arf! Arf! Arf!*

"Almost there, Little Buddy," Casey called over his shoulder. "Don't worry. We'll only stay a few minutes and then we'll get ice cream."

Dylan swiveled and scratched the front screen so fast his paws burned. *Stop!* He turned around and saw the bag teetering on the edge of the roof. *No, no, no!*

Casey turned into Jake's driveway and parked under a big tree. Sumo slid his bike to a stop next to Casey's.

Dylan gave the paper bag one last look. *I'm exhausted. I need ice cream bad.*

"Oh man," Casey said when he got off his bike. "We almost lost the posters." He slid the poster bag back under the bungee cord. "You should've said something, Little Buddy."

Grr.

"That was close." Sumo took off his bike helmet. "If we'd lost the posters your mom would've been mad. She said they were really expensive."

No joke.

"But we didn't. Let's go see Jake."

Dylan trudged behind Casey and Sumo. When they reached the front door Dylan lifted his muzzle and caught the summer breeze. Scents of flowers drifted his way. *Nice.* Dylan flicked his ears. He heard a sputtering sound and sniffed the air again. *Water. Strange.*

Casey started to ring the doorbell but stopped when the front door was yanked open.

"What are you doing here," Jake hissed. "My mom just came home."

Sumo hooked a thumb over his shoulder. "We're going to Brea's Ice Cream. Want to come?"

"Not going to happen. Captain Rizzoli called my parents last night. She told them everything. My parents went ballistic. The only reason I'm still alive is because I didn't get arrested."

You didn't get arrested because you ran away.

"Are you going to be at Dream Big K-9 Academy tomorrow?" Casey pointed to Dylan and Sumo. "We need you."

"Are you nuts? I'm grounded for the rest of the summer. Maybe for the rest of my life."

"Can you talk to your parents tonight?" Sumo asked. "Tell them it's really important."

A woman's voice called out from inside the house, "Jake, where are you?"

Panic shot across Jake's face, and he yelled back, "Coming, Mom." He leaned closer and whispered, "You've gotta go."

"Sorry," Casey and Sumo mouthed.

Casey picked Dylan up. They sprinted down the front walk and over to their bikes.

"No!" Casey and Sumo cried.

No!

The lawn sprinklers were in a watering frenzy. Flowers, hedges, and trees were getting drenched. They heard a hissing sound followed by a popping sound before the sprinklers turned off.

"Our bikes!" Sumo and Casey groaned.

Water dripped from the bikes and Dylan's bike trailer.

And the bag of posters.

Lawn sprinklers. That's the sound I heard. Dylan leaned

against Casey's chest and whimpered. *What are we going to do?*

"Okay, okay, okay," Casey chanted, holding Dylan close and walking in circles. "Don't panic."

"I can't help it! I am!"

Me, too. Dylan kicked out a back paw. *Slow down. You're making me dizzy.*

"Stay here, Little Buddy." Casey put Dylan down and whipped his T-shirt off. He started wiping down his bike and Dylan's bike trailer. When he got to the drenched paper bag, he opened it and bit his lip. "These posters are a goner."

"Are you going to tell your mom?"

Casey, Dylan, and Sumo thought about that one.

"No way." Casey ran both hands through his hair. "I have an idea."

"Your last idea got us arrested."

Yup.

Casey scowled at Sumo. "We got arrested because you didn't tell me about the security room."

Sumo jabbed a finger in Casey's face. "Because you never asked!"

"Want to hear my idea or not?"

Say no.

"What is it?"

"It's genius."

I don't think genius means what you think it means.

"It's so simple it's guaranteed to work." Casey slowly peeled the delivery label off the soggy paper bag and shook it out. "I'll pretend to be my mom and email Brea Office Supply to order more posters. *She'll* tell them it's a rush job. *She'll* say she's sending us over to pick them up." Casey nodded cheerfully. "Then we'll take them to Brea's Ice Cream."

"Won't they ask why it's coming from your email address and not your mom's?"

Yeah, Casey.

Casey studied the delivery label. "The order number is on the label. I'll include it in the email. No problem." He slid a look at Dylan and muttered, "I hope."

"How are we going to pay for this?" Sumo checked his pockets. "I don't have enough money."

"Hmm." Casey frowned and then he brightened. "*Mom* will tell them in her email to add the charge to Cranston's bill."

"Oh man. That's like forgery or stealing or I don't know what." Sumo scrubbed both hands over his face. "But I know we're breaking the law again. That's two days in a row."

This is getting to be a habit.

"We're not breaking the law because *Mom* is ordering this stuff." Casey unzipped Dylan's bike trailer and looked inside. "It's a little damp." Casey used two fingers to hold up Dylan's cushion. A river of water ran off.

Dylan sidestepped the puddle. *That's a lot of water.*

Casey wrung out the soaked cushion. "That's better."

No, it's not.

He motioned for Dylan to get in.

No.

Casey gave Dylan's rump a little nudge.

Dylan stepped onto his cushion one paw at a time. Water squished up between his toes. *Eww.* He wrinkled his snout, turned around twice on the mushy pillow, and faced front. *I'll stand.*

When Sumo took his T-shirt off and started wiping his

bike down, Casey got busy writing the email. He read it over and pressed Send. "That'll work."

Sumo slipped his wet T-shirt over his head and got on his bike. "We'll find out."

Casey shrugged into his shirt and called over his shoulder, "Hang on, Little Buddy."

Dylan spread his legs and braced himself. *Go slow.*

Forty-five minutes later they were leaving Brea's Office Supply with a bag of posters.

"Told you this would work," Casey said, sliding the bag under the bungee cord.

"What if they call your mom?"

Yeah?

"They won't. Mom orders stuff from them all the time." Casey zipped up the screen on

Dylan's bike trailer and got on his bike. "Quit griping. You're just hungry."

"I'm twelve. I've got a rap sheet. Living a life of crime makes me hungry."

Dylan's stomach growled. *Me, too.*

Sumo swung his leg over his bike. "When we get to Brea's Ice Cream, I'm ordering double of everything."

I'm sitting next to you.

After Casey pulled into Brea's Ice Cream and parked, Dylan pawed at the front screen. *Hurry up. It's wet in here. My fur is frizzing.*

"Okay, Little Buddy."

Dylan charged out, stretched forward on his front legs, and shook out his damp ears. *I need the sun.*

"Hi, guys!" Crystal came out of Brea's Ice Cream and walked over to them. "Your mom called."

Of course, she did.

Casey undid the bungee cord and handed her the posters. "Yeah, we dropped by to see Jake."

"I heard you broke into The Sledgehammer's house yesterday." Crystal shook her head. "That was a dumb thing to do. The guy is bad news."

"Yeah," Casey and Sumo mumbled.

"I'm not surprised about you two," she bent down and cupped Dylan's muzzle in her hands, "but what were you thinking?"

Good grief.

CHAPTER THIRTY

Dylan leaned halfway out of his bike trailer and felt the sun beat down on his shoulders. *Hot!* He took two steps onto the blacktop. *Yip!*

"Hold on Sumo. The parking lot is too hot for Dylan to walk on." Casey tucked Dylan under his arm. "When we get to the grass, Little Buddy, you can walk."

I like being up high. Dylan's head swiveled left and right, taking in the sights. *You can carry me all day.*

"Lisa said the Brea Cadets are assigned to Admissions." Casey scanned the grounds. "We need to check in with her."

"Over there."

They headed toward Lisa and five other cadets working at two long tables. People were handing over their plastic and the cadets were feeding the credit card machines. Every guest walked away with a Dream Big bandana and wearing a big smile.

"It's not even nine o'clock," Casey said. "Look at all these people lined up to get in. Every kid in Brea is here."

Dylan wiggled and Casey put him down on the grass.

"When does Roger have to pay the money?"

"By midnight tonight." Casey straightened out Dylan's Dream Big bandana.

Sumo let out a low whistle. "That's cutting it close."

"If he doesn't pay, Dream Big K-9 Academy belongs to The Sledgehammer."

Oh-no.

Volunteers wearing Dylan's Dog Squad T-shirts hustled around the large exercise field setting up portable grills and arranging picnic tables. Brea's Ice Cream was under a white canopy and already doing a booming business. Crystal was working the cold case, scooping ice cream and Dominick was arranging the ice cream fixings with lightning speed on a long table.

Dylan lifted his snout and sniffed. *They have vanilla ice cream. Yum.*

"Hey, guys." Lisa waved them over. "We're packing them in. Everyone loves the free bandanas. Your mom has the best ideas. Speaking of ideas," she shook her head, "it's all over the police station how you broke into The Sledgehammer's house." She shot both hands into the air and exclaimed, "The guy's a crook. He's a criminal."

Dylan cocked his head. *Crook sounds worse than criminal.*

"You're lucky the police caught you instead of The Sledgehammer. When people cross him, they disappear," she looked left and right before leaning in close, "permanently."

Yikes! No one explained it to me that way.

Casey and Sumo shrugged.

"Talk about dumb." She reached down and stroked Dylan's ears. "As for you, what were you thinking?"

I wish people would stop asking me that.

Lisa straightened up. "You need to get started. People are already in line for photo ops with Dylan."

"Where do we go?"

"Anna is set up near the parking lot." Lisa pointed to the Dream Big canopy. She adjusted her aviator sunglasses and searched the faces in the crowd. "Jonah was here." She tried again but gave up. "He's writing a story for the *Orange County Register*. In a few minutes, he'll be doing an interview with Ms. Langdon and Bailey."

"Where?" Sumo stretched up on tiptoes and looked around the exercise field packed with people. "We can stop by before Dylan gets started."

Dylan lowered his head and tried to see. *No hairy legs. No big flat, feet. No, Bailey.*

"Here." Lisa tapped the screen on her iPad and then giggled. "Bailey is so cute. No wonder he and Dylan are BFFs."

Dylan pawed Casey's leg. *What's a BFF?*

"Best Friends Forever."

Dylan pawed Casey's leg again. *We're BFFs.*

"With two celebrities," Lisa sighed happily, "today will be a success."

Casey waggled Dylan's leash. "We're really hoping Roger can pay off The Sledgehammer. Right, Little Buddy?"

Arf! The Sledgehammer's a bad man.

"Roger has been training the Brea Police dogs for years," Lisa tossed her long black braid over her shoulder, "so all the cadets are happy to help. Dylan's Dog Squad volunteers have been here since six a.m. This is a lot of work but Dream Big K-9 Academy is worth it."

Casey nudged Sumo with his elbow. "Every kid out

there is holding a recipe. Mom said Brea's Best is delivering the steak at eleven o'clock."

Sumo perked up. "I hope Ms. D ordered a lot of steak."

I hope I get to eat a lot of steak.

"I'm in charge of," Lisa pointed to the sign above her head, "Cash Admissions and Donations. This is so terrific." She pulled a cord attached to a large ship's bell mounted on a sturdy tripod next to her. A deep clanging erupted.

Sumo clapped his hands over his ears. "How often do you do that?"

"Every time someone makes a cash donation." She rang the bell again.

Dylan dropped to his stomach and covered his ears with his paws. *Make her stop.*

Lisa beamed. "We've already taken in about fifteen thousand dollars in donations." She patted the cash box. "You're definitely the social media guru, Sumo!"

"Grillin' With Dylan and Friends has gotten like a zillion hits so far. Everyone is excited to meet Dylan and Bailey." Sumo nodded happily. "I bet Dylan's Dog Squad gets a bunch of new cases from this."

Casey grimaced. "Did you say we got arrested and have to do community service?"

"Uh-uh." Sumo grinned. "I left that part out."

Lisa laughed. "Why let a few facts get in the way of a good story?"

"Hey," Sumo jabbed Casey with his elbow, "your mom says that."

"Only when I'm in trouble."

Dylan rolled his eyes up to Casey. *Mom says it a lot. Whine.*

"Mark Twain might've said it first." Casey glanced around. "Where is my mom?"

Lisa went back to her iPad. "She was here a few minutes ago with Mayor Matias."

"I'll text her." Casey got his cell phone out. "How long is Dylan doing photo ops?"

"Only until ten o'clock. You can hang out until Brea's Best arrives at eleven with the steak. Then the grilling contest will begin."

Arf! When do I begin eating?

Casey, Dylan, and Sumo said goodbye and joined the people slowly making their way across the lawn. Everyone was having too much fun to be in a hurry.

Roger stepped in front of them. "What are you doing here," he growled.

Nice to see you, too.

"Saving Dream Big K-9 Academy for you," Casey smirked. "You can thank us later."

"I heard you broke into The Sledgehammer's house. Stupid stunt." Roger put two hands covered in bites, scrapes, and bandages on his skinny hips. "Dylan could've been hurt."

Dylan's head shot up. *You called me by name. Since when do you care?*

"I see you're still making dog friends." Casey pointed to Roger's hands. "How much do you shell out on bandages?"

"Don't get arrested today." Roger waved them off and disappeared into the crowd.

Roger didn't even thank us. Dylan pawed Casey's leg. *Why are we doing this again?*

"Roger is a hard guy to like," Sumo muttered. "He's lucky all these people came to help him."

No kidding.

"Dream Big K-9 Academy is a good school. It's done a

lot for dogs." Casey waited for a woman with three kids to pass by.

Dylan noticed each kid was wearing a Dream Big bandana around their neck. *Where's your dog?*

"If it wasn't for Dream Big K-9 Academy, I'd never thought of becoming a dog trainer. Right, Little Buddy?"

Right!

"Besides," Casey smiled, "everyone likes Jean."

Adults and kids were in front of Rachel and Bailey, shouting out questions and clamoring for their attention. Bailey was holding Rachel's hand, but his shiny black eyes were darting around. Off to the side, Holly stood with her hip cocked, earbuds in her ears, chewing gum, and glued to her cell phone.

"Looks like Holly is the same unhappy kid," Sumo said.

Dylan studied Holly. *Yup.*

Casey wondered, "What happened to going to Environmental Camp and saving the world?"

Sumo snorted. "Maybe they wouldn't take her."

Rachel looked over, saw them, and waved. When Bailey spotted Dylan, he started tugging on Rachel's hand, trying to get free. She bent down and whispered something to Bailey. He stepped back and gave her a huge yellow teeth grin.

Uh-oh. Bailey didn't like that.

Rachel sighed and flashed a big smile to her audience. "Excuse us. We'll be right back. Bailey wants to say hello to his friend Dylan. Holly, are you coming?"

Holly rolled her eyes at Rachel but managed a limp wave in their direction before going back to her cell phone and ignoring the world.

I think that's a no.

Two celebrities were too much for the fans to pass up.

Cell phones were raised high. Eager fingers snapped photos and started videos rolling. The air hummed with delighted voices.

"So sweet!"

"Oh look!"

"That's Dylan." A kid showed the woman next to him a recipe card. "He's judging today's grilling contest. I'm gonna win."

The woman placed a hand over her heart and sighed. "I heard Dylan and Bailey are best friends."

"That's true," a tall, thin man in a Dylan's Dog Squad T-shirt confirmed. "Dylan was Bailey's bodyguard at the San Diego Zoo for the new primate habitat ceremony. Dylan and Bailey even went on a Skyfari Tram ride together."

"Really!"

"Thanks for coming, Rachel," Casey said when she joined them.

"After all you've done for us," Rachel smiled, "we wouldn't miss this for the world."

Bailey was sporting two Dylan's Dog Squad bandanas. He patted them, touched Dylan's bandana, and gibbered to him.

Arf! We match!

Then Bailey gave Rachel a big yellow tooth smile, crossed his long arms over his chest, and turned away from her.

Sumo slid a look to Rachel. "What's the matter with Bailey?"

"Bailey's pouting. He doesn't want to do the interview. He wants to be with Dylan."

Dylan pranced on four paws and shoulder-bumped Casey. *I wish we could do photo ops together.*

"The photo ops go until 10 o'clock. Then we're going to hang out until Brea's Best arrives with the steak." Casey tapped Bailey on his shoulder. "You can hang with us."

Bailey gibbered, closed a hairy hand with his index finger extended, and touched his mouth. His hand moved forward and down. Opening his hand up he rested it on the open, up-turned palm of his other hand, signing Promise."

Hey! That's good.

"You bet, Bailey.

Bailey gave Casey and Dylan a happy tight-lipped grin.

"We'll be over there, Bailey." Sumo pointed to the Dream Big canopy.

"I'll wave to you when we're done," Casey added. "Watch for me."

Bailey clapped both hands together. He made a fist and rocked it back and forth, signing Yes.

"Great. We've got to go Rachel. Right, Little Buddy?"

Arf!

Dylan fell into step beside Casey. *This is the best day. We're helping our friends and we get to be with our friends.* On the way, he checked out Brea's Ice Cream.

Crystal and Dominick saw them and shouted, "Hi, guys!"

Save some ice cream for me.

"Casey! Sumo!" Anna stood on tiptoes and waved both hands over her head. "Here." When they got closer, she bent down and ran her hand down Dylan's back. "How's my favorite model?"

Tickles. Arf!

She straightened up and aimed her Sony camera at Dylan. She checked something, squinted up at the cloudless sky, and then put something silver on her camera. "It's bright today. I'm glad we have the canopy."

"Where do you want Dylan?"

"Wait until you see this." Under the Dream Big canopy was something bulky covered with a red velvet drape. She whisked the drape away. "Ta-da!"

Dylan stared at a gigantic heavily carved wooden chair with a huge red velvet cushion. *It's the size of Mom's SUV*.

"I'm not going to ask where my mom found this," Casey murmured.

Anna told him anyway. "Brea Community Theatre. They have a Shakespearean Festival coming up in August. Do you like it?"

Dylan went over and sniffed at the carved wooden legs. *Awesome*.

Sumo had his cell phone up. "Dylan, try it out."

Casey put Dylan in the chair. "Plenty of room for two."

Dylan kicked out his back paws and then rolled over onto his side and snuffled the thick cushion with his snout. *This is better than my bike trailer cushion*.

Anna got serious. "Sumo, can you chat up our location on social media? After people go through Admissions, they should come to us before the barbecue begins."

"Yeah, sure." Sumo's fingers were already tap dancing on his cell phone and he was humming happily. "I'm the social media guru."

"Excuse me," a lady called. "Is the blond doggie ready?"

"First customer, Little Buddy." Casey rolled Dylan back onto his stomach and fluffed out his ears.

I was just getting comfy.

The woman, wearing big hoop earrings and too much perfume, wedged herself in beside him. "Are you the little doggie that teaches the beginning dog training class?"

That's me.

"I follow you on social media."

That's Sumo.

"Look this way." Sumo waved his hand to get the woman's attention and brought up his cell phone. "I'll post it today so you can show your friends."

The woman patted her hair. It was glossy black like a bowling ball. "Ready."

Anna brought her camera up. "Say Dream."

The woman squeezed Dylan close to her and gushed, "Dream!"

Uh, Casey!

"Don't do that." Casey hurried over and reached for Dylan. "It makes him barf."

The woman jumped up like she was on fire and took off.

Sumo started cracking up and dropped his cell phone. "Oh man."

Kids and adults came by nonstop.

Anna would wait for them to settle and then announce, "Say, Dream!"

All obliged. "Dream!"

I'm dreaming of ice cream. How much longer, Casey? Dylan swept his eyes over the next man in line, watching him shuffle closer. The man had a lived-in face and wore a cowboy hat, a faded plaid shirt, and scuffed boots. The man stopped at Dylan's chair but didn't sit. Slowly he stretched out a wrinkled hand and let it rest on Dylan's shoulders.

"Had me a dog once," the man drawled. "Ranger was his name."

That's nice.

"What kind of dog?" Casey waited.

"Best kind. Mine." The old man's hand lingered. "He's gone now."

That's sad. Dylan sat up straight so the man wouldn't have so far to bend.

"Yup. Me and Ranger worked cattle ranches from Montana to California."

"Would you like your picture taken with Dylan?" Anna stepped closer.

The old man touched a tanned index finger to the brim of his hat and smiled, showing very white teeth. "Thank you, ma'am, but that wouldn't be fair to Ranger."

"We get it." Casey stroked Dylan's back. "Don't we, Little Buddy?"

The man touched his finger to the brim of his hat again and ambled off.

Dylan watched him go. *I would never leave Casey.*

"It's almost ten o'clock." Casey looked over his shoulder. "One little girl left."

When Dylan peeked around Casey, he saw a van with a picture of a poodle wearing a crown on its head cruise into the parking lot and park. *The Sledgehammer! Arf!*

A moment later, a man with sandy hair got out of the van. He gave a quick look around, slammed the driver's door shut, and headed toward Admissions.

We've got trouble! Arf!

"The girl will only take a minute." Casey rubbed his stomach. "Ready for ice cream?"

Arf! Arf!

"Thought so." Casey turned around and gave a big wave to Rachel and Bailey.

When the little girl sat down in the chair, Dylan hopped over her. He got up on his hind legs, pawed Casey's arm, and tossed his head back toward the parking lot. *The Sledgehammer is here! Grr!*

The girl shrieked. "Mom!" and bolted from the chair.

"What?" Then Casey saw the Royal Treatment van. "Sumo, call Uncle Rory!"

"Why?" Sumo's eyes darted around.

We need help.

"Just do it. Tell him The Sledgehammer is here." Casey picked Dylan up. "Tell him to get to the parking lot."

Sumo was hunched over his cell phone, his fingers working the screen. "Where are you going?"

"We're going after him!"

CHAPTER THIRTY-ONE

Dylan's head bounced like a rubber ball as Casey's long legs ate up the lawn and raced toward Admissions.

"Comin' through." Casey tightened his hold on Dylan and dodged parents and kids. "Sorry!"

"Slow down, kid."

"Watch where you're going."

Casey ignored the shouts and picked up speed. When he reached the parking lot, he slammed on the brakes. "Where did he go, Dylan?"

Dylan's head snapped forward and he bit his tongue. *Ow!*

"We couldn't have lost him." Casey turned slowly searching for The Sledgehammer.

Arf! There!

"Hold on!" He hugged Dylan close and took off.

The Sledgehammer was taking his time, walking with the crowd heading to Admissions. He nodded at a man carrying a sleepy toddler before falling into step beside a woman with two small boys.

"He thinks he's so smart showing up in the Royal Treatment van. No one would think twice about seeing a groomer's van here."

He's trying to blend in. That's what criminals do.

"Good job, Little Buddy. You spotted him."

A loud clang pierced the air. Heads turned and saw Lisa ring the ship's bell a second time.

The Sledgehammer heard it, too, and walked in Lisa's direction.

"We have another cash donation!" Lisa announced and clapped her hands.

Dylan saw The Sledgehammer zero in on the Cash Admissions and Donations sign above Lisa's head. *This isn't good, Casey.* Then he saw a smug smile spread across The Sledgehammer's face. *This really isn't good.*

"I see him." Casey searched the area. "Where's Uncle Rory? He should've been here by now."

The Sledgehammer said something to Lisa. She smiled and turned to point to the sign.

That's all The Sledgehammer needed. He grabbed the cash box and made a break for it. "Stop, thief!" Lisa shouted to the other cadets, "Get help." She catapulted over the table, grabbed The Sledgehammer's shirt from behind, whirled him around, and landed a punch to his nose that sent him staggering. He snarled at her and used the back of his hand to wipe away the blood gushing from his nose.

"Stay here." Casey put Dylan on the ground. "Lisa!" he shouted and ran toward her.

Lisa turned when she heard Casey call her name. The Sledgehammer's left hand grabbed her long braid and wrapped it around his hand. He reeled Lisa in, holding her in front of him like a human shield.

"Don't anybody move!" he warned.

Lisa came down hard on his instep and shot an elbow to

his gut. The Sledgehammer clocked her on the side of the head with the cash box. Lisa crumpled to the ground and lay stretched out on her side. Blood oozed from her right temple.

Casey charged up and crouched low in front of The Sledgehammer, ready to fight.

The Sledgehammer sneered, "Think you can take me, punk?"

Get away, Casey! Dylan pranced in place and whipped his head around. *Where's Uncle Rory?*

"Yeah."

No!

The Sledgehammer laughed, snagged Casey by his T-shirt, and got him in a chokehold. With his free hand, he reached into his waistband and pulled out a Glock nine-millimeter handgun.

"Gun!" someone shouted.

"Get down!"

Sirens wailed. Police cruisers raced into the parking lot, squealing tires, and stopping on a dime. Doors opened and officers took cover behind them. Doors slammed shut and officers pounded the asphalt, getting closer and dropping into ready position.

"Back off," The Sledgehammer ordered.

"This is the Brea Police Department," Rory announced and pointed his gun at him. "Drop your weapon."

You've got to save Casey!

Dylan watched Casey struggling to use both hands, trying to loosen The Sledgehammer's hold. *You can do this. Whine.*

Earsplitting bell clanging tore through the air. Holly was madly ringing the ship's bell. The sound was deafening.

Heads swiveled and hands covered ears. Bailey stood next to her, baring his teeth.

"Knock it off, kid," The Sledgehammer shouted.

"Bad guy, Bailey! Save Casey!" Holly ordered.

Bailey bounded over the Cash Admissions and Donations table and streaked toward Casey and The Sledgehammer.

The crowd gasped. "Is that Bailey?"

That's Bailey!

People kept one hand on their ear and brought cell phones up with the other. This was instant news, and they would be the first to let the world know.

A thin siren screamed through the air. Seconds later an emergency vehicle pulled into the parking lot. Two paramedics got out and unloaded a gurney.

The Sledgehammer's gun danced between Rory and the paramedics. "Tell them to stop or I will."

"Theo Sledge," Rory called but he held his hand up, signaling the paramedics to stop, "Cadet Chen needs medical treatment."

"She'll get it when I'm gone." The Sledgehammer shuffled Casey forward. "Grab the cash box, kid. You're coming with me."

"Get it yourself."

Dylan fell in beside Bailey and they shot forward. Bailey went in high, and Dylan went in low. Bailey plowed into The Sledgehammer, knocking him on his butt. The gun flew out of The Sledgehammer's hands, and he lost his grip on Casey. Casey rolled to his side.

Bailey bared his teeth, screeched, and moved aside for Dylan.

I've got this. Dylan sank his teeth into The Sledgehammer's arm.

"Stupid mutt! Get off me!"

I'm not stupid. You are. Dylan worked his way up and latched onto The Sledgehammer's neck. *Grr. Grr.*

The Sledgehammer howled in pain.

Good.

Bailey wasn't to be left out. He dropped to the ground and pinned The Sledgehammer down with his big hands.

"Hey, what is this beast?" The Sledgehammer called, struggling to get away. "I'm being attacked here."

The crowd cheered, eagerly rooting for their heroes.

"Bailey!"

"Dylan!"

Casey got to his hands and knees. "Good job, Little Buddy."

Dylan kept going. *I'm not done. Grr.*

The Sledgehammer twisted out from under Bailey's hands and sent a vicious punch to Dylan's head.

Ow! Dylan came back for more.

The Sledgehammer scrambled backward, grabbed the gun, and fired once.

CHAPTER THIRTY-TWO

"Dylan!" Casey shouted.

Hey! The bullet whizzed by Dylan missing his ear by a breath. *That creep tried to shoot me. Grr!* Dylan heard Casey call his name again. *Your voice sounds weird. Kind of fuzzy.* Dylan shook his ears out. *Worry about that later.*

Dylan launched himself into the air. He made a four-paw landing on The Sledgehammer's chest, knocking him off balance.

The Sledgehammer fell backward cracking his head on the ground. "You lousy miserable mutt!"

"Dylan!" Casey and Uncle Rory yelled.

Dylan sprang forward snake fast. The Sledgehammer turned over onto his stomach and Dylan clamped his jaws around The Sledgehammer's neck. *I'm not a mutt. I'm an American Cocker Spaniel.* Dylan shook his head back and forth, taking The Sledgehammer's neck with him. *Grr! Grr!*

"No, Little Buddy." Casey tried pulling Dylan back.

Grr! Let me go. He hurt you and Lisa. Dylan shook harder.

Casey used both hands and pried Dylan's jaws off The Sledgehammer's neck.

Dylan hauled his head back, trying to wiggle free from Casey. *Let me at him.*

Bailey gently pushed Casey and Dylan aside. Then he sat down hard on The Sledgehammer's back, knocking the air out of him.

"My back's broken!" The Sledgehammer squirmed underneath Bailey and flailed his arms out to his sides. "Get these wild animals off me!"

"Okay, Bailey. That's enough." Rory held his hand out and helped Bailey stand up.

Grr! Grr! Good job, Bailey!

"You, too, Dylan." Rory moved in and cuffed The Sledgehammer. "Theo Sledge you're under arrest. Penal Code 211, Robbery. Penal Code 245, Assault With a Deadly Weapon. Two counts of Penal Code 207, Kidnapping and Penal Code 664, Attempted Murder."

That's all? Dylan plunked his buns down. *The guy nearly shot my ear off.*

Bailey agreed and bared his teeth.

"Big deal." The Sledgehammer curled his upper lip. "I've got lawyers." He sneered some more. "I *own* lawyers. I'll be out by dinner."

Don't count on it. Dylan lunged, showing all forty-two teeth.

Casey caught Dylan in midair and pulled him close. "It's okay. Uncle Rory's got this."

It's still my turn.

"You don't want Uncle Rory to look bad in front of the other officers, do you?" Casey whispered. "Let him do his job."

Dylan gave it one more grr. *Okay.*

"Oh, it's a big deal," Rory assured The Sledgehammer and hauled him to his feet. We've got you on five violent felonies. Using a gun is an enhancement and makes the charges more serious. You're looking at twenty-five years to life."

Good. Dylan wagged his little tail. *How long is that in dog years?*

Rory gestured toward Lisa where the paramedics were at work. "You'd better hope Cadet Chen makes it, or we'll be adding Penal Code 187, Murder."

"She broke my nose." The Sledgehammer tried sniffing up the oozing blood. "I'm gonna sue."

"Good luck with that one." Rory motioned an officer over. "Palermo read him his rights and take him in."

Palermo nodded and stepped in. "You've got the right to remain silent."

"Yeah, yeah, yeah."

Palermo continued reciting the Miranda warning over The Sledgehammer's protests and steered him to the police car.

The crowd hooted, hollered, and cheered.

Two officers nodded to Rory and got busy. One officer started taking pictures of the scene. Rory waited until the other officer bagged the gun before turning his attention to Casey, Dylan, and Bailey.

"Good job, guys," Rory said. "We've been after Sledge a long time."

Holly broke through the officers holding the crowd back and raced over. Her face was flushed, and she was breathless with excitement. "Hey!"

"Thanks for doing the bell thing and distracting The Sledgehammer." Casey turned Dylan to him and rubbed his ears. "That's got to be the loudest bell on earth. Right, Little Buddy?"

Dylan shook his ears out. *No joke.*

"This was so much fun. This is like the greatest day ever of my life." Holly giggled. "I've decided I'm going to be a cop."

Casey and Dylan stared at her.

Who is this happy kid?

"What happened to going to Environmental Camp and saving the world," Casey asked.

"Forget that." Holly made a face. "Too slow. Fighting crime is where it's at."

The criminals won't stand a chance.

"You're so lucky, Lieutenant Kellan," she bubbled. "Being a cop is like the coolest job ever." She rubbed her hands together. "I can't wait to go after bad guys and drag them into a cell with no windows and lean on them until they squeal." She nodded smugly. "I know I can get 'em to roll over on their friends." She put her hands on her hips and cocked her head. "Can I be a cop right away or do I have to do the whole cadet thing first?"

Rory's eyebrows went up and then they came together in one long line. "I'll talk to your mother."

I hope you're kidding, Uncle Rory.

"Great!" She leaned forward, gave him a huge hug, and hung on. "I can't wait to get started! You'll let me know?"

"Sure." Rory peeled her arms off and took several steps back. He cleared his throat and continued. "Today was a good day. We couldn't have gotten Sledge without everybody's help."

"I was so worried when Dylan went after The Sledgehammer." Casey hugged Dylan close. "You could have been hurt, Little Buddy."

You're my buddy. I'd do anything for you.

Casey started laughing. "The best part was when Bailey sat on The Sledgehammer." Casey shifted Dylan in his arms and held up his right hand. "High-five, Bailey."

Bailey slapped his big hand to Casey's, gave several tight-lipped smiles, and shuffled his big hairy feet back and forth.

"You and Dylan are a great team," Casey said.

Bailey gibbered and held his hand up to Dylan.

Dylan looked to Casey. *What?*

Casey leaned Dylan closer to Bailey. "Give Bailey a high-four, Little Buddy."

Dylan touched his paw to Bailey's hand. *You saved Casey. Thanks.*

Thunderous applause from the crowd filled the air. More cheers and shouts rang out. Cell phone cameras didn't miss a thing.

Holly's cell phone vibrated, and she checked the screen. "Bummer." The happy new Holly had disappeared. She shoved her cell phone back into her pocket and frowned over to where the officers were doing crowd control. Rachel was in the front row, smiling and waving.

"Holly! Bailey!" Rachel called. "Over here!"

"The party's over," Holly muttered. "C'mon, Bailey."

Bailey didn't wait for Holly. Just dropped to all fours and ran into Rachel's outstretched arms.

The crowd ate it up and called his name.

"She was happy for a while," Casey said. "Do you think she'll really become a cop?"

"We'll see," Rory said. His face said no way.

"All clear, Lieutenant," an officer called out to Rory.

"Thanks." He gestured to the officers holding the onlookers back. "You can let them through."

"Hey, guys." Sumo jogged up, waving his cell phone. "That was so cool! I got the whole thing. Social media is burning up."

"Hello, Sterling." Rory stepped closer, zeroing in on Sumo's cell phone.

"Uh, uh." Sumo immediately jammed his cell phone into his shorts pocket. "Hi, Lieutenant Kellan."

Rory spread his legs, put both his hands on his gun belt, and nodded. "Been busy?"

Sumo hitched a shoulder and let it fall. "The usual."

"Casey! Dylan!" Mom shouted and ran to them. "Are you okay?" She hugged them both.

"Yeah." Casey stepped back. "Dylan and Bailey are heroes. They did all the work."

"I saw!" Mom grabbed Dylan's face with both hands and kissed him on his topknot.

"Theo Sledge has been sidestepping the law for years, Sis. His arrest is going to make Captain Rizzoli's day. Still, you could've been hurt." Rory ruffled Dylan's ears. "You're lucky the bullet missed you."

Dylan leaned into Casey. *Casey needed my help.*

They watched Officer Palermo open the patrol car, put his hand on top of The Sledgehammer's head, and guide him down into the backseat. Palermo slammed the door and went to the driver's door.

Roger and Jean were watching from the sidelines. They waited for the patrol car to drive away and then walked over to join them.

"Thank you." Jean was clutching the cash box to her chest. "I'm so grateful," her lower lip trembled. "Dream Big K-9 Academy will be saved."

Arf!

"Never thought we'd see the cash box again. Thanks," Roger mumbled.

Casey, Mom, Sumo, and Rory were too stunned to speak.

Wow! Roger said thanks. Dylan blinked. *He's been in the sun too long.*

Jean shivered despite the heat. "Why would Mr. Sledge steal the cash box?"

"He knew," Rory began, "people were making cash donations today."

"How?" Mom asked.

Rory slid his cop eyes to Sumo. "Grillin' With Dylan and Friends has been on every social media site nonstop for the last two days."

"That's stupid." Roger sliced a scarred hand through the air, brushing it off. "What idiot pays attention to that garbage?"

"Believe it or not," Rory laughed, "even criminals follow social media."

"Lowlife creeps. Too much time on their hands," Roger muttered. "They should get a job."

"Roger, be quiet." Jean closed her eyes and sighed. "So many people could've been hurt today."

"That's what happens when you do business with a crook," Sumo smirked.

"Sumo!" Rory and Mom warned.

You're not helping.

Casey pointed to the cash box. "Can you pay The Sledgehammer back now?"

"I can't wait to count it." She shook the box and grinned. "Feels heavy."

Mom wouldn't let it go. "This seems so outrageous. Petty thieves pull stunts like this. The Sledgehammer is an experienced criminal." She shook her head. "If he wanted the money why not wait until Roger paid him?"

They thought about that.

"Maybe," Casey reasoned, "he didn't want the money."

"Of course, he did," Roger snorted. "I owed him a hundred grand and he was charging fifty percent interest. That's a hundred and fifty thousand bucks."

"How much is Dream Big K-9 Academy worth?" Casey asked.

"Casey!" Mom gave him The Look.

Sumo was already logged into the real estate app and scrolling across his cell phone screen. "Whoa! Dream Big K-9 Academy is nine acres. This says the land is worth millions!" Sumo looked up. "I bet a real estate developer would do anything to get his hands on nine acres."

The truth clapped louder than thunder.

"That's it." Casey grabbed Sumo's arm. "Captain Rizzoli said real estate was one of The Sledgehammer's businesses."

"Right." Rory crossed his arms over his chest. "A lot of new homes could be built on nine acres."

"A lot of new homes mean a lot of buyers with lots of money," Mom added.

"Don't you get it, guys?" Casey's words tumbled out and picked up speed. "The Sledgehammer didn't *want* Roger to pay the money back. That's why The Sledgehammer took the cash box. He wanted to make sure Roger *couldn't* pay him back by midnight tonight."

"Then Dream Big K-9 Academy would be his." Mom mused. "Getting land worth millions of dollars in exchange for a hundred-thousand-dollar loan is a great deal."

"That's cold," Sumo said.

That's scary.

"Okay," Uncle Rory nodded, following along, "but the money in the cash box wouldn't be enough to pay back the loan."

"Lisa had fifteen thousand in donations before Grillin' With Dylan and Friends even started. I bet it's twice that amount now. Add the paid admissions to that." Casey was on a roll. "Don't forget Cranky Pants paid Roger big bucks to rent Dream Big Academy. Then there's all the money people paid when they signed up for classes. Right, Jean?"

"That's true. Business has been good since summer started, so we already had some of the money."

Casey summed it up. "When The Sledgehammer heard about Grillin' With Dylan and Friends, he panicked. His big idea to get the land for cheap was suddenly falling apart. When he got here, he saw we were raking the money in. He was desperate and that's why he took the cashbox. He wanted to *make sure* Roger *couldn't* pay him back." Casey hugged Dylan. "Thanks to Dylan and Bailey, he's going to jail instead."

He's a bad man. Dylan nuzzled Casey's cheek. *I'm glad we caught him.*

Jean put her hand over her heart. "We can't thank you enough."

A loud honk came from the parking lot and Brea's Best rolled up.

"You thank them." Roger scowled. "I'll take care of the steak delivery. I've got to do everything," he griped and walked away.

"Roger is such a charmer," Mom murmured.

I don't think charmer means what you think it means.

"Would it kill him to say something nice?" Casey rolled his eyes.

Jean laughed. "That was something nice."

The excitement was over. People drifted to the portable barbecue pits, ready to get down to the business of grilling and eating.

Dylan whined. *When do we eat?*

"Mom, we're starving." Casey bounced Dylan in his arms. "We're going to get ice cream."

Arf!

Mom checked her cell phone. "Okay but be at the judge's table in an hour." She looked up. "We can't have a Grillin' With Dylan and Friends contest without our favorite judge."

"No problem, Mom. Dylan's excited about being a judge. Right, Little Buddy?"

Dylan thought about tasting steak. His innards hummed and his mouth watered. *Right!*

Casey turned to Sumo. "Want ice cream?"

"You bet."

"One moment, boys." Mom reached out and brushed Dylan's topknot out of his eyes. "When you knocked Mr. Sledge over, that was smart thinking."

Dylan's chest puffed with pride. *About time someone says I think smart.*

She smiled. "I hope you really hurt him. The man is such a villain."

"Villain?" Casey snorted. "Really, Mom. Where do you come up with these words?"

She gave him a patient smile. "Reading improves your vocabulary."

"Oh man." Sumo had his cell phone out and his digits were dancing across its screen. "Dylan's Villain. Good one, Ms. D. Social media will love this."

Arf! Dylan gave a forty-two teeth grin and slurped a

canine kiss on Casey's cheek. *Dylan's Villain. I like it. Catchy!*

"But," Mom brought her face close to Dylan's, "if you ever do something like that again, Dylan Easter Donovan, you won't get vanilla ice cream for a week."

Aw, Mom!

The End

ACKNOWLEDGMENTS FOR DYLAN'S DOG SQUAD

Dylan is my inspiration every day. He's always loved a good story and now that they are about him, he loves them even more. I thank him tremendously.

Many thanks to Gina Capaldi, award-winning illustrator, author, and friend, for not once complaining about the zillion photographs, I sent to her of Dylan. Her cover designs for *Dylan's Dilemma, Dylan's Dream,* and *Dylan's Villain* are perfect and I can't thank her enough. They make my heart sigh.

Many thanks to my best friend Robyn Matias for her constant support and never telling me once that I should stick to my day job.

Many thanks to my incredibly talented writers and illustrators' group: Teri Vitters, Priscilla Burris, and Gina Capaldi. Their work leaves me speechless.

Many thanks to Marjorie McCowan, my awesome friend, and writer, who always asks me to read one more chapter to her.

Many thanks to Retired Detective Lieutenant Kelly Carpenter, Brea Police Department, for patiently answering my endless questions about police procedure.

Many thanks to Matt Baldwin, creative consultant, and private pilot, for providing detailed flight and aircraft information.

Many thanks to Deborah Halverson and her invaluable editing comments.

Many thanks to Kami Wiley, my favorite creative consultant, who always looks forward to reading each new *Dylan* book and is always disappointed when she comes to The End.

Many thanks to Jonathan and Jynafer Yanez for guiding me through the boggling process of getting my book published. You are truly the best.

Many thanks to Rockelle Henderson, Rock Inked, for her patience and wisdom, and for steering me through the muddy waters of commerce and distribution.

I couldn't have done this without you.

SIMPLE SIGNS/HAND COMMANDS

- Applause/Yay/Hurrah: Hold your hands in the air and twist them a couple of times.
- Come: Extend both hands with index fingers pointing forward and up.
- Then bend your arms at the elbow, pull your fingers in toward your body.
- Dad: Open your fingers and place your thumb on your temple.
- (Directions) Left: Raise hand and show thumb and index finger only. Motion to the left.
- (Directions) Right: Raise hand, show index and third fingers only. Cross index and third fingers. Motion to the right.
- Down: Point your index finger down and move your hand in a downward direction.
- Go: This is done by 'throwing' the index fingers forward. The index fingers trace the air. Throwing the index fingers to the side is popular, too.

- Hi: Open hand to forehead and quickly move away in a salute.
- Hippo: Extend your index finger and little finger on both hands, and open and close them, having both hands meet in the middle—like a hippo's mouth.
- I Love You: Show your little finger, then your index finger and then your thumb.
- Jump: Make one hand flat. With your other hand, extend your middle and index fingers to make a 'little man' and have him jump up and down on your flat hand.
- Mom: Open your fingers and place your thumb on your chin.
- Not me: Point index finger to chest and shake your head no.
- (Are you) Okay: Point the index finger on your dominant hand toward the person and then quickly withdraw your index finger. With your thumb straight up, make a couple of quick circles.
- Please: Put your dominant hand on your chest with your thumb sticking out and your fingers extended. Move your hand in a circular motion (clockwise) two or three times.
- Promise: Closed hand with index finger extended and touching mouth. Move hand forward and down while opening to rest on open up-turned palm of other hand.
- Quiet: Bring your index finger to your lips.
- Show Me: Open left hand with fingers separated. Then point to the center of your palm with right index finger.

- Sit Down: Have one hand flat/palm up. Take your other hand with index and middle fingers extended together in a slight hook to make the person's legs, and then sit them on your open palm.
- Stay: Use your thumb and little finger in a palm-down 'Y' shape. The movement is a forward thrust, not a downward slap. You are shoving the knuckles forward and a bit down.
- Stop: Extend your left hand, palm upward. Bring your right hand down to your left hand at a right angle.
- Watch: Use your index and third fingers. Thrust them forward.
- Work: Close both hands into fists in front of you, then tap your right fist on top of your left fist a couple of times in the wrist area.
- Yes: Take a hand and make it into a fist and bob it back and forth.

RESPONSIBLE DOG OWNER'S PLEDGE

I will be responsible for my dog's safety.

I will properly control my dog by providing fencing where appropriate, not letting my dog run loose, and using a leash in public. I will ensure that my dog has some form of identification (which may include collar tags, tattoos, or microchip ID).

ABOUT DYLAN EASTER TROY

Dylan was born on Easter in Daejeon, South Korea. His first owner bought him from Walmart.

At that time, I suggested basic dog training, but his first owner didn't think training was important. Dylan immediately destroyed his owner's apartment by chewing his way through electrical coverings, baseboards, and furniture. When Dylan ate the interior of his owner's BMW, his owner decided having a dog was too much work and didn't want him anymore.

I said I would take him.

Dylan spent twenty-seven hours in cargo hold to get to California. When I picked him up at Korean Air, Los Angeles International Airport, he was eighteen-months old, didn't know his own name, nor was he housebroken. We immediately started training and Dylan thrived. He loved agility training and competing with other dogs. His first big step came when he became certified as a Therapy Dog. Dylan enjoyed this but when he became American Kennel Club Canine Good Citizen certified, he went into service dog training and became a Hospice Service Dog for people actively dying.

Additionally, Dylan's accomplishments include:

• Bilingual understanding: English and Korean

• Five hundred word and phrase vocabulary

• Ability to contact 9-1-1 with a special device

• Count to ten

• Television appearances

• Recognized in a feature article in the *Orange County Register* for his accomplishments

• Recognized by Baskin-Robbins for his accomplishments and his love of their vanilla ice cream

• Mascot for Cypress College in Cypress, CA.

Dylan is proof that there are no bad dogs. In fact, he's the smartest, best dog I've ever had or ever trained. Dogs need love, guidance, companionship, and a sense of purpose. At the end of Dylan's workday, he receives a bit of Baskin-Robbins vanilla ice cream.

He deserves it.

ABOUT THE AUTHOR
KATHLEEN TROY, JD; PHD

Kathleen Troy is a published author, children's book publisher, movie producer, writing and law professor at Cypress College, and former Director of Education and Development for the Archdiocese of Los Angeles. Kathleen is an active member of Sisters in Crime and Society of Children's Book Writers and Illustrators and has won several awards for middle grade and young adult books. Dog training is Kathleen's passion, and she has achieved recognition, most notably for training service dogs for hospice work.

Kathleen welcomes hearing from you. Please get in touch with her at www.kathleentroy.com.

STAY INFORMED

I'd love to stay in touch! You can email me at kathleen@
kathleentroy.com

For updates about new releases, as well as exclusive
promotions, visit my website and sign up for the VIP
mailing list. Head there now to receive a free story

www.kathleentroy.com

Enjoying the series? Help others discover _Dylan's Dog
Squad_ by sharing with a friend.

CPSIA information can be obtained
at www.ICGtesting.com
Printed in the USA
BVHW092304051022
648789BV00002B/130